There came a new sound, in the distance.

Indira heard it through the soles of her feet and up into her bones, just as she had heard Ma'adim's speech; but this did not feel like tremorspeech, and it was far louder. In fact, it was so loud that she'd have sworn she very faintly heard it through the nearly nonexistent *air*.

Paul knew what it was.

His already awful fear turned to unmitigated horror.

A white shape, streaked with stripes of gray, undulated over the snow. It was so big that at first Indira mistook it for one of the famous Martian duststorms. Yet this was solid, a living white shape that surged over the wastes, implacable as a glacier. Through the spray of frost, she could finally make out that it resembled a vast ivory caterpillar. The thing named itself and the world drowned in a repetition of the noise she'd heard a moment earlier. It vibrated through her skeleton, through her skull, through her soul:
***HOOOOOOOOONNNNNNNNN***

## Also by Jim Cleaveland

## THE INEXPLICABLE ADVENTURES OF BOB!
## Comics Anthologies

*Chronicling the adventures of Bob Smithson, who was the world's most average man until the day he inexplicably became a magnet for the bizarre.*

### *The Penn State Years:*
*The 1990's stories originally printed in the Penn State Science Fiction Society newsletter!*
"The Fickle Finger of Fate"
"Boxhunt"
"Molly's Tale"
"The Return of Princess Voluptua"

### *There But For the Grace:*
*Sweet-tempered Molly the Monster meets a mysterious doppelganger — Galatea's origin!*

## COMING SOON! --

### *Love And Space:*
*The love triangle between Bob, Jean, and Voluptua gets heated while the evil Fructose Riboflavin attacks Butane, Planet of Dragons!*

**Read the original comic online at**
***http://bobadventures.comicgenesis.com***

From the creator of *The Inexplicable Adventures of Bob*

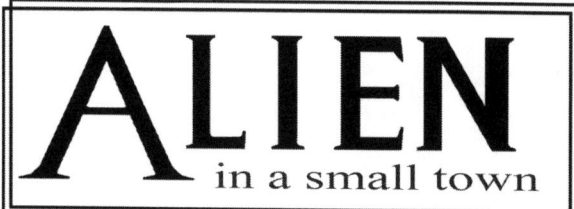

# ALIEN
## in a small town

=== *Jim Cleaveland*

**BobAdventures Prod.**

Copyright © 2014 by James Brower Cleaveland

2nd EDITION – 2015

This book is a work of fiction. Any similarity to actual situations or actual persons, living or dead, is purely coincidental.

Scripture quotations on pp. 61 and 125-126 taken from the New English Bible, copyright © Cambridge University Press and Oxford University Press 1961, 1970. All rights reserved.

Cover art by Acacia Torres.

ISBN: 978-1-5116-3579-0

# ACKNOWLEDGEMENTS
(a.k.a., the Thank You Page)

I'd like to thank Brynne Chandler and the regular attendees of her writing group for their feedback and support: Vaughn Johnson, Sara Hanley, Karen McCarthy, and Todd McCaffrey. In particular, thank you Brynne for pointing out that Indira should be the first person Paul meets in the story, and for prodding me to go an extra mile in giving him a believably alien psychology; and Todd for pointing out that my first method for depicting Paul's native language was too gimmicky, and encouraging me to take a different approach to it.

Thanks as well to my friend Adam Kuppersmith for his feedback on the mechanics of said language.

A big thank you to one of my favorite science fiction authors, Alexander Jablokov, for first conceiving the idea of communication by sonar images in his novel *A Deeper Sea*, and for then being gracious enough to give a thumbs up to my own approach to the concept. Thank you, sir!

Thank you to Acacia Torres for a gorgeous cover painting. It's exactly what I wanted.

My thanks to Brad Linaweaver and Jessie Lilley of *Mondo Cult*, Fred Coppersmith of *Kaleidotrope*, Wesley Kawato of *Nova Science Fiction Magazine*, Mark Sachs of *Hostigos*, and E. Bernhard Warg of *Explosive Decompression* for publishing my early work and for general encouragement.

Thank you to the readers of my webcomic, *The Inexplicable Adventures of Bob!* for sticking with me through my other main creative endeavor these past eight years.

An enormous thank you to my parents for their love, support, and patience through this process, and to my brother Peter for fostering my love of science fiction in the first place.

Lastly, thank you so much to Jen Atkinson for shepherding me through the final stages of this and making sure I actually get it to press. Thank you, Jen, for everything (and, of course, for stuff).

# 1

On a warm June evening, clad in cape dress and hooded bonnet in the manner of centuries earlier, a woman sat and fished at the edge of a lake in a Pennsylvania wood. Just shy of thirty, dusky skinned, with curly black hair and an aquiline nose, she was weary of her day's labors and now reclined against an old willow. She wore her hair in a bun, held in a white cap with white straps indicating she was unmarried, and a dark blue bonnet over the cap. She gazed through half-dozing eyes at her unmoving fishing line. The silver water shimmered in the sun, lingering late in the summer sky. She'd had no bites, and suspected none were forthcoming.

Her fishlessness frustrated her less than she might have expected. She considered herself an impatient person, but she was in a patient mood now. The day's labors were done, the soft lake breeze was glorious after the heat of the fields, and she knew that at this rate she would soon be asleep and welcomed it. She'd been angry and depressed for so long, it felt good to feel good. Perhaps she was finally getting used to this place again.

# 2

*No... not really,* she decided. Her mood shifted, as she'd made the critical mistake of becoming aware she was happy. Her muscles ached because she'd spent the day doing *farm work*. How had that happened? She'd loudly forsworn this mode of life a decade ago.

As this new sense of gloom congealed, she grew dimly aware of a sound of movement in the trees some distance behind her. Indeed, the noise had gone on some while and been growing louder, but she'd been too absorbed in her half-somnolent ruminations to notice. Unlikely though it was that a large bear had appeared out of the woods with intent to eat her, she conceded it was possible, and so she probably ought to look. With a grunt, she shifted around and beheld an extraterrestrial.

It resembled a stony gray cone of rock the size of a small car, supported on three elephantine legs, and with three tentacular arms sprouting from the cone's apex. Two of these arms terminated in three-fingered "hands" like a brittlestar's tendrils. The third arm supported a shining, jet black eyesphere like an oversize bowling ball. This eyestalk was held upright, while the handed arms brushed tree branches out of the creature's way as it advanced. The ground trembled at its approach, not in time with its footsteps, but rather as through the thing were growling in a voice so deep only seismographs could hear it plainly. The tentacled hulk moved awkwardly through the trees, but it would none the less be upon her in moments.

When it was near her, she addressed it. "Evening," she said, and yawned.

"Hello!" the alien said, coming to a stop so his massive bulk loomed over her. "I wasn't expecting to find anyone out here. I hope I'm not disturbing you," he said. The voice was not the alien's own, but came from a decoratively jeweled translation vocoder strapped to the base of his eyestalk tentacle. He wore a broad, green belt around his midsection, as well.

"You're disturbing the fish," she said, pointing at the lake. "I felt your tremorsounding as you walked up. They probably heard it half a kilometer away. It explains why I couldn't catch anything." Again, she was surprised she wasn't more annoyed about that. She supposed the alien's unexpected appearance had made for a welcome break in her routine. That, and that the vibration of his sonar through the ground was actually rather soothing. She stretched, sleepily.

"What? Oh!" The ground vibration ceased abruptly. "I hadn't even noticed I was sounding. I thought I'd broken that habit years ago. Above ground, in daylight, there's no need for it. I'm sorry. I didn't mean to disturb them, either," said his vocodor. He probably understood English, the woman reflected, but he was physically incapable of speaking it.

"I'm sure they'll get over it," she said. "My name's Indira Fenstermacher. I take it you're not from around here?"

"Not that far away, actually. I live and work at the Jan Consulate in Lawrenceton," he said, pointing a finger tendril at the horizon where, if not for the trees, the city's towering spires would be visible. "Though I do some freelance writing on the side. My name is," and the ground trembled again almost imperceptibly as he tremorspoke his real name, "but on Earth I go by Paul Dwightson."

The Jan were not Humanity's first alien contact—there were several competitors for that title, dating from Man's earliest forays into interstellar space: the *Kimson's* encounter with the T'sor-Konapites, the *Ad Astra's* violent run-in with the Ploogs, the legendary lost ship

# 4

*Ograe Nyha*—but the Jan were the first to have established open diplomatic relations with humanity. Earth's governments had allowed them to set up a colony on Jupiter's moon of Callisto—a barren rock of no interest to any human except geologists and miners, but comfortable for a silicon-based race—in exchange for their aid in establishing mankind in the interstellar community. It was hoped an Earthling embassy could be opened on planet Faldor soon—the main obstacle being the distance, of course, but with relativistic-speed travel and a modicum of patience, this was hardly insurmountable.

He extended a tendril and shook her proffered hand. To her, his skin felt rough but not especially hard, like the bark of an old sweetgum tree. Her own hands were callused. To any human, they'd have felt hard and rough; but to Paul, nearly all living things on Earth were soft. "One of Dwight's many offspring, eh?" she said. "So that'd make you... under fifty, right?"

"I'm fifty years, two months old by Earth's calendar," the alien said. "I was born in this solar system, and was part of her first brood when she became fertile."

"Well, it doesn't show. You don't look a day over forty," Indira teased.

Paul laughed in response to what he recog-nized as a 'joke,' wondering as always whether it was dishonest to perform that gesture, as he had but poor grasp of Earthly humor and was incapable of laughter without the vocodor.

"Your English is excellent," she said. "How much of it is handled by the vocodor?"

He'd delivered this explanation many times. "Only the enunciation itself," Paul said. "I am fluent in

Proxy." Human and Jannite speech had little in common, as the Jan communicated through ground tremors, much as Earth's elephants do. Further, Jannite tremorspeech relied more on three-dimensional sonar images than on discreet words. Automatic language machines could give very basic translations, but this was slow, and much was inevitably lost in the translation. To truly speak an Earth language, a Jan had to learn a proxy vocabulary of pronounceable tremorwords, which corresponded to English words on a one-to-one basis. The vocodor would then enunciate the English words for him. Proxy-Mandarin would use nearly the same vocabulary of tremorwords as proxy-English, but would follow Chinese grammar. The same was true for Hindi, Spanish, or what have you.

"But first you have to wrap your heads around the idea of one word standing for each idea, right? Instead of the sonar pictures you normally use with each other. That sounds hard to learn," she said.

"It was," he said, not even bothering to try to decypher the odd phrase *wrap your head around*. He inclined his eyestalk to better regard the small human before him. Even after all this time on Earth, the little bipedal bloodbladders still all tended to look alike to him. The ground hummed for a moment as he took a sonograph of her, giving him a flash image of a delicate calcium/phosphorus understructure, wrapped in a flexible form-fitting sack of goo. It was truly miraculous that such an... *object* could be a conscious being.

In the thin Callistan atmosphere, his sonar would have been dependent on indirect echoes transmitted through the ground and up through her body—which would have been perfectly adequate for a clear image; a Jan's brain could decypher such input as easily as a human brain could reconcile a single stereoscopic image from two eyes—but in Earth's thick atmosphere, he could sonoproject along a direct vector, straight through the air to her body, which gave a very clear image.

He wiped condensation off his cold eyesphere, ruminating that while Earth's brutal heat was difficult enough, *humidity* was something he would never get used to; he would always need salves to prevent it corroding his hide. The humidity was better or worse depending on one's location on Earth, just as the painfully high air pressure was better or worse depending on elevation. Thus far, he'd found Appalachian Pennsylvania in summer to be unpleasant, but bearable. He frequently ached from atmospheric oxygen levels so high that dry objects ignited with only minimal prompting (humans had discovered fire absurdly early in their civilization's prehistory). In his belt he wore specialized filters to chill ambient $O_2$ into a liquid form he could respirate and which would help cool his body. It still felt strange to have no need to drink oxygen because he was walking *around* in it. *Just as fish never feel thirst,* he thought, pleased at the Earthling analogy. He regretted having bothered the swimming creatures with his sonar.

For what seemed the billionth time, he asked himself why he was subjecting himself to this, and for the billionth time the answer came: because he deserved it. Enduring gawking stares from the aborigines was as necessary a part of his penance as his physical discomforts. The absence of such a reaction from this human intrigued him. "If you'll pardon my saying," he said, "you seem remarkably at ease with my appearance. I'm surprised."

"'If you'll pardon my saying'?" she parroted him, and then made the barking sound humans called laughter.

He wondered if perhaps he was going to be mocked after all. "What planet *are* you from?"

"Callisto, originally," he said. That was common knowledge, surely.

Indira giggled. "No, no. It's an expression. An idiom. And I was making a joke. It means you're acting weird. I've just never met a... courteous Jan before."

"Oh," he said, comprehending. "You mean that we have a reputation for rudeness."

She waved her hands in the air in a gesture Paul recognized as a *shrug*. "Don't get me wrong. I know you guys don't mean anything by it. It's the whole honesty thing."

Paul bobbed his eyestalk to imitate a nod. "Yes. Symbolic communication is difficult enough for us to grasp. Duplicitous communication is even more difficult."

"That's so strange. Isn't lying a survival advantage?"

"My ancestors were not predators, like yours. They were prey."

"Like I said," she said.

"Cooperation was all they had to keep them alive," he clarified. "Well, that and our Warrior caste."

"Oh. Anyway, what kind of predators would eat you guys? You're freaking huge."

"You've never seen a great striped *hoon*," he said.

"Who wha?"

"Millions of years ago, Earth's animals were much bigger than they are now. On Janworld, they remained that big. My people are *not* large creatures. What lions, bears, and sharks are to your symbolism, a *hoon* is to ours. Perhaps times ten. Our great sacred nightmare. When we colonize a planet, naturally we bring samples of many of our native organisms to help adapt the environment to our needs. We make sure every colony world has some *hoons*."

"What? That's crazy. Why? They *eat* you!" she said.

"Not if we stay alert. That's what they're for," he said. "It's the same reason we limit our technological conveniences: to prevent decadence."

"This is Dutch Country, so I'm all for that, but doing it at the risk of getting *eaten* is going too far," she said. "And anyway, I'd think speaking Earthling languages would make lying easier, not harder. If you have to pick and choose your words, doesn't that make it simpler to hide your meaning than if you just project full sonographic images at each other like you normally do?"

*Don't lecture me on the temptations of deceit!* he restrained himself from snapping, and then reflected, in amazement, that he'd just now been thinking verbally. His language skills were clearly better than he'd thought. "Withholding information isn't lying. It's secrecy. There's a difference."

"Lying is forbidden in your culture, but not keeping secrets?" she asked.

"Yes, although we try to keep it to a minimum," he said, making sure his intonation out the vocodor did not sound snide. "Our neurology doesn't even lend itself to deceit. And the selective withholding of purely subjective opinions which would be potentially insulting to the listener is what humans call tact. I have endeavored to learn tact."

"You've done a good job," she said.

"Thanks," he said.

"You're pissed off, aren't you?" she said.

Paul hesitated before answering. "I... beg your pardon?"

"Pissed off," she said. "Angry. It's another idiom."

"I'm familiar with it. I just... I thought I was hiding it better than that," he said.

"Your whole body is tense like you've got a bug up your ass the size of Wyoming. You're not actually lying, I guess, but just being passably polite is taking everything you've got." It was downright comical actually, but she respected him for trying.

"That's... That's very true. I was thinking that I was hot and uncomfortable, and that I hated having to overthink my every word to make sure I didn't offend your lying, paranoid, human sensibilities."

"Me? How am I lying?" she asked.

"I..." It was true. She wasn't lying. At least, she'd told no lies such that he could tell. There was none of the usual human false veneer of politeness here. His passive sonar told him that her heartrate was polygraphically steady. By human standards, she was being mildly rude, saying he had a "bug up his ass," but with no evident malice behind it whatever. Paul found it quite refreshing. "You're the first human I've encountered who has so accurately gauged my emotional state. I'm also surprised to hear the use of obscenity. I was under the impression that linguistic taboos were stronger in this geographic area."

She laughed again. "Oh they *are*. Believe me. I grew up in Eppleberg, just outside Lofthaven," she said, pointing the opposite way from the tree-hidden spires of Lawrenceton. "I don't know if I've ever fit in well here, though, even back in the day. And since I've been away and come back, I feel even more like a fish out of water." She caught herself in another idiom. "I mean, I feel out of place. Different."

# 10

"Where had you been, that you acquired enough experience with Jan to read our body language?" Paul asked.

"Felice Station," she said, pointing straight up (though the orbiting city would actually be in the southern sky, Paul reflected). "I was an engineer up there more than ten years. Believe me, you meet all types of people in a port city. I certainly met my share of Jan. Downright gentle, in their way, but they never pull any punches when they talk. You always knew just where you stood with them. Maybe that's because they weren't using that proxy-English you were talking about, just relying on their autotranslators to approximate their meanings. But believe me, that frankness is nothing to be ashamed of. I liked it."

"So, am I offending you by being polite?" he asked.

"Nah, you're cool," she said, and she began gathering up her fishing gear.

"Is that a weapon for killing fish?" Paul asked. He hadn't recognized it at first.

She shrugged again. "That was its original purpose. I was doing 'catch and release' with an adherance pad instead of a hook, so I suppose that makes it just a tool for... scaring and annoying fish."

"To what purpose?" Paul asked.

"Mostly just to give me an excuse to sit and stare at the water."

"Why?" he asked.

"'Cause it's pretty," she said, thinking he sounded like a toddler asking "why?" to everything.

Paul looked at the lake—curiosity about which had drawn him here in the first place, for outside of recordings, and having seen the ocean pass below him in a shuttle, he'd never seen a standing body of molten water before. Callisto had liquid water, of course, an enormous amount in fact, but it mainly lay in that worldlet's depths, untouched by Jupiter's light. Here, light danced across the undulating silver surface and sparkled through the dark green leaves, all of it filtered through the moist and heavy Earthling air. Such a bizarre sight, and yet she was correct that there was an eerie beauty to it. He could feel the movements of the gently convecting water and the creatures swimming in it through his three feet. The utility of bullying the fish eluded him utterly. Yet he was astonished to realize that—taking in these ethereal surroundings and talking to this funny little blob monster—all of a sudden, he felt more at ease in an Earthly environment than at any other time since he'd first set foot on this Godforsaken rock six years ago.

There was a pause. "That's very kind," Paul said. "What is Eppleberg like?" he asked, an idea forming. He'd been so antipathetic towards humans when he'd first come that he'd shunned Earthling company these past six years, living at the embassy and rarely leaving it. Such behavior was utterly contrary to his purpose here, and he knew it was long past time he corrected it.

She cocked her head. "Quiet and peaceful. I don't know how I'd compare it to a Jan warren, but in human terms, I'd say it's quiet and peaceful. The people are mostly Mennonites, which means... Well, Mennonites are a pretty diverse bunch, but in our *local* case, it means, among other things, that they're not strict luddites like the Amish are, but they take a pretty minimalist attitude toward technological conveniences. They're old-fashioned farmers. You guys can relate to that, right?"

# 12

After the Genomic War had raged between the various genetically engineered subgroups of man, and then the Android Uprising a generation after that, luddite movements had grown in popularity—such as the Amish and Mennonites among the religiously inclined, and the Neohippies among the nonreligious—and the term had ceased to be a pejorative. Two centuries ago, there had been a diaspora from this land, when Alfheim's forces had occupied this section of North America in the Genomic War. When the Dutch had returned at war's end, they, like the Hebrews returning from Babylon, were somewhat changed—and outsiders followed them, seeking the kind of peaceful life the long war had denied them. More outsiders had followed in years since, and the Plain people were today a far more ethnically varied group than they'd once been.

"Yes. It's one of the main reasons I came to this area," Paul said. The Earthlings' culture was too young for them to have found a level of technology with which they could be reasonably content, and most humans' decadent Arachnean technophilia repulsed Paul. Luddite movements of any sort attracted him. His own dependence on life support technology to survive here was a source of consternation to him.

"Of course, that makes *me* kind of an oddity," she said. "I'm planning to open a fix-it shop for what few gizmoes people *do* use. Transmitters, tractors, the odd nonsentient robot. I've been helping out at my Pa's produce farm, but..." Then she changed subjects. "What *are* you doing on Earth?" she asked. "You said you work at the Consulate, but that can't give you much to do in Center County of all places... although I guess Lawrenceton is still considered a major city. Just wanderlust?"

Honesty competed with shame in Paul's mind as he cobbled together his response. This was a matter about which he preferred to remain silent even among his own kind, let alone among the congenitally dishonest endoskeletal blob monsters of Earth. But he was growing to like this particular blob. "I promised God I would try to learn to better understand humans," he said. "Please don't ask why. The reason is private."

It wasn't an answer she'd been expecting, and she was startled. "I don't know much about the Jannite religions," she said, which was true.

"Actually, I'm a Christian," Paul said. "I haven't settled on a denomination yet. I may pick Mennonite. I need to better familiarize myself with them before I decide."

That *really* threw her for a loop. "Um......... O-kay, Brother Paul," she said. "Glad to have you with us!"

"Are you being sarcastic?" he asked. He was familiar with the concept—to say the opposite of one's actual meaning, but to make it clear through intonation what the actual meaning *was*. It was frequently used as a means of derision. He was not confident of his ability to recognize it.

Another shrug. "Maybe a little," she said softly. "I mean, I'm happy about it. I just wasn't expecting it. Do you know from 'irony'? It means kind of the same as 'funny.'"

"Yes, I'm familiar with Morisette's lyric on the subject," Paul said.

Indira thought back to her school days. "Morisette... Oh! Those things aren't ironic, they're just sad." *Which is ironic, which is genius,* a lit professor's voice droned in her memory. "No Paul, I'm happy to have you among the flock, I completely am. It's just amusingly unexpected because you're a tentacled rock monster." She did not stop herself saying this, since the other side of Jannite tactlessness among their own kind was that they were difficult to offend. "You're a perfectly *nice* tentacle monster. A perfectly gentlemanly tentacle monster."

Paul grasped humor only imperfectly, but supposed he could see the absurdity of it from a human perspective. "Yes, and you are a very charming bipedal bladder of fluid," he said.

"Nicest thing anyone's said to me all day! Thank you!" she said, grinning broadly. "Actually, Paul, I need to get home. My pa will be wondering what happened to me."

"Shall I carry you?" Paul asked. The courtesy gesture was automatic, for the Jan were a communal people. He was used to one-g gravity by now, and he figured that the little human and her fish-bullying equipment could not be very heavy.

"I..." she began to protest and then stopped. The spectacle of riding this critter through the center of town would be priceless. Spectacles were frowned upon, of course, but she found she really didn't care about offending such ones of the local yokels as were likely to raise a stink about it. "If you don't mind. I mean, people will stare."

*Good,* he stopped himself from saying. He didn't want to speak of his desire for humiliation. Christ had said that it was sinful to boast while fasting, and Paul agreed. And yet, did the wanton display of his grotesque alien form in public constitute a sort of backhanded boast? He hoped not. He wondered when he would become used enough to the human form not to find it equally repellant.

He lowered his massive arm, and her soft, moist, brown appendages wrapped round its dry, rough, gray surface, and she clambered up it like a tree limb. And so, with her legs dangling on either side of his eyestalk, and a hearty, "Heigh-ho, rock monster! Away!" she directed him out of the woods, his black wrecking ball eye doing its best to shift branches out of her way without breaking them.

She noticed with a start that she was hanging directly above his central mouth, used for burrowing, which was now shut. *Good thing it is shut!* she thought wryly. *Swallowing a big sack of water like me would probably poison him.*

The alien was radially symmetrical, having no front, back, right, or left. He spun as he walked (though he tried to minimize it for her sake), leaving her dizzy and making a challenge of directing him. "Just follow the brook up the way. We're one of the first farms you'll come to. The one with the big red waterwheel."

To his self-recrimination and surprise, she was getting heavy. He'd spent years exercising in preparation for Earth's gravity, and had continued in his years at the Consulate, but even *now,* he continually underestimated the weight of even small objects. He knew that Jan were perfectly capable of adapting to higher gravities than this, but a lifetime of low Callistan gravity had spoiled him, and it would take him time to toughen up. He was grateful when the wood and brick village of Eppleberg, surrounded by farmers' green fields, hove into view.

Although it was an old community, dating back nearly to the days of William Penn, Eppleberg wasn't much of a town: just a few roads and hoverpaths among a handfull of small houses, surrounded by farmers' fields or pastures full of dairy cattle, while other folk tended to small orchards, from which the town took its name. For most of its history, the nearest community had been the town of Lofthaven (originally Lufthafen, maintaining the longstanding Dutch tradition of unintentionally funny town names, though only a German-speaker would note its similarity to *Flughafen,* "airport"), but Lofthaven had finally been annexed by the city of Lawrenceton. Paul found that it was pleasantly quiet here, as she had said. And the air was pleasantly scented with methane...

"Sorry about the reek of cow shit," Indira said. "It's kind of everywhere."

"I don't mind," he said.

"I know you're too big for the sidewalks, but be careful on these hoverpaths," Indira warned. "We don't get much traffic, but I don't want a hoverlorry smashing into your big silicon-based tush." It was probably a needless precaution, she supposed, since Amish horses and buggies still trotted by here periodically and everyone knew to drive slowly. Of course, the Amish had the sense to put reflectors and transponders on their buggies. Paul was solid gray, and it was twilight.

"My tush contains both silicon and carbon," Paul said.

"That's nice. Make a left here."

The townsfolk did stare as Paul tromped through town, Indira riding astride him with a childlike grin, her arms wrapped round his eyestalk like a little girl climbing a slim tree. The adults at least tried to be polite and minimize their gawking, but the children gaped openly, some hiding, while others laughed and ran after them. There may not have been any great prejudice or suspicion against the Jan, but it was still akin to riding an elephant down Main Street. Earth's alliance with the Jan had been in place for over a century, and they were generally well-trusted, but it was rare to see one on Earth, let alone outside of the polar regions where they were most comfortable. Most Jan in Earth's solar system lived on Callisto, which they'd terraformed (or janniformed, rather) to resemble Janworld, many light years distant.

It was past sunset by the time they arrived at the simple Fenstermacher farmhouse. Out front was a wooden seat suspended from chains so that it could swing back and forth freely; Paul wondered as to its purpose. Tromping over a path of paving stones designed for tiny human feet, he came to a wooden door. Its white paint was peeling a bit, revealing the absence of the self-repairing nanites found in commercial paint. He towered over the door. Indira had climbed down from his eyestalk by the time Jawaharlal Fenstermacher opened it to greet them.

He was a swarthy, lean, severe-looking man, with a clean-shaven square chin; his garb was simple and monochromatic, a white shirt with black pants and suspenders. His moods were difficult even for other humans to gauge, so Paul stood scant chance of doing so. He stared at the Jan for a moment, his eyes a bit wide, but otherwise showing little reaction. "Good day to you, sir," he said. "Daughter?"

"Hi Pa. This is Paul. He followed me home. Can we keep him?"

Paul said, "I hope that I haven't intruded, sir."

"Not at all," Jawaharlal said. "I don't suppose you'd be wanting a bite of supper?" he added, a mite sardonically.

Paul fidgeted his tendrils. "Well, if you have a brick or a bit of loose masonry, that would be lovely. Thank you."

Jawaharlal didn't bat an eyelash. "Daughter, go and find your friend a brick."

"Um... Okay," she said, and trotted out to the workshed.

"Your house is..." Paul began to compliment the house, but then faltered at how to do so. He couldn't call it beautiful, for (as well as he grasped human aesthetics) it was in fact very stark. No adornments to speak of and the barest of furnishings. Very empty. Though not of all-Dutch ancestry, Fenstermacher was clearly a traditional Plain sort. Paul completely respected that, and felt suddenly conscious of the jewelry on his vocodor, though he doubted Pa Fenstermacher had noticed it. "...very traditional," he finished.

"Yes, I suppose so," Fenstermacher said.

"I wish that I could fit through the door to enter," Paul said, with heightening embarrassment.

Jawaharlal nodded. "I'm sorry about that."

"Oh, that's fine," Paul said. Not a very social man at all, Fenstermacher stood there, silently examining Paul while trying not to seem rude about it. Paul fidgeted in a slow, heavy sort of way.

"Here you go, Paul," Indira said, returning with a cinder block. She was strong for her size.

Grateful for her return, Paul hefted it in his hand/mouth easily, and took a taste. It was a little bitter, but not bad considering its origins. "Well, thank you," he said. "And good night, I guess. It was very nice to meet you both."

"Thank you for the lift," Indira said. "And please keep in touch! Our contact info is on the public service."

"I will," Paul said, gallumphing away into the night, rovolving slowly as he did so.

# 2

"Hello, Mr. Paul," Ambassador Kwan said. The appellation "Dwightson" was of little use at the Consulate, since a large percentage of the Jan there were also Dwight's sons, so he simply went by Paul. "I've come for the signed documents regarding the new Jannite reception terminal at Beijing Spaceport," she said.

"Yes, Ambassador Kwan. I'll have those documents for you posthaste," Paul told the Earthwoman before him. He regretted that he'd never learned Mandarin (let alone Proxy-Mandarin) and was grateful that she was using English for his benefit.

Trundling off to fetch the papers, he regarded the anteroom of the Jan Consulate; it was hard to believe he would finally be leaving this place after so many years. The room was an odd amalgam of Jannite and Earthling decor, intended to seem exotic yet inviting for Earthling visitors, while still comfortable for the Jan who worked there. The floor was concrete with a carpet of soft silica-moss, for tender human feet, but the moss was a white variety, resembling the frosts of home. The room was lit by standard Jannite lamp plants, their glowing crystalline vines clinging to the walls in baroque patterns—but far more of them than the subterranean Jan themselves had need for. Artistically grown stalactites hung from the ceiling in a myriad of hues, although only a few of these had been permitted to form corresponding stalagmites on the floor. Rectangular doors led to rooms intended for humans, while round tunnel entrances led down to the Jan workers' apartments and offices. Rectangular tables and small, four-legged upholstered chairs seemed out of place but were there for human convenience.

His time here had not been a waste, he reflected as he upended himself and crawled top-first into one of the round tunnels. He had learned a great deal about interacting with humans, far more than most Jan ever bothered to learn. Yet he wondered whether he had conquered his old prejudices.

He made a right at the tunnel fork, and emerged at the entrance to his superior's office. Among humans, Paul's boss called himself Bill. He was an old Worker, having been a passenger on the original Jan mission to Earth, along with Dwight and the other Matriarchs when they had still been motile. Bill liked human company well enough, but like many Jan, he was somewhat agorophobic, and preferred not to venture above the tunnels if he could avoid it. Bill's office was done in shades of brown, with colorful stalactites and a single crystalline glowmelon planted in the center of the ceiling. Very tasteful. There was a faint aroma of crystal-thorns in petroleum paste. Bill had just had lunch.

Bill tremorspoke a greeting to Paul, simultaneously using Paul's Jannite name and also projecting a sonar image *of* Paul. The "images" of Jannite speech were not perfect reproductions of the sonar echoes which would reflect from the actual object being described, but a sort of loose sketch of the object, bearing roughly the same relationship to it as an onomotopoetic English word like "slam," "bark," or "gasp" has to the sound it represents. By controlling the volume and delay of the sound emanated by each of the three feet, a sonar echo of an object could be imitated, with its size scaled up or down to roughly match the size of the Jan speaking. A mention of the scale of the object relative to the speaker was added as a prefix when speaking. Simple "words" did exist, mainly as conjunctions and the like, and there were also words to describe emotional states.

Paul caught himself before he forgot, and performed a one-third genuflecting arm gesture with eyestalk bob for his superior, with a two-ninths-resonant greeting tone. Bill chastised him for his slowness. *Acknowledgment,* Paul said without taking offense (at least not much).

Bill projected the sound for *query,* followed by another image of Paul, and a scaled-down image of Bill's office. Bill wanted to know why Paul had come. Bill had a very calm, uninflected tone of voice at all times. Paul found it irritating.

Paul answered by projecting an image of a human with its hand outstretched in greeting ("ambassador"), an image of a globe with Asia highlighted ("from Asia"), followed by the Proxy notation for the letters K-W-A-N. Then an image of a sheaf of paper, and a rough scaled-down image of a spaceport.

Bill gave acknowledgment. He trundled over to a printer and soon had the documents in his tendrils. He handed them to Paul. Bill then projected *"query,"* an image of an exit tunnel, and an image of the embassy, *"soon?"* He'd asked if Paul would be leaving the Consulate soon.

Paul confirmed this in Proxy English. "Yes, I will be leaving soon," Paul said. Bill had been among the first Jan to master human languages, both written and spoken, and had been one of Paul's tutors in the skill, and so Paul felt it right to demonstrate his facility with it now.

Bill made a sound roughly correspondent to a human's "hmph!"

"Do you object to my leaving?" Paul asked, neutrally.

"No," Bill said, in Proxy. "You do mediocre work. It is not for lack of skill with human languages. Indeed, you have a great aptitude for them. But you are lazy."

Paul knew of his linguistic aptitude and was pleased about it. Where once he'd thought of images and then hesitated as he tried to think of corresponding words, now the words came swift and imageless, almost unbidden. He'd been told by humans that he commanded a fairly impressive vocabulary. He hoped this did not constitute pride, and he was grateful to his teacher, but that did not lessen his desire to leave. "I am sorry. The work I do here does not interest me at all." Paul tremorspoke, *"Apology. Annoyance. Impatience. Gratitude."* He sonoprojected an image of piles and piles of paper, followed by *"Loathing."* "I came here to learn about the Earthlings, so that I can now live among them."

"That is probably folly," Bill said, "but I eagerly anticipate your replacement." Bill projected an image of a Jan worker shuffling papers with ease and enthusiasm.

"I doubt the *existence* of—" and Paul projected back the same image of the hypothetical worker shuffling papers enthusiastically.

"Earthlings invented paper," Bill observed.

*"Alas,"* Paul said.

Bill handed Paul the papers and urged him to get a move on. He projected a rough image of Ambassador Kwan tapping her foot. At least Paul was fairly sure the image was supposed to be her, specifically; Bill was better at telling humans apart than Paul was.

"The foot-tapping body language denotes impatience?" Paul asked.

"Yes," Bill said.

"Thank you, teacher. *Gratitude.*"

*"Go! Slow! Bad!"* Bill said.

Paul headed back toward the tunnel. En route, he encountered "Tommy," a member of the six-armed Warrior gender. Paul did not want to deal with him (the male pronoun was preferred in English for the sterile Warriors, over the more accurate but depersonalizing "it").

Though superficially quite different, a Warrior had the same basic anatomical structures as a Worker, just in different proportions. Tommy lacked an eyestalk, his black eyesphere being flush with the top of his torso, a far more secure location for the eye in combat; and his torso was somewhat flexible. What would be a Worker's arms were truncated so the hands were fused with the body, while the finger tendrils were elongated to form *six* tentacle arms ending in pickaxe-like hooks, these arms splayed in a flower-like ring around and below the eye. It always seemed to Paul that the arrangement ought to hinder vision whenever they raised their arms, but they seemed to cope. Lacking a Worker's hand-mouths, the finger-arms could nonetheless produce digestive acid for attacks. Instead of a central burrowing mouth, the ring of arms had a wide gap on one side that was taken up by a huge mouth used for attack as well as eating; this broke the radial symmetry, giving the Warrior a proper "front."

Tommy had always struck Paul as obsequious, and he was now reinforcing that impression. He genuflected with all his arms again and again and again, then approached Paul with fighting hooks held tight against his torso to present as unthreatening an appearance as possible. His attack mouth was shut tight, and even the stalkless eyesphere atop his body quivered nervously. In tremorspeech, he asked if he could help Paul with anything. Tommy had asked the question incessantly since Paul started here six years ago.

"No," Paul said.

"*Acknowledgement! Acknowledgement!* Yessir! Yessir," Tommy said.

Paul told him to stop the repeated acknowledgements and to stop being such a... it took him a moment to remember the Proxy English term... a "suck-up."

Tommy responded with a rough topographical map of Valhalla on Callisto, followed by an image of Paul. *"Fear. Relief. Gratitude. Caution."*

*Ohhhh!...* So, that's it. After all this time, finally Paul understood the reason for Tommy's behavior, and he was awash with conflicting emotions regarding it. He reassured Tommy that he had no intention of exiling the office-bound Warrior back to Valhalla.

*"Gratitude!"* Tommy said.

*"Alas,"* Paul said and entered the tunnel upward.

Unnerved by the encounter, Paul returned to the anteroom and handed the documents off to the ambassador. "Here they are," Paul said.

"Thank you, Mr. Paul. I'll see you later," she said.

"Perhaps not. I will be leaving the Consulate soon," he said.

"Oh? Are you being transferred?" she asked. "I have to admit, I can't make any sense of your people's appointment systems." While Jan society was run by their handful of breeding females, the Matriarchs, everything below that was a vast bureaucracy. It had been Paul's experience that humans from Asian cultures tended to be more appreciative of the worth of a well-run bureaucracy than North Americans, but Jannite bureaucracy was considered impenetrably complex by almost all humans.

"No. I have quit," Paul said. "I bought a house outside Lawrenceton."

"A *house?*" the ambassador said.

"Actually, it is a barn. I will use it as a house."

Her facial expression was unreadable to him, but her heart rate increased slightly. She made a small sound which he suspected to be a giggle. She wished him a good day, bowed, and left.

His business with the ambassador completed and his work shift over, he stepped out into Sol's light and gazed at Lawrenceton. The sun glittered from thousands of windows on hundreds of towers (population size having long ago forced the Earthlings to embrace vertical housing, and they disliked living underground if they could avoid it). Hovercars flowed through streets in vast numbers, and still more in the elevated tubeways above him, while planes and aircars flew above all. All these images swam blurrily before him in the thick air.

Paul and Indira had indeed kept in touch in the months following their meeting. As early as September,

Paul had purchased a disused barn in Eppleberg, which was large enough to serve him as a living space.

He received a stipend, for his people were of a fairly socialist bent; but that alone would not cover the great expense of maintaining his home and his health in this inhospitable environment, so finding paying work was essential. "I plan to be a writer," Paul informed her over visiphone one day, when she'd inquired how he intended to make his living outside the Consulate, where he'd been a minor middle management bureaucrat. "I have contacted an editor who says he likes my work." He owned an oversized keyboard, but he preferred to use an audio-controlled text transcriber, for his fingers were frustratingly slow for typing.

"I thought you couldn't handle fiction. It's like lying," she said. She was using the public visiphone at Hochleitner's Diner, since her father only owned an audiophone, and she didn't own a portable comm these days. She fingered the straps on her cap, and watched absently as Barney the waiter bused a table.

"I will be an essayist," Paul said. "As a Jan among humans, and with a fluent command of English, my point of view should be of interest to others."

"Hm. I can see that," she said.

"And I'll be a stone mason in my spare time."

She chuckled at this. "You *do* realize the two jobs have absolutely nothing to do with each other."

"Yes, of course. But, I had been taking masonry commissions even when I was a middle management translator. It was a useful means of compelling myself to deal with the world outside the Consulate. A biotic or nanoform building can be grown to specifications with little effort; but for aesthetic reasons if none other, there's nothing quite like good stonework, and it has been my experience that humans appreciate it. At risk of boasting, few humans can build with stone as well a Jan, and very few Jan are willing to endure the harsh conditions of Earth to work here in that career."

"How are you doing with those 'harsh conditions?'" she asked. The Jan were born space travelers. As burrowers from a big, geologically dead world (meaning Paul's ancestors could dig as deep as they liked without striking magma), they were comfortable at a wide variety of depths, gravities, temperatures, and atmospheric pressures. The deeper they'd dug into Janworld, the lower the gravity and temperature, and the higher the air pressure. And vice versa. Hence, they could endure the high accelerations needed for relativistic speed travel, and when they arrived, they could live quite comfortably on a little chunk of rock with just a whiff of atmosphere.

"When I moved here, I wasn't used to Earth conditions, but I knew I was fully capable of adapting to them, and I have," he said.

Indira regarded him; she knew he was over-stating his case a bit. Silicon life was extremophile in nature, needing extreme cold or heat to function at a chemical level. Jan were only partly silicon-based, their carbon-based component giving them a far wider range of endurance than they would otherwise have, but only up to a point. Earth's temperate zones were *endurable* for him, but she knew he was still miserably hot, the air pressure was too heavy for him, and he would never be able to safely travel into the tropics without life support gear. The gravity wouldn't bother him much, though; Jan got stronger, heavier, and slower as they aged. Still, she nodded. "So. Masonry. Is it true that you use your own poo as building materials?"

"Yes, actually," he said in some surprise. "They... are effectively bricks, and there are no organisms in your biosphere to decompose them. They're mostly silicon oxide from my respiration. Where did you... learn that?" he asked.

"Like I said, I've *met* other Jan," she said. "And it's sweet that you actually understand tact well enough *not* to come up to a human being and start talking about excrement."

"Yet," he pointed out, "*you* brought up the subject of excrement with *me.*"

"You *are* a Jan," she said. "Don't tell me you're offended?"

"No," he said. "The excrement taboo is a human convention."

"Well then," she said. "Besides, nobody's ever accused me of tact."

Paul hesitated again. "All right," he finally said.

"I'm glad you're coming back," she said. "You're fun."

"I poo bricks," he said.

"Life doesn't get much more fun than that," she said. "So... you plan to convert that old barn into your home?"

"It is my intent," he said.

"Wait." Her eyes widened in sudden excitement. "So you're going to need... systems to regulate air pressure, gasses, temperature... I can even put in some gear to simulate the UV radiation on Callisto's surface, if you want."

"*You* will?" Paul asked.

"Sure. Please! It's been so long since I've had a chance to work on any equipment even remotely interesting."

"Jannite life support equipment is interesting?" he asked.

"Everything's relative!" she said. "Come on. I installed life support gear for Jan quarters on Felice all the time. It's a piece of cake."

"Cake?"

"Idiom. I mean it's easy. I'll ask my friend Barney to help me lug heavy stuff." She watched Barney's blue and silver form wiping down an unoccupied table, squirting cleaning fluid from his index finger. "He's a freewill robot, and a nice guy. Very strong. I don't think he'll mind," she said.

"*I* can lug heavy stuff," Paul said.

"You're *not* gonna do heavy physical labor in Earth's heat with no place to rest," Indira said. "I'll make a list of the equipment. If you can come up with it and get it shipped, I can have it put in place by the time you want to move in."

Paul was taken aback. "That's exceedingly kind."

"Feh. You're doing me a favor. You have no idea how bored I am," she said.

By the time Paul arrived to take possession of the barn, Indira had already seen to the installation of a central cooling unit and vents, as well as solar collectors on the roof and a windmill to provide power (the Plain people always preferred self-sufficient power sources independent of the outside world's infrastructure). The walls and door were sealed to make them reasonably airtight, and the cooling vents could then be adjusted to pump air out of a room until it was unlivable for a human but cozy for a Jan.

After all this was seen to, Paul himself then set to redesigning the interior. He tore out the existing wooden structures for the stabling of horses and cattle, reinforced the walls and second floor with stone from the local quarry (Bebi Tsi's Gravel Pit, down Totter's Lane; visiting the rocky place, he was pleasantly reminded of his homeworld), and finally excavated a roomy cellar underneath to satisfy his racial yen for the subterranean. It was the heaviest labor he'd had since his youth, when he'd pulled his compulsory stint excavating tunnels with the Youth Mining Corps on Callisto; in fact, this was harder, because of the much higher gravity. But that was a good thing, in his opinion, since it would finally help build up his strength for an extended sojourn on Earth; he'd been far too idle at the Consulate these past years.

He intended to keep himself fed with his own small plot of Jannite crops. There was no risk of their spreading beyond his garden and causing ecological damage, since it would take constant care from Paul to make them grow at all in Earth's hostile environment. And, of course, he'd be able to supplement his diet with handfulls of the landscape itself, though that would not have been nutritious enough to live on.

Paul's arrival was the talk of the quilting bee at Eunice Lajevardi's house, as several of the local womenfolk prepared a quilt for Eunice's recently married daughter Shiphrah . Though not nearly so homogeneous a group as their ancestors had been, nor so isolated as their neighbors the Amish, the Lufthafen Conference Mennonites were not without elements of xenophobia, both in its classical sense of "fear of outsiders" and its modern sense of "fear of extraterrestrials."

The Lajevardis' waterwheel creaked and splashed in the background as they sewed. "So. We got an alien now," Adah Chan said in a disapproving voice. "I don't know what this town's turnin' into. I really don't."

"Adah, come now," Ruth Hochleitner said.

"He fixed up Kinshoffer's old barn real nice," Leah Baumgartner said. "Paid Old Yonnie Kinshoffer right well for it, too. You seen it?"

"I saw him workin' on it," Adah said. "Tentacles holding a paint roller. Thought I'd have a heart episode right then and there."

Ruth laughed. Eunice's dog Chaukidar perked his head up and barked at something. A small brown rabbit materialized from the grass and fled.

"Tentacles! That does give me the shivers, a little!" said Leah. "And he is so big!" She laughed at herself.

"It ain't funny. It ain't," Adah insisted. "What ever happened to 'be ye separate?' Now look, we're not the Amish, we all got English friends, but we have to be different from the World *somehow,* don't we?"

Ruth shrugged. Adah had raised exactly the same complaints when Ruth had hired Barney as a waiter at her diner. In fairness, a robot like Barney was technology *incarnate,* but Barney couldn't help that. "He wants to join the church," Ruth said. "You're *not* gonna tell him he shouldn't, are you?"

Adah accidentally pricked a finger with her needle and winced. She sighed. "You know well as I do, all the time, some youngster comes the city out," she said, gesturing vaguely in the direction of Lawrenceton, "and wants to 'go luddite' or whatever they call it. They don't last. Why, last one I remember staying the course was poor Ingrid, Lord rest her soul, and then her daughter up and left anyway, soon as she was old enough to do it."

"You say that as if Indira wasn't livin' here now again," Ruth said.

"Mm," Mrs. Chan conceded. "So, so now we got this... alien. From *space*. It's just silly. How's it going to...?"

"Now I spoke with him, just quick mind you," Leah Baumgartner said, "and I thought he seemed very nice. Kind of surprised me, but, you know. Talked just like a person, and so polite! I say let him join if he wants. Ain't no harm in it. Not like he brought his spaceship with him."

"Hmp," Adah said.

"I think it's gotta be real hard for him," Leah continued. "Tryin' to fit in on our planet. He's probably lonesome."

"Hm. Poor... what's his name?" Eunice asked.

"Mr. Dwightson," Ruth said.

"Hm? Oh, 'Dwight's Son.' I getcha. Ain't that a thing, 'Dwight's son.' Hm. Like... whoositz up there in space," Eunice said.

"Dwight?" Ruth asked.

"Yes! Him!" Eunice said. Dwight was the single most well-known Jan in the Sol system, having been their first ambassador as well as the first to receive a pronounceable Earthly name.

"Her," Ruth corrected.

"Eh?" Eunice said.

"Dwight's a her," Ruth said.

"Oh! Well. Poor Mr. Dwightson, all lonesome," Eunice said, bemusedly. "I could bring him a ham pie. Bet he's never had a ham pie. Up in space, y'know."

"I think he eats rocks," Ruth said.

"Eats rocks!" Eunice said. "He doesn't eat rocks. Nothing eats rocks."

"The aliens do," Ruth said. "They're like... worms."

"Worms?" Eunice said.

"Mm-hm," Ruth said, realizing she was uncertain herself that she knew what she was talking about. "Worms eat dirt. And dirt is just little rocks."

"A *worm* wants to join our congregation?" Adah demanded.

Eunice and Leah both laughed.

"He's not a worm!" Ruth said. "He just... eats rocks." And she chuckled, too. "Come now! We mustn't make fun of him."

"I think he'd *like* a ham pie," Eunice said. "Gotta taste better'n rocks!"

"Eating rocks ain't natural," said Adah.

"He's natural enough where he comes from," said Ruth. "The Good Lord made him, same as He made us. And he's young Indira's friend," Ruth emphasized, "and that's good enough for me." She could remember when Indira had come home from outer space, so incredibly upset, tears welling up at anything and everything, and seeming to be without anyone in the world. Ruth knew what rejection was like. So Ruth had resolved that she would stand up for Paul against any objection because Indira had identified him as a friend, and Ruth believed Indira needed friends.

When Paul's customization of his barn/house was finally complete, Indira came to visit him with a housewarming present of "stone soup," served in an insulated bucket. She hoped she'd followed the recipe properly at her machine shop, using her chemistry expertise to make the normally foul-smelling dish not stink. It was sometimes called "tar soup," since most of the ingredients were petroleum products. These were mixed with solvents to keep it liquid when served freezing cold, with small stones of different types floating in it like vegetables.

She was startled to find that, though it resembled a barn on the outside, the interior walls of Paul's home were all molded, gray-white stonework. Odd scalloping and swirling patterns were carved into the walls, as well as many abstract bass reliefs which she took to be Jannite writing. Luminous silicon-based plants created patches of light which she supposed would appeal to a Jan's sensibilities but were somewhat disorienting to her. So this was to be his little piece of Callisto, she supposed, with the exterior of the building still conventional-looking enough to avoid being a spectacle.

Indira was further surprised to find him reading a conventional, paper codex book. It was oversized, but even so, she figured he must be having trouble reading it. A Jan's 360° vision was not well-suited to two-dimensional images, not even text. Even Jan who could read Earth languages typically used text readers that projected the letters above the screen in a 3D form. The Jan's native writing resembled abstract bass-relief carving corresponding to sonar images, and was mostly indecypherable to a human without computer assistance.

This one room, a foyer he could use to entertain guests, was quite large for a human, but probably not for him. A Paul-sized round-arched doorway led to the airlock to the refrigerated interior of the barn.

"What are these in this alcove thingy in the wall?" she asked, seeing row upon row of lumpy, rainbow-colored glass plates.

"Icecrawler shells," he said. "I used to collect them in my youth. They're animals that look a little like Earth's crabs, but with nine legs. They're translucent. At least, I think to a human's eyes, they'd be translucent.

They shed their carapaces as they grow, and I would find them scattered on the ground. The animals themselves could never survive in this heat. Their insides would boil. I was a little afraid that the shells would be damaged in local conditions, but they seem fine."

"Hm. They're very pretty," she said. She stole a glance at the book he was reading. "That a Bible?" she asked.

"Yes," he said, closing it and setting it down on a stone table. "Oh, thank you for the food!" He dipped a hand/mouth into the frigid concoction and began slurping. It was a little bland (it didn't need anything fancy, maybe some shreded mica for texture, or granulated feldspar to bring out the flavor) but he appreciated the effort and he wasn't going to quibble. He'd gotten very tired of the Consulate cafeteria.

"You're welcome," she said, setting the bucket down on a small column she took to be a table as he set to chowing down on it. She was amused at the fact that, since the mouths in his hands were not used for speech, he could hold down the conversation while happily slurping away with one hand. His third large mouth, at the apex of his tendrils, was used for tunnel-digging, and she assumed he had used it to help excavate the earth under the old barn. She wondered how the taste of Earth dirt compared to Callistan dirt. She noticed he'd swapped his old green life support belt for a black one, and his new vocodor was unadorned.

He'd set the book down open, so she checked what section he'd been reading. She laughed a little. "The Song of Solomon is a very beautiful passage," she said, "but I'd be afraid that the metaphors would be lost on you."

"The metaphor of the two lovers representing God and Israel?" he asked.

"No," she said, "I meant the more basic metaphors. Of doves and pomengranites and stags representing... well... what they represent."

"Oh, yes. Mating," he said, "Well, I suppose that is beyond my ken. Love, romantic love, is an alien concept to my people. Children are born from the Matriarchs and raised communally. Our genders are so different that to a human they must seem like different species. Couplehood does not exist for us."

"That's kind of a shame," she said.

"God's plan for us is clearly different. We *have* friendship," Paul said. "Human love seems like it must be a burden as often as it is a blessing."

"Well it's..." she trailed off. "You know, I was going to try and convince you that love is a beautiful thing, but, you know? I've... In my life... Let Solomon do it. He's better at it," and she left it at that. She looked around the room. Most of the furnishings were stone, as she supposed they would be on Callisto Colony.

One of the main reasons for the Jan's success as a widespread interstellar race was that, as a silane rather than organic race, they preferred to live on cold, rocky worlds that few other races were likely to *want*, which saved them from most territorial conflicts. Callisto's gravity was light for them, but they could deal with it, as they were naturally able to adapt to a wide variety of conditions. By rights, Indira thought, no critter that was used to conditions on Callisto—even an environmentally engineered Callisto—could survive *easily* on Earth, and she again wondered what ghastly manner of air filters and other aids poor Paul must be using nearly continuously.

She suspected that the life support gear in his belt projected into orifices both natural and surgical. It had to be uncomfortable as hell, she thought.

Well, he'd requested that she not ask his reasons for his mysterious oath to come here, and she supposed she ought to respect that. His use of a paper codex Bible was particularly curious. Why was he trying to "go native" like this?

The Jan were a spiritual people. Earthlings had been surprised when the first contingent of Jan colonists to arrive in Earth's system a hundred years ago (following a hundred years of clumsy long-range communication by radio and gravitic transmitter, further hindered by the language barrier and time dilation effects of the Jan's spacecraft approaching at relativistic speeds) had turned out to be such a culturally diverse lot, even within just a handful of colony ships. Though perhaps this ought not have been a surprise. The Jan had made a conscious decision to include representatives of as many of their different cultural and ethnic groups on the colony ship as possible, just as Earthlings would likely have done.

Many people were annoyed to learn the Jan practiced religions, and still more were annoyed (or, at the least, surprised) to find that they had religions *plural*. Atheists were dismayed that these aliens had creeds at all, and religious folk were surprised at the plurality of said creeds. There were also Jan atheists and agnostics of several stripes. So nobody on Earth got their philosophy of life particularly validated or invalidated by the visitors from the stars. Many humans felt cheated by this.

A bastardized amalgamation of several mutually contradictory Jannite religions called Astroism spent a good twenty years as the cool religious-cult-to-annoy-your-parents-with-du-jour. Even Jannite missionaries (and they did have them, in varying flavors) became irritated with it. In the nature of such things, most of these cults fizzled out in less than a generation. Some human cults had even formed worshipping the Jan's ruling Matriarchs—a phenomenon which the Matriarchs themselves loudly condemned but which still persisted at some level.

"Oh, Mrs. Lajevardi brought me a ham pie earlier," he said. "I told her that I couldn't eat it, but she insisted I take it, and I did not want to offend her. I'm afraid it's cold."

"Eunice Lajevardi's ham pie? Oh, lemme at it! No way it's spoiled in this icebox you call a house."

"Are you cold?" Paul said, handing the pie to her.

"I'm okay," she said. She tried not to shiver. He kept this foyer chilly, but perfectly tolerable for humans. The other rooms were kept to Jan standards, and unendurable for a human.

"Does it require flatware to eat? I don't have any forks or knives or spoons," he said.

"Don't sweat it," Indira said, clawing out a chunk of cold pie with her bare hand and reveling in the chance to act like an unmannered trog with impunity, even with someone watching; *I miss college,* she mused. She shoved it in her mouth messily and grinned. "Mm, that's good! She puts curry in it. Only woman in town who knows to do that. My grandma used to do it that way."

"I'm glad it won't go to waste. And I'm glad I had some food to offer you. That is customary here, isn't it?" he asked.

"Hm? Yeah, yes it is," Indira said after swallowing. "You know what you should do, if you want to meet people?"

"What?" he asked.

"Invite them to dinner. Ruth Hochleitner's diner could cater it for you. No, scratch that. *I'll* cook it for you. It's been forever since I cooked anything big." She looked bemusedly again at her stony surroundings. It would be like dining in a cave.

"That's very generous, after you already helped prepare my home," he said, touched. "I want to be a good neighbor. Your family's friends would, of course, be welcome as well."

"Our family friends," she said, chuckling ruefully. "Um...." She trailed off.

"What?" Paul asked.

"I should've... Yeah. We're misanthropes, Paul. Pa and me both. Honestly, I don't know who we'd invite. We're practically hermits." At this last word, Paul visibly shuddered. "What?" she asked.

"Don't worry about it," he said, hurriedly. "A dinner with just the two of you might be preferable, actually." he said. "I am surprised, though. Not about your father. But *you* seem... more gregarious than that."

She shrugged. "Maybe around you, I do," she said, quietly. "You're a little more interesting than most of the folks around here. I don't mean to sound like a snob by saying that."

"You don't," he said. "I'd be surprised if I didn't seem different from the local populace."

"Well, yes, of course," she said. The she appended it, "But you're not *that* different. I mean... You've gone native pretty thoroughly, *Paul,*" she said, emphasizing the name. "It's... weird."

He wasn't sure what to say to that. It was indisputably true. He decided to try to make a joke. "Not in my choice of decor, surely," he said.

"Well, no," she said, twirling around with her arm extended to indicate the room. It was a surprisingly graceful motion, he thought. "Turning a barn into a cave is sure weird enough." She was surprised there wasn't more of an echo off these hard walls. She noticed the strange manner in which the stone surfaces were roughened and scalloped, and figured it might be to muffle the sound. If so, it was a neat trick.

Indira said, "Hey, we can invite Pa's hired hands, Amos and Thrym. I can't imagine either one of them turning down a meal."

Paul attended a worship service at the local meetinghouse. It felt uncanny to him to finally be doing this, and though an Anabaptist service was far simpler an affair than most church services would have been, he had attended no others to which to compare it. He'd had to enter through large delivery doors in back, and he stood in the back of the sanctuary where there was room for him if he bent his eyestalk over. Indira and Jawaharlal sat near him, as did Ruth Hochleitner and the robot, Barney Estragon. The congregants attempted not to stare at him and failed utterly.

There was a capella singing of hymns, and talk of church business. Then came the sermon, which was about the book of Jonah, the prophet who shirked God's command to preach repentance in the wicked city of Ninevah, lest He destroy their city. Instead Jonah fled by boat. He was swallowed by a huge fish, miraculously survived inside it for days, and was then vomited back onto dry land. The Lord having made His point, Jonah then reluctantly completed his mission (the fish was of course frequently cited by cynics as one of the most outlandish stories in the Bible, but be that as it may).

The Ninevites listened and repented their sins, so the Lord spared Ninevah.

Yet—and here lay the crux of the story—Jonah had *wanted* God to destroy Ninevah. He had refused his task not out of fear of the Ninevites or fear of his own shortcomings, but because he'd known God would forgive them if they repented. And He had. So now Jonah went into the desert to sulk. A plant sprouted to shade his head, but then quickly withered. Jonah complained about the plant's death. God then told Jonah how absurd it was for him to bemoan the death of a plant, and yet complain that God had spared the lives of the thousands in Ninevah. The preacher concluded, "The Lord loves His creations. He wants us to love, forgive, and look out for one another, even as we ask Him to do for us."

Afterward, the congregants met to chat outside. Many wanted to speak to Paul, and he felt overwhelmed and did his best to keep up with the chattering and curious creatures. He was soon brought up short by a small child attempting to *climb* him. The boy hadn't gotten much further than his leg, due to lack of proper handholds, when his mother scooped him up and apologized. Noticing Barney approaching, Paul thanked him for his work on his home.

Barney said, "The preacher talked about Jonah. It makes me think of something. My first time here made me feel like Queequeg."

"Like what?" Paul asked.

"Queequeg is a man in a long book. It is called *Moby Dick.*"

"Oh. Fiction," Paul said, rather dismissively.

"You do not like made-up stories?" Barney asked.

"I'm... predisposed against it. I'm a Jan, and fiction is lying," Paul said.

"No. Fiction is parable. Christ used parables. Do you know about them?"

"Yes, although it's an idea around which I had a hard time wrapping my head," Paul said, pleased at his use of the new idiom.

"It is a thing that is like another thing. So people can understand," Barney clarified.

"I suppose that's true," Paul said.

"I like to read books. Books are good."

"All right," Paul said, becoming mildly impatient. He wondered why the machine spoke in such an odd fashion.

"Queequeg is a cannibal."

"Cannibal!" Paul said. His own race of prey held any sort of predation to be beastial, so cannibalism was particularly horrific.

"He has tattoos, and he is purply yellow. He comes to a church, and the sermon is about Jonah. Queequeg is nice, but he looks scary. When I came here, I felt like him. Do you feel like him?"

"I suppose I do," Paul conceded.

"I think it will not be as hard for you to fit in as it was for me," Barney said. "I am not human, and people are used to me now. Besides, people did not make you."

"Make me? What...? Oh! But... you are *conscious,* aren't you?" Paul asked, not sure he saw the problem. Barney was an Earthling, after all, not an alien. The Jan rarely made artificial beings of Barney's sort, but sensible law and tradition held that if a robot were made with ability to think and feel, it should be treated fairly. Humans had similar laws, but prevailing sentiment was often another matter. Still, that the prejudice against conscious artifacts should be greater than that against aliens surprised him. Then he remembered where he was, in a land where advanced technology was anathema, and Barney's point made perfect sense. "Oh, I see, of course. Have you been accepted here, finally?" Paul asked, sympathetic and also concerned about how Barney's experience might speak to his own future here.

"Yes. They do not like people to make robots. But they know I did not make myself. Other people made my body and my brain. Just like a mommy grows a baby inside her. I think God made *me inside,* my soul. The town people like me now. I am glad. I am happy I am here. But I am shy. So I sit in back," Barney said.

"I stood in back because there's room there," Paul said.

The obvious question Indira expected from her father was not long in coming. "Why don't you ever cook like this for your own household?" He didn't say family, since their family was only the two of them, but "household" included Amos and Thrym.

"Because it's a big dinner with guests, Pa," she said. "When is the last time you invited a bunch of guests over to eat?" She did enjoy cooking. Just a different sort of engineering, really. She dashed about the kitchen as Jawaharlal could remember her mother Ingrid having done, long ago. It made him very wistful, but his stoic face was unchanged.

More and more as he aged, Jawaharlal found himself recoiling instinctively from any strong feelings—even joy could be frightening in its intensity, such that he forcibly shoved it down to his usual equibrium in which he could function. And if joy was unpleasant, how much worse sorrow, loneliness, horror, loss... he thought of Ingrid, the special one person who had loved him and whom he'd loved in return, and now she was gone—gone to heaven, but still gone from his earthly existence—and all he had left was the daughter who until recently had scarcely acknowledged him.

Yet Indira *was* here, now.

Jawaharlal's father Saul had been a mean man. When Jawaharlal's older sister Nahal had left to marry an outsider, Saul disowned her. The last that Jawaharlal had heard, she had moved to Alpha Centauri. Thanks to starflight time dilation, his older sister was now surely younger than he was. He missed Nahal almost as much as he did Ingrid, who had been the fresh air of his life. Jawaharlal had determined, when he'd seen the first signs of prodigality in his daughter, that he would not treat her as Saul had Nahal, and he was certain that he had not. He loved her deeply and thanked God she was home.

He smiled despite himself. The kitchen was warm and smelled delightful. "Do you *want* me to invite guests over to eat?" he asked mildly.

She was caught off-guard and said, "No."

"Hm," he said.

"And we're Pennsylvania Dutch. *Aye, arre daedi!* And Dutch folk do all their socializing by eating. It's why a lot of the people in town look like walking pickle barrels with hats and bonnets."

"Daughter, do not speak ill of others," he said for the squillionth time in a voice like a rolling millstone.

"All right, not 'a lot.' Some. A non-negligible *some*. And all I'm saying is that people here like to eat. It's not a criticism, it's just an observation. There's a difference!"

"Hm," he said.

"You know, the fact that you don't extend invitations is one thing, but how do you avoid receiving them? Do you know how hard it is to be an introvert around here?" *Not that I've ever had trouble doing it,* she thought ruefully. *Yay for heredity. Yay for it.*

"Hm."

"Hm!" she imitated him. "For the amount of arguing we do, you're not very good at it!"

He crossed his arms and leveled his stony gaze at her, and she knew she'd lied. Her father was a sufficient master of debate that he needn't even open his mouth to do it.

"Anyway," she muttered, "I need vinegar for the potato salad."

"I'll fetch some," her father said.

"Thank you for this food, and for the effort it represents." Paul said and then added, "Why are you helping me so much?"

Indira shrugged while she pulled more containers off the wagon. Samson, the Clydesdale that had pulled it there, regarded Paul uncertainly, whinnied, and shook his mane. "'Cause this town needs a little color. And I like you."

"Oh. Thank you," he said. "'Color'?"

"Diversity. Spice. Excitement. Something to break the monotony," she said.

"Oh," he said. "I thought that was exactly what people here *didn't* want."

She smiled wickedly. "Yeaaaaaah."

"Perhaps my coming to this community was a mistake," Paul said.

"No! No," Indira said as she put the bowl of baked beans down on the grass and took his huge arm in her hands. "I'm only teasing you. People here are nice. It'll be fine. They'll like you, you'll like them, everybody will gain five kilos, and it'll be a swell dinner. Just um... try not to... loom."

"Loom?"

"You're very big. Don't hover over people like a boulder that's about to topple. Remember that we're little, and little people are afraid of getting squished." She patted the skittish horse's huge neck and said, "Nobody gonna squish you, boy, nuh-uh." Samson snorted.

Paul agreed to forebear looming as best he was able. Upon entering, Indira was impressed at the obvious effort to which Paul had gone to make his odd dwelling place hospitable to his Earthling guests since the last time she'd been inside. He'd brought in a long wooden table with chairs and had fed the glowing crystal-plants special tinted solutions to light the place nicely. He'd arranged candles on the table—again, impressive, since many Jan were unnerved by the close presence of open flame. It was also redundant, with the lamp plants, but the place was too big to rely on candlelight alone. He'd purchased good silverware, she noted. *Oh yeah,* that'll *make a good impression on a relentlessly Plain guy like Pa,* she thought, with a wry grin of sympathy. The tabecloth was of local make with a floral pattern.

Indira had invited Ruth Hochleitner, who operated the diner near the edge of town. Ruth had been a friend of Indira's mother Ingrid. She was Indira's notion of what a Mennonite ought to be: cheerful, friendly, virtuous, content, and to all appearances at peace with both God and her fellow man, at least as much as any mortal can reasonably aspire to be. She was vaguely aware Ruth had intended to marry and have kids, but some youthful romance had failed and no other had come along to replace it. There was a lingering sadness in her eyes from that, if one knew to look. But her eyes were generally merry. She'd taught school, and as caring for the young came naturally, it was she who had most helped Indira's mother, newly fled from the city, in learning Plain ways, till she had finally settled down with Mean Saully Fenstermacher's sullen boy Jawaharlal.

Ruth was puffing a bit from the walk. She was a hefty person. She handed Indira a flower-painted tureen full of tuna something-or-other that smelled wonderful.

Next came the Fenstermachers' two farmhands. Amos Baumgartner was a big, beefy, blonde-haired fellow in his early twenties, with wide blue eyes under pale eyebrows. None too bright a fellow, Indira felt, but cheerful and good-natured enough. His family had lived in this area since Billy Penn's day. Pretty handsome guy, actually, but he was too young for her and immature even for his age.

Thrym Scyllaschild was a grumpy old Tesk man, the Tesks having been bioengineered as cannon fodder by Imperial forces during the Genomic War two centuries ago. He was gaunt, wiry, and strong, with cat-slit eyes that caught light in darkness, jaundiced-looking skin that could withstand intense radiation, and pointed teeth. He was short and broad-shouldered for a Tesk, their race usually tending toward a tall, lean, hard musculature. His hair was an iron gray. Like many of his kind, he'd led a hard life, there being prejudice against Tesks on Earth even today; and he had now settled into a surly senectitude, though his engineered genes gave him more than enough strength to keep doing heavy farm labor.

Jawaharlal was his usual stoic self. A certain amount of stoicism was endemic to his people, and to this land, but Jawaharlal took it to a far greater extreme than most.

She saw her father had noticed the silverware, but his scowl only lasted a moment and was replaced by blank politeness. She smiled. *Surrounded by extraterrestrial weirdness, and he takes exception to the fancy silver. That's my Pa...*

"Thank you for coming," Paul greeted them, fluttering about the room as best that so unwieldy a being could be said to flutter. "I hope you enjoy the meal." Paul himself had a large plate of fine, amber-colored crystalline organisms that he'd grown in his garden. They all sat at the table, except Paul, since Jan do not sit. The table was absurdly low for him, and Paul towered over everyone else. *I am looming,* he sighed to himself.

The humans chattered a bit about people Paul didn't know. He surmised that this was "small talk," and his understanding was that it served roughly the same familiarizing function that nonverbal tremorspeech did among Jan, or that grooming one another's fur did among apes.

"How's Barney?" Indira asked.

"Oh, he's fine," Ruth said. "I told him he was welcome to come, but he felt shy because, y'know, he doesn't eat. I'll tell him you were asking after him."

"Pa, if you'd say grace," Indira said.

The elder Fenstermacher nodded and claspsed his hands. "Father, we thank you for this meal and for this day. Please bless this gathering and guide us in all we do so that it may be acceptable in Your sight. We thank you for Your love and for the sacrifice of Your Son, Jesus Christ, in Whose Name we pray. Amen." It was the same prayer he'd said, with very little variation, at every meal Indira had ever eaten with him. But it wasn't a bad prayer at all.

As the guests began passing the platters around in a circle to serve themselves, Ruth inquired about Jawaharlal's crop this year, and Jawaharlal answered very gravely, and Indira rolled up her eyes because her father always sounded grave when discussing the crops as if he expected blight and locusts at any moment. Thrym kept eyeing Paul, strangely.

Jawaharlal then turned to Paul and directed the conversation to something that had been all over the news recently. "So Paul, what can you tell us of these new aliens out in the, um, the Oort?" Few Eppleberg locals followed outside news reports closely, but it was impossible to avoid recent news about new creatures at the Solar System's edge.

Paul, still standing, shuffled his feet. "Please bear in mind my youth—I was born after Callisto Colony was established, and I've never traveled outside Earth's solar system, so I have no more firsthand knowledge of them than you do. My people's records about the race your press has named the Arachne have been made public."

"Well," Jawaharlal said, "you probably know more about it than we do."

Paul moved his tentacles in approximation of a human shrug. He'd worked in the Consulate long enough; he could deliver a news report. "Well, we've told you about them for a long time, so I don't think your solar system's governments are *surprised* that the Arachne have shown up. It's true that the Arachne didn't give advance notice of their coming, as my people did, but that's typical. From what I understand, they're not a very considerate lot."

"Are they a threat?" Thrym asked tersely.

Indira mused as she regarded old Thrym. He was such a stereotypical Tesk, seeing everything in military terms. She often wondered what he was doing in Dutch country. Still, there was a lot of such talk these days. Fear of alien invasion dated back as far as H.G. Wells, and it was well known that the friendly Jan were not the only civilization Out There.

"Not a military one," Paul answered him, "but perhaps a cultural one. They're in your Oort Cloud now, which by most local interstellar treaties would be considered unclaimed open space, since the comet clouds of different solar systems overlap one another. I doubt they'll cross into your Solar System proper without your permission. They prefer living in low and zero-g environments like comets, asteroids, and their own space platforms, so they typically don't covet other people's planets."

"The same way you guys don't get in anyone's way, because you like living on barren rocks instead of warm squishy worlds like Earth," Indira said.

"Exactly," Paul said. "Even ignoring the fact that they're not very warlike, you needn't fear an attack from them because Earth simply doesn't have anything they'd be likely to want. Not even the planetary real estate itself."

"What's the cultural threat you mentioned?" Thrym asked.

"Can I have some more of the baked beans?" Amos said.

"Here they are," Paul said, lifting the serving dish over to him.

"Thanks!" Amos said, trowling a large serving onto his plate. "Aw, there's no bacon in them."

"Shush," Ruth said.

"Cultural threat?" Thrym pressed.

"Right," Paul said. Actually, he was rather enjoying this. He'd feared he'd be treated as a freak. Instead, he was a learned authority. His dinner party was going quite well! He saw Indira smile and nod for him to continue. "Well," he said, "the Arachne's attitude toward technology is almost diametrically opposite the Jan's. We practice restraint in use of technology for personal convenience, because we believe doing otherwise encourages decadence and a sense of purposelessness. The Arachne revere technology. Their very bodies are artificial. Their race's original body shape has been virtually forgotten after eons of bionic and biological engineering to give individuals whatever body type they feel like at any given time.

"Even their brains are mutable to such tinkering, reducing their personalities and identities to an inconstant haze as they change their inmost selves in accordance with their every passing whim. And the irony is that, despite the appearance of embracing technology and constantly advancing, their technology is at a virtual standstill because they lack the patience or attention spans necessary to improve anything." Paul realized he was reciting Jannite policy as surely as Jawaharlal had recited his memorized prayer. But, as with the prayer, it was a statement of policy that Paul agreed with.

"That so bad?" Thrym asked.

"The Arachne arrive and promote the glories of heavy body modification. In time, a whole race might body mod itself out of existence, becoming physically indistinguishable from the Arachne. And this has happened, repeatedly. The Arachne are not a single species. They're an amalgam of many." Paul suddenly stopped and said, "I must sound like a bigot. Please understand, I'm sure they're as varied a group of individuals as any. Moreso, in some respects. But I find their culture distasteful."

*And since their culture defines them physically and neurologically, they* are *their culture,* he thought, but he did not say it. He was trying to learn tact.

"Hnh. But you guys... you're *perfectly* benevolent. That right?" Thrym said.

Paul was unsure if he detected sarcasm. "Well, not perfectly. But we have tried to be good guests here," Paul said. "We're grateful for your hospitality in letting us colonize a world you weren't using, and we've tried to help y..."

"Why *are* you here?" Thrym interrupted.

Indira glared at him. What was the codger doing?

Paul said, "Well, apart from the motivation of simple friendship, our greatest strength has always been our network of alliances. There are far more powerful civilizations than the Jan in space, but it's known that to attack us is to attack all our allies, and so such attacks rarely come. It is completely to our advantage to have friends. It also allows for meaningful cultural exchanges since, like humans, we see fellowship and cooperation as desirable for their own sake."

"Mmh-hm," Thrym said, nodding. "Answer me straight. How do we know you won't take us over one day? The Mayas welcomed the Conquistadores."

"Aztecs," Indira said.

"Whatever! How stupid was that? Aren't we doing the same thing?"

Jawaharlal, amazed at his rudeness, said, "Brother, have a care!"

Amos said, "Mm? Oh. I'm sorry, Brother Jawaharlal," either apologizing for Thrym or mistakenly thinking he'd made some error of table manners.

While this sort of talk would have been wholly unremarkable among Paul's own kind, Thrym's directness seemed out of place here, and might mean hostility. Uncertain whether or not he ought respond, Paul said, "As I recall, Cortez showed his hand pretty quickly," and hoped he'd used the idiom right. "We've been among you as friends a hundred years now. Maybe I should be flattered that you think us so patient. But we have no motive other than those we've always given. I do not know what better proof of our trustworthiness I might give you than the near-universal acknowledgement among the races of space that my people do not lie. We've our faults, to be sure, but from the shackles of dishonesty we are virtually free."

Indira was smirking. Paul realized he'd been showing off his facility with English and was ashamed. It was clear she heartily approved, though. She quipped, "From the shackles of grandiloquence, though?"

At that moment, Paul would have laughed, were he able. Jawaharlal did laugh, which was a rare thing. Amos didn't seem to get the joke, Ruth seemed a little fuzzy on it but laughed anyway, and Thrym ignored it.

Thrym said, "We shouldn't've given up Callisto. When it comes to the Solar System, I believe in manifest destiny. We're Esau, trading our birth-right for a bowl of soup."

Indira said, "What Esau did was foolish, but it was also God's will. And if you remember the story, he and Jacob both made out okay, and they reconciled at the end. As for the Solar System being God's gift, surely His gifts are meant to be shared. And the Jan have given us more than soup."

"That right?" Thrym said, "What'd they give us? Any fancy technology? Any big, world-changing philosophies? Zip! Nada."

"We told you from the first that we were withholding technological information," Paul said. "We never lied or misled you about that. For the most part, we withheld technologies from you which we ourselves avoid using."

"Yes, but you still know how to *make* the stuff," Thrym said, "even if you don't like to *use* it. Don't you trust us?"

"No. We don't trust ourselves with it, either." Paul thought this was a good retort, but he didn't like being thrust into the position of apologist for Matriarch policies. He really wasn't a part of that world anymore, anyway.

"Don't pull that 'white man's burden' crap with me," Thrym said. Indira winced as Thrym swore at the dinner table with her father, and Ruth gave a little gasp. Thrym continued, "I been reading about a place called Elavia. You pen the natives in like pets!"

"That's a damned lie!" Indira had never heard Paul curse before. It frightened her. "Elavians can come and go freely. I've heard there are a few here on Earth. They're not an expansionist people. They've never shown much interest in leaving their planet."

"And I wouldn't guess you boys have encouraged them to stay there, eh?" Thrym said.

"It's their planet. We maintain a military presence there with their blessing," Paul said.

"Bullshit!" Thrym said, as Jawaharlal's eyes widened to the size of saucers, baffled as to why his normally taciturn farmhand was suddenly behaving this way. "Anybody could have seen this coming a hundred years ago! We're nothing but a damned protectorate!"

"We have sponsored your entry into the wider interstellar community," Paul said. "Surely *that* is of some value."

"Yeah, and now it's attracted more little green men to our borders," he said, invoking the age-old pejorative term for alien races. "Even if *you* guys are nice as you say you are, it's only a matter of time till someone shows up who *isn't,* and who *isn't* shy about showing off their technology. Then we're dead. And it'll still be your fault for bringing them here!"

Paul said, "No, it will be Edison and Marconi's fault for inventing the radio and sending omni-directional broadcasts into space. That's what attracted us here, and it will attract others in time. Surely it's to your advantage to have diplomatic relations with us and with Faldor and other nearby societies so that you aren't caught unprepared when that happens."

Indira was impressed with how Paul acquitted himself but was concerned that he was letting Thrym bait him. She'd always known Thrym was disagreeable, but she'd never expected this or she wouldn't have invited him.

"So you admit that there are hostiles out there!" Thrym said.

"Yes, the universe has its share of jerks!" It dawned on Paul, with some surprise, that he was extremely angry. He'd finally encountered a human who *fit* his early stereotype of humanity—even if Thrym wasn't, biologically speaking, a mainstream human. "Case in point!" he muttered.

Ruth tried to suppress a smile of amusement at this.

"Brother Thrym, Brother Paul," Jawaharlal interrupted, weightily. "Stop it!"

Jawaharlal was right, of course. Her smile just as quickly gone, Ruth gave Thrym and Paul both an absolutely glacial schoolteacher glare that reminded Thrym of his first drill sergeant many moons past, and he quietened.

"Yeah, hush up, Scyllaschild," Amos said, unnecessarily.

Thrym then said, "Well if you're not going to take this seriously, maybe I'll just leave."

Jawaharlal said, "What? Thrym! Don't go. We're guests, and can't we have a nice, peaceful supper?"

Instantly, Ruth changed the subject by launching into a long dissertation about her second cousin Haifeng who had recently married a fish farmer—"Nice boy, but he always smells like herring!"—and Ruth's audience and Ruth herself feigned fascination with the subject. Thrym sulked. The rest of supper was relatively uneventful.

Afterward, Indira apologized profusely to Paul for Thrym's behavior, and afterward she spoke to her father about him. "Why don't you fire him? He's such a jerk."

Jawaharlal said, "That's not like you, daughter. All Tesks have a temper. And even today, it is hard for them to find work. I will not fire him, but I will make it plain that he may not insult friends of our family."

Indira said, "Then... you *do* consider Paul a friend?"

Jawaharlal seemed surprised. "Yes. He is your friend, and so he is my friend."

"Thank you," Indira said.

# 3

Fall has come, and harvest.

Indira, small, lithe, strong, rides upon a cart, pulled by a horse. She has dropped off vegetables at the open air market, and is headed home. She has her repair shop now, but still runs odd errands for Jawaharlal. Her father prefers the horsecart over powered cars for such short trips. She took issue with it in her youth but is more amenable to it now. She likes the scenery and takes the ride slow. Even though it's hot. Humid. Dark eyes sting with sweat, and black hair under bonnet itches. Insects drone.

The horse, Samson, born when she was ten, now he's nearing twenty. He's a huge animal, his head droops, his mane in his eyes. He's hot, too.

The wagon is oak, painted black. Its surface is hot, when she lets her callused hands touch it. Well-made and well-maintained, it creaks only a little. The cobblestones are loud.

A breeze in heavy air carries rhubarb pies alongside the methane scent of cattle. Paul likes the latter. *He's welcome to it,* she thinks, smiles ruefully.

Heat and moisture and scents and the sound of insects and clop of hooves and rumble of wheels give a dreamlike quality to the morning; her mind drifts. She traveled this road countless times in her youth, and the fields and houses are scarcely changed. Green of trees and unripe grain. It is very beautiful.

Behind her, round and verdant mountains loom. Soon, they will be red, gold, amber. In winter, they'll be frosted, sparkling, stars come to Earth.

Days, the sky is blue, the waters separated from the waters, and among the pious farmers she is content. Yet nights, the stars beckon, space's siren song. Her heart is cloven.

An old bioblimp scuds the sky waters. Its hide glitters decadent in the sun. High overhead, product of a bygone age—but not so far bygone as her town's world—a rainbowed, opulent, mindless fat flying fish carrying passengers in a gondola on its belly. She thinks of Jonah. Relic of biotech's heyday, two hundred years back. She wonders if this blimp may be that old, as wrought flesh is less subject to time than men's flesh, or if it was grown more recently for nostalgia. She doesn't know, but prefers the former. Iridescent like a hummingbird wing—albeit a fat, fishy hummingbird wing—it veers slowly toward the nearby metropolis hidden from her view by sweetgum and oak.

The sound of handsawing from Stodt's carpenter's shop. *A carpenter's shop.* Just beyond these hills stand towers forged molecule by molecule, and others grown living like the crops in the fields, while here she rides a horse-drawn wagon past a carpenter's shop. Sometimes, she loves the simple self-denying anachronism of this place, and other times detests it. She usually feels both at once, and she supposes that is how most people feel about where they were bred. Behind blue sky, the stars sing, call. She wonders if it be piety to shun them.

Tears form. She holds them in. Kills them in their ducts.

Little town where nothing changes. Stasis is encouraged. Monotony made manifest. She sighs.

They know her for an odd one. In a stricter community she would be in danger of Shunning for past actions and beliefs. But she is not shunned. *Do I shun them?* she wonders. She attends Sunday meeting, of course, but what else? Social stuff is a Mennonite community's lifeblood. She takes far too much after her father, she knows. Hermitic old fart.

This can't be all there is to life. She knows from experience that it is not all life is or can be. That understanding is central to Plain thought. Those things the World-with-a-capital-W deems desirable are mere distractions from the pursuit of holiness.

Her mind reiterates, this cannot be all her life has become. And it must not be all that it remains. She groans in frustration.

The blue sky becomes a smothering blanket. The muffled stars behind it no longer sing, they howl and jeer. All the universe is her enemy, its components roaring at her as one, and she silently cries to God for succor and is unsure He hears her.

Panic seizes her, as all the landscape about her seems to convulse in almost hallucinogenic fashion. Not a convulsion that she can see or hear, for it is not truly hallucination, not sensory... but she feels it, she *feels* it.

She sees a groundcar drive past, and in her mind's eye, she sees the engine driving it, the chemical combustion in the engine, the molecules combining and breaking, the waves of energy passing and coalescing. The sense of how all the machines going past work. The sense of how all the matter around her is put together. Of all the waveforms of spacetime that constitute their particles. Her own particles. Her body and all matter just so many waves in cosmic fabric, and that fabric just part of something vastly larger beyond her comprehension, stretching on and on into what might be only the most minor of passing thoughts flitting through the infinite mind of God. Which isn't to say a minor thought might not be important to Him, since surely God does not have insignificant thoughts.

Why, when she looks at the trees and grass and wheat, does she feel apart from them, even as she stands in their midst? As though separated from their world by glass. She feels the urge to leap down and hug a tree just to feel, at that instant, intimate connection with it. With something. So hideously, solipsistically alone. She wonders *why.*

Her throat tightens. The faces of these people. All going about their damned business.

Always just one stimulus away from pitching off the deep end into frenzy, which often as not is so self-contained that no one else knows the wild panic going on behind her eyes.

She reaches Paul's house. Had she been headed to Paul's house? No, she led the horse here unconsciously.

Paul greets her. A simple word of hello, and the universe settles back into shape. Giving no outward sign of her inner turmoil, she returns his greeting, nonchalant, monosyllabic, casually smiling.

He asks why she is upset. *Only he could tell!* Tremorsense that hears the blood rushing in her veins. *How dare he!* For a sliver of a moment she is angry at his perception.

*What is he thinking?* She can't tell. He can't smile or frown.

He has no "tells."

He could be thinking anything.

She finds this hugely calming.

She grasps her arms around his torso and clings tightly as to a rock face in a storm.

"Why are you crying?" he asks.

"I'm all right now," she says. "I'm all right."

They were inside Paul's foyer, now. She welcomed its starkness, its differentness. No more clanging repetition and sameness. She sat in a simply upholstered chair.

"I hope I'm not a burden to you, coming over here."

"Not at all, not at all," Paul said. He lifted a tea kettle from the hotplate which he kept for those occasions when he needed to prepare human food. A fire or stove would have been more in keeping with the local culture, of course, but he wouldn't abide that kind of heat in his own home. He had once allowed Indira past the front anteroom he maintained for human visitors into his refrigerated living quarters. She'd had to wear a heated pressure suit, but she'd been fascinated by the weirdly curving alienness of the room. It reminded her of Crystal Cave in the Poconos, a little bit.

She sipped at the tea. It wasn't very good, but she knew of course that Paul himself couldn't taste it. It relaxed her anyway, and she was grateful for it. "My thoughts... race. Especially when I'm upset." She'd rarely even tried to explain this to anyone. Her father had never understood, although melancholy was hardly unknown among the Dutch. "'Tis a gift to be simple. It'd be a gift to be *able* to be simple! To shut off the overanalyzation for just a minute and work Candide's garden in peace like all my hayseed neighbors. I envy them."

The *Candide* reference went over Paul's head, he being largely oblivious to fiction, but he believed he got her gist. "The ability to analyze the problem is itself a gift," Paul said, hoping that was helpful. He wasn't sure he understood precisely what was troubling her so, but he would do his best.

"I guess," Indira said. "A centipede can't walk if he thinks about how he does it. If I could just *live*. Just experience. And not over-damn-think every fucking thing."

Paul said, "You'd be an animal."

Indira said, "And they die in the cold dark woods. They're probably no happier than us, and wouldn't know it if they were." Indira said, "I always used to blame my neuroticism on stir-craziness. There was nothing here to mentally stimulate me, so my mind went off on wild, strange tangents. So why didn't leaving home for Felice cure it? I feel trapped here, and I feel adrift out there. I'm like a dog that can't decide which side of the door it wants to be on."

She continued, "My Ma was an outsider. She came here voluntarily, joined a luddite community, wanted to be closer to God. It worked out for her. I totally respect that. But she couldn't help passing on her love of learning to me. Certainly couldn't help doing it biologically, regardless. It's in my blood."

Paul said, "Knowledge can lead to wisdom, and wisdom can lead to virtue. But knowledge, in and of itself, is not virtue, it is power. And while power can be used for good, it can very easily lead to wickedness." It was a standard Jannite belief.

"So you're recommending willfull ignorance?!" she said, incredulous.

*"No.* Ignorance is weakness, and there's no more inherent virtue in weakness than there is in strength. Besides, knowledge can be a path to wisdom, which *can* lead to virtue."

"Scripture says we're supposed to be innocent as doves *and* wise as serpents," Indira quoted. "I got no use for dumbth."

"I've never heard that word," Paul said.

"Shaddap," she said. "I'm probably just bored. If idle hands are the devil's plaything, an idle mind is his playground. There's nothing around here I can really concentrate on, not for long."

Paul said, "A pastoral life suits you, but only up to a point. Your mind needs challenges."

Outside, the sun set. The two of them stepped out to look at the stars. In the darkness—and the night is very dark in a land without powered lights—she reached out and took his finger tendrils in her small hand, and she held to it very tightly, for over a minute. Then she said, "I really do need to get this cart and horse back home. Pa will worry. I should go."

"All right," Paul said.

"Thank you," she said.

"Sure," he said. She clambered into the cart, and the horse clopped away into the night.

# 4

Stargazing became habit for the two of them.

Paul liked night. He had never adapted to a 24 hour sleep schedule for entering torpor, nor desired to do so. The night was marginally cooler, and the stars became hazily, twinklingly visible through Earth's crushing air. In his early days on Earth, he'd also cherished the solitude of night. He'd been a misanthrope (or misjan?) among his own kind, and in a planetwide hive of shrill-voiced Earthlings, solitude was doubly welcome. But now that he had friends—and one friend in particular—his wakeful nights did sometimes feel lonesome.

One night, when Indira was feeling insomniac and since she'd known he'd be wide awake, she had come to visit him. They sat out front and watched the stars together.

Paul tried to pick out Janworld's star for her, but it was too dim to see through Earth's sea of air, not even as a twinkle. "On very clear nights, I can make it out." His ancestral home, where he had never been and would probably never go.

"You know, in ancient times, people thought the sky *was* a sea," she said. "It's even in the Bible. God separated the waters from the waters."

"Your atmosphere is like a sea to *me* at least. I can feel it all around me. I imagine that it feels a lot like swimming in water does for a human," he said.

It was cicada season, and the seven-year locusts were droning away with a vengeance. Indira claimed she actually liked the sound. A comforting drone, not unlike Paul's tremorvoice. "Beautiful night," she said.

"Hot, though," he said. She knew he was sensitive to the heat.

She told him, "I've always... had a mixed relationship... with the stars. I miss them. I miss being up there. But... you can't look out into all that and not have your insignificance rammed down your throat. It makes me feel agorophobic and claustrophobic at the same time."

Paul said, "I always feel closest to God when I can see the stars. They remind me that the universe is a very big place, and that all my problems, all Jankind and mankind's problems... If you can just stand far enough away to see them in perspective, they're nothing. Looking at the stars, I get a sense of the divine order of things. The celestial clockwork. So, why did I make a pilgrimage to a place where I can't see the stars clearly?"

"Mm-hm," Indira said. "It is kinda warmish."

"Weren't you listening to...?"

She punched him in the side.

"I barely felt that," he said.

She laughed at him. "I really should leave this town," she said. "It's all just the tail end of *Candide*. We've seen the world, concluded the world is mad, and we're working in the garden for the sake of having something, something relatively safe and stable, to do.

Maybe our doing it isn't going to make the world any saner, but... well, maybe it'll keep us a little saner. But I think I won't hide. I think I'd rather go mad."

"You're being unfair to them," he said.

"By thinking about leaving?!" she said, suddenly defensive.

"No. You're being unfair in your evaluation of what they're all about. They're trying to be closer to God, and to remove any unnecessary distractions from that pursuit," he said.

She said, "You write those essays about human society. Well let me tell you, it doesn't make any sense, the way we run things. None of it makes any sense. Just all of us doing jobs that don't make us happy just to live on, and even when we get the things we think will make us happy, they never do."

"Well, isn't that why these people are *here*? To seek God? To pursue something above and beyond all you're talking about?"

She took a long, shuddering breath. "Yes. Yes I guess," she muttered. She didn't like being so unguarded around anyone. He was seeing her raw, unprotected inner self. Yet she looked up... and there was no face. No human eyes staring. And as before... that kind of made it okay. A little okay. Because she'd always felt people staring. She didn't know why. It's not as if they really had stared all that much. Just this constant, raw self-consciousness. Even when she shut her eyes, she could feel the eyes of God upon her. Sometimes that was a source of comfort, but much of the time the thought of it just made her want to cry out like Ezekial at the sight of God, "Alas! I am undone!" But she could confide in Paul. She didn't know why. And she dreaded the all-but-inevitable day that he must surely lose patience with it.

"I have to get out of here," she said. "But there's nowhere to go. Nowhere to go." It had become a mantra for her. She said it all the time. She couldn't remember if she'd ever said it out loud to anyone before.

"Why do you say that?" he asked, a little startled.

"I'm not cut out to be a farmer. For farm country. I came back here when I was at loose ends, and then it turned into a permanent thing," she said.

"How did that come about, exactly? You never have said. Why did you come back here? To live with your father on a farm?"

She sighed. "A broken heart." She paused, and then said, "God, how mundane an answer is that?"

He vaguely understood what the term meant. A failed courtship with a potential mate. "How did it happen?" he asked.

"On Felice Station, I was an engineer and general spacehand. For years. I was good at it. The fix-it lady people came to when something broke. And... This is... This is pretty embarrassing," she said. "Look, you have to play, too. What *is* your motivation behind all this? Being on Earth? If I'm opening up, you have to do it, too."

Paul hesitated a long moment. The cicadas' droning seemed louder for his silence. "What was it Elijah told Elisha? 'You have asked a hard thing.'"

"I'm not asking for a double portion of your spirit," she said.

"I'm not sure you'd *want* that," he said. "I worry that my faith is a pretty feeble thing."

"I'd just like to know what you're doing here, is all," she said.

Finally, he said, "All right, I will. But tell your story first."

"Okay," she sighed. "God, I can't believe I'm telling you this. Now I feel like I've got to... Ah piss."

"You have to urinate?"

"Piss the interjection, not piss the verb."

"I've never heard piss used as an interjection," he said.

"Well you have, now!"

"You were saying..."

"Yes I was," she said. "Ungh. Um, abadabadaba.... Okay. Growing up in this town... It's not a good place to be chronically pissed off."

"An adjective now?" he asked.

"Yeah. Such is the nigh-infinite variablity of piss," she said.

"It's a pity I can't produce any," he said.

"You guys basically shit bricks, don't you?"

"Yes. I sometimes use them in my stonework."

"Oh *God...!* I'd managed to forget that," she said. "I'm sitting on one, aren't I?"

"So you grew up here, pissed off," he dodged the question.

"Yeah. Never fit in, not very well. Tranquility's the watchword here, and I reveled in rocking the boat. Blame my mother. She was an outsider originally."

"You mentioned her name was Ingrid. Isn't that a German name? I assumed she was local."

"Well, Lawrenceton," and she pointed in the general direction of the city, "but that's not *local* local. Even though she'd chosen a Plain life for herself, I think she encouraged my nonconformist streak, maybe even unconsciously. Some of the kids backhandedly admired me for being kind of a rebel, but I didn't have many friends. Pa never understood me, so when Ma passed away, I just got out of this endless sea of farmland and went to Rinstillor

University in Lawrenceton and took every technology course I could get my hands on."

Indira said, "My mother told me about the outside world. She had her reasons for leaving it. I think she was sick of it. But she would get wistful for some things, and listening to her I got wistful for things I'd never seen and desperately wanted to."

"And then you went to Felice, and became the fix-it lady," Paul said.

"Yeah. It was a good life, but very strange for a farm girl. Childish of me to be homesick after a lifetime of complaining about this place, but I did get homesick. You do meet a kaleidoscopic variety of people on a space station... Hell, I sound like a travel brochure. But it's true. But... Well, at the end of the day, it's a big city and I'm a country girl, and it took me years to finally admit that to myself."

"That's why you came back? I have to admit, you don't seem contented here, either."

"No," she said. "There was a reason."

Felice, the most vital port city in the Solar System, was a long and broad revolving cylinder in geosynchronous orbit about the Earth, and on its inner surface dwelt a busy citizenry and countless visitors and passers-through. This city had its mansions and slums, restaurants and theaters and parks, seedy bars and garbage processing plants, and districts built to be hospitable to baseline humans, cyborgs, androids, robots, Jan, and a few aliens other than the Jan. The botanical Plandarites had opened an embassy recently, though it housed only half a dozen representatives, four of whom could be counted on to be in photosynthetic hibernation at any given time.

As a general spacehand, Indira Fenstermacher had been over and seen to the maintainence of nearly every inch of the place over the years. She knew the workings of the life support systems for every sentient form of life and cybernetic animacy known to man. Plumbing and power systems, air vents and cleaners, gardens and yeast vats, and nanoforges built to manufacture textiles, alloys, finished products, and edible foodstuffs. She could make at least patch repairs for most common problems that human-made spacecraft were likely to encounter, as well as a few Jannite craft. Doing this work was fulfilling, felt like what she'd been made for. She'd spent her entire early life rising up long before the sun for farm work, and she'd maintained that habit now. She labored round the clock, near obsessively.

She did have trouble finding time for her boyfriend of the past five years, Aleksei Callahan; and she regretted that, for he was a good guy. She was grateful for his patience; and judging by his performance in the sack when she could reward that patience, he appreciated her company.

Everything was going so well. She'd escaped her home town and was making a good living with her skills in one of the most fascinating places in the Solar System. Life was fine.

Except at the moments when she stopped moving long enough to feel the universe lying on her like a blanket of lead.

She was tense, always. She blamed the slow-paced world of her youth, figured it had crippled her mind so it could never adjust to a wider, faster universe. No, that wasn't it, she decided. She felt *stagnant* out here, and in a completely different way than she had felt stagnant at home. She remembered when she'd first left home for college. Everything had been wondrous. Awe-inspiring. Big and wondrous and cool. Where was the cool wonder now? She had gotten used to it, and now the outside world just seemed like an endless cascade of trivia and sensualism that never ever shut up, and she hated it when it *did* shut up because then she could hear herself think. Like everyone she now knew, she was an addict to constant stimulation, unable to deal with quiet, even as she longed for it.

Words came to her unbidden, from her youth, from Ecclesiastes: "All things are wearisome; no man can speak of them all. Is not the eye surfeited with seeing, and the ear sated with hearing?"

She'd slowly but inexorably become aware of this new discontent—seemingly antithetical to her old discontent, yet eerily similar to it—and tried to hide it, but she believed it was becoming visible. Aleksei said recently, "You always look like you're about to throw yourself out an airlock." She'd brushed this off with some blithe response she couldn't recall now—probably to the effect that her melancholy artist boyfriend was hardly Mr. Sunshine himself. In fact, she felt a frightening apathy toward her own welfare. Not suicidal, but there was one time she was working on the third tier hydro-correlator core, and it had shown sudden signs that it might burst, killing her instantly. She had stopped it, but what struck her most was that she had not been *frightened*—had on some level thought, *"Well if it blows in my face, so what?"* and afterward, if she allowed herself to think about it— and she tried not to—it frightened her deeply that she had not been frightened, that she should love life so little.

She remembered the last party they'd been to together. It had been at Kaffi's place. His apartment always smelled of scrubber nanites working endlessly to remove stains and odors and never quite succeeding, so it always smelled like a blend of sweatsock and nanite. That she could smell the scrubbers meant by definition that she was inhaling them, which didn't please her much.

There'd only been one kreghead there that time, which was a peculiar mercy. Instead, just a bunch of people, most of them on frash, dancing to music only they could hear on their internals rather than the music that was actually blaring; several couples weren't listening to the same song, so their movements weren't in any kind of sync. Others played neurovid games, running and jumping in place and shooting their fingers at invisible adversaries. Usually she would have joined in with a VR link (she had never gotten an internal; she'd have been hard-pressed to say why she didn't want one, but she didn't), but she'd had an exhausting week, so she just sat reading a bookslate in a corner and tried to enjoy the isolation that so often comes of parties. She tried to ignore the sounds of the small crowd doing something loud and orgasmic in the back room; she was pretty sure the multiple-limbed guy Octo was back there. Regrettably, as more attendees kept wandering to the back, it kept getting louder. She wondered if Aleksei would have joined in, had she not been present. She told herself she would have been fine with that, and tried not to think about it again.

The guy on kreg, whose name she wasn't sure of, was at least having a *quiet* high, sitting in the corner giggling at nothing. Did he know his legs were bent at that angle? She sighed, set down the slate, and went to straighten them out for him. He kicked her hard in the face and never realized he'd done it. She swore like a thesaurus with Tourette's for a few seconds, hoped it wouldn't bruise, and wished to God she could have been surprised at the occurrence. She looked over at Aleksei, swinging an invisible sword. She considered joining his game, then considered downing another beer so she might be less aware of how crappy she felt, then went back to her book.

That was one of the *better* parties, she now thought. Aleksei loved them; he claimed they provided insights into the human character that he could use in his art. *That's what Dostoevsky said about a Siberian prison,* she thought. The parties had never done much for her, but lately she'd left them feeling... scathed. Numb. She supposed young people were supposed to find profundity in their loins and bellies. *Am I that young any more?* she wondered. *Was I ever?*

Now they were having dinner at their favorite falafel joint, a week or so after the face-kicker party. The decor was Schiaperelli Martian Colonial, all white and silver. She spent so much of her day in cramped spaces overflowing with tangled cables, that she liked the wide-open clean-lined aesthetics of this place; stark, after the fashion of old colonies, but starkness meant home to her, even if this starkness was predominantly white and silver rather than black and brown.

With a trim, fit build, longish blonde hair and shortish blonde beard, Aleksei was handsome. It would have been odd if he weren't, as he'd been completely genengineered from the ground up. It was rare to be *completely* predesigned, as he was; he shared no heredity with his mother, the woman who'd commissioned him. His genome had been assembled from catalogued fragments from countless donors, with countless more modifications. She hadn't even carried the pregnancy herself, and he had been born out of a gestation tank like a biological android. Aleksei's eyes were large and earnest in his chiseled face, but perpetually bored. He was apathetic, or at least feigned apathy, about everything. He wrote poetry. She thought it was very good. She thought he'd make a good philosopher, but he insisted on being a singer or artist or poet or whatever other artistic thing struck his fancy and seemed vaguely profitable that morning. He was a bright, capable artist but very needy, and she was young enough still to find neediness charming.

"Fensty, we need to talk," Aleksei said ominously. It was his pet name for her.

"About what?" she asked. She ran her fingers through her hair. She kept it short these days; couldn't risk it getting caught in equipment. "Lex, I'm sorry, but I can't stay long. Rivka's expecting me to overhaul the filtration system on Whitman, and that's gonna take all night. I already told her I'd do it, so I can't back out." She looked at his plate. "Are you going to eat those beets?"

He smiled. It was their custom when they ate here that he always let her have his pickled beets, since she liked them and he didn't. A million little customs like that. He forked them over to her plate, and she grinned like a little girl. Damn, he'd miss that smile. "Yeah, well, that's kinda it. There's no time. There's never time," he said.

She stopped the fork on its way to her mouth. "Oh." She sighed. They fought about nothing a lot, lately, but she thought that in a way, that might be a sign of a maturing relationship. "Look, I'm sorry babe, but it's my job. I have to do this. It's kinda not even about the money, although Lord knows that oughtta be enough. But... Fix things I must, y'know? You knew that when you met me."

He sighed. On a vague level, he thought he should be feeling something more than he was. Mostly, he just wanted this dinner to be over.

He'd felt under tremendous pressure since birth. He was as close to being an übermensch as the law allowed since the Genomic War's end. There should have been no opportunity denied him, his life a limitless vista of potential. He'd been told this so many times growing up—and had so many times and in so many ways inevitably failed to fulfill his mother's colossal hubristic expectations for him—that he now lived his life in an indeterminate state between self-reverence and self-loathing (the two faces of self-absorption being close kin). He believed himself a loser who should have been a king. Not that he'd ever really seriously wanted a throne, but he felt guilty for not wanting it. So now he just scribbled some poems and art, partied as damn hard as he could, and said fuck-all to his supposed unfulfilled potential. He was ashamed of all this, even though he figured it was exactly what Fensty liked about him.

Indira fascinated him. Here was this brilliant woman, totally self-made, professionally successful, with no biological enhancements at all. Raised *Amish,* for God's sake. She entranced him, and yet the more time he spent with her, the more her very presence made him feel crapulous by comparison. More so because *she* didn't consider him a loser. She saw him as an artsy, anti-establishment aesthete with an enlightened dismissiveness of the world's priorities. That was how he tried to present himself, and even he believed it part of the time, but he knew he was just shirking off of... well, everything, really. He'd finally decided he needed to get away from her, because she intimidated the hell out of him.

Envy of her accomplishments, intimidation by them, that wasn't the only problem, of course. She had a hair-trigger temper that would intimidate anybody, and he was very, very tired of dealing with that.

She knew none of this..

He averted his gaze, coughed, and said, "There's someone else. I'm..." He picked his words carefully. *"Very sorry?" "Deeply regretful?"* No. *"Terribly."* Yeah. "...terribly sorry," he chose.

Her whole body froze for a moment as she tried to take in this new information, her mouth hanging open, a falafel ball still on her fork in midair. "You... *What?!*"

"Look hon, I'm sorry. But it's not working out. You can *see* it's not working out. And Kim makes me happy," he said.

"Wh... H..." She still hadn't quite processed this. It was all so damn sudden. "Well good for Kim!" she said. "Who is *Kim?*"

"You don't know her."

"Why?" she asked. She could feel hot tears starting.

"'Cuz... Hell, I dunno babe. You're always busy, and you're always cranky." He usually tried to sound more erudite around her than this, but there was no point now. "And... Eh, I dunno. It's me."

"You just said it was me," she said.

"Eh, I dunno," he said. "I need... more. Something else."

"'More,'" she parroted. "How long?" she asked.

"Not long," he said.

*"How long?* How long have you been hitting some slut behind my back?"

"Not long," he said.

"You're not even defending her. I just called her a slut, and you're not denying it. What, are you actually paying her money for it?"

"Here, see? *This* is why I'm leaving. This is what you get like when you get mad, and you get mad like every ten minutes."

"Of course I'm mad! You just told me you've been two-timing me with some hooker, and you won't even tell me how long you've been doing it!"

"She's not a hooker! Damn it, she's... She's better than you. When you get like this," he said.

"You drop a bombshell like this and you expect me to be calm? You're out of your mind!"

"I'm going," he said. He got up from the table, waved his debitor in front of the sensor to cover their tab, and walked out the door without looking back, taking half her adult life with him. The emptied woman sat and stared at the space where he had been.

After a long time, she got up and left the restaurant.

She wandered through Market Zone, keeping off the moving sidewalks, attempting not to blubber in public and ultimately failing. They'd been together for—she added it up—five years! Sure, he was kind of an ass sometimes, dragging her to parties full of kregheads, but she'd always figured he'd grow out of it when the two of them settled down. They could travel the Solar System when they got married. Maybe settle on Mars, finally. She'd always wanted to see Romulus City, visit the Phillips Memorial, then maybe Kyvadia (more partying; at least he'd like that), and Olympus Mons of course. Now all of it was up in smoke.

Deafening, kathumping pop music pounded at her, while garish floating holographic advertise-ments clashed and threw themselves at her. Light and colors, everywhere colors, bright and blinking and trying to crawl beneath her eyelids (and they *could* get under her eyelids with an AR link, which she wasn't using at the moment). She glanced at a holotheater she passed. Every title floating above its placard was either a love story or at least had a romantic subplot. *Damn it, don't they have* anything *else to make stories about?* If she took time to make out the lyrics, all the skull-shaking songs blasting from the speakers over-head were about love, or at least sex of every permutation the mind could conceive or the body execute, with or without cybernetic assistance. Considering how easily the sex and pleasure and even *companionship* centers of the brain could be massaged by artificial means, she supposed she ought to find it reassuring that the sex act was surviving at all.

She ducked in a shop, bought a noise filter, and stuck it on her shoulder. It synced with the Market's audio systems and the infernal music stopped, so all she could hear now was the crowd noise. She considered filtering that too, but she didn't like being deaf to the world.

Turning *insensible* to the world for a while held some appeal, though. All her long-standing pent-up frustrations about her life suddenly came to the fore, and she was as deeply miserable as ever she'd been. She decided she wanted to get very, very drunk. Wiping tears and snot on her workshirt sleeve, she called Rivka on her comm, let her know she was taking one of her many unused days off *right now,* filtration systems be damned, and set out to find a source of ethyl alcohol.

There was no shortage of bars and pubs on Felice, but she'd never been one for the bar scene, and so she headed someplace classier than that. She hopped on an express slidewalk, sat on a bench, and headed uptown. The Mercury Unicorn was the best restaurant on the station.

She'd always wanted to go there with Aleksei, but somehow they'd never made it. You needed a reservation for a table, at least a good table, but she wasn't after a table.

It was a nice place. She'd been inside to do maintenance before. Holographic effects twinkled in the chandaliers, and live waiters and busbeings puttered between the tables. A Selenite woman (easily recognizable as Moon-born by her height) in a slinky blue dress was crooning a torch song to piano accompaniment, infinitely preferable to the purile racket in the Market; Indira supposed the singer was probably wearing a support harness to help her deal with the gravity, but it didn't hurt the curves of her dress at all. Nice, calm, attractive place. The furnishings looked like real wood. Indira actually smiled a little. She made a beeline for the bar, ordered a honeyed venusburg, and got started.

She'd moved on to bad Tharsis vodka that tasted like ionized plasma cut with napalm and lost all track of time when she noticed the two of them eating together at a table.

The woman with Aleksei was *shockingly* beautiful. Honey blonde with a teeny tiny waste, toned and smooth limbs, luminous blue eyes that shone across the room, and a quite senselessly large bosom; and wearing a small black dress that tastefully but very effectively displayed all the aforementioned, particularly the bosom. Indira was feeling undesirable already, but next to this... goddess, she felt positively repulsive. *No way any of that's natural,* she snarked, inwardly. *Probably a geneng like him. And had nanosurgeries since then and...*

*Wait...*

*The movements of the arms. The hands. The head. Are they...*

*Moving on smooth trilateral compound arcs like Figsbuy pivots.*

*Oh... hell...*

Indira got off her barstool. She fumbled for her debitor and then headed for her ex's table.

"Indira?" Aleksei said stupidly.

"That's an android," Indira said, pointing an accusing finger at the pulchritudinous cybernaut. Strictly speaking, the term would be *gynoid*, but nobody was that pedantic. It wasn't a biological one, either, but a clockwork mechanical robot. Granted that this "woman" might be a free, sentient droid... but that wasn't Indira's first guess.

As she said it, she realized that Kim might just be a cyborg, in which case Indira had just made a fool of herself, but...

"Wh... How did you know?" Aleksei said. She felt incongruous momentary relief that she'd been right. And good, he wasn't denying it, which would have actually made her more pissed, if that were possible.

"I'm an engineer, and I'm not blind! Her small muscle movements, body language... Are you sentient?" Indira demanded of it, trying to keep her words from slurring. "Are you free?"

Indira hoped that the machine would not be programmed to react to sudden disclosure. Sure enough, it turned its improbably big eyes on Indira, flashed a demure yet perky smile, and said, "No, I belong to Aleksei!" and hugged his arm. He looked embarrassed, (he had ordered this *moe* personality interface, after all) as well as a little terrified of Indira.

"Oh God," Indira said. She could have forgiven dating a free robot. That would have been a little kinky, but not much different from dumping her for a human woman. But *cyberslavery?* It was legal on an international station like Felice, but it was beneath contempt. Of course, even that assumed the droid was sentient and programmed for subservience. If, on the other hand, it was a "hollow" nonsentient robot... the notion that she might have been dumped for a mindless sex toy was an even viler possibility.

She was surprised at how quiet her voice was. "You... vomitous.... piece of..."

"Fensty... It's..."

"...toaster-fucking shit. You... and this thing..."

"I'm not a thing," the thing said pouting, and seemed genuinely resentful. Again, Indira wondered if it was sentient. It could be very hard to tell, even if she took the time to converse with it (the old Turing Test was a joke; the parser program ELIZA had done a fair job of making a mockery of it only sixteen years after the test was proposed, and modern "hollow" behavior simulators could ape human speech quite well while lacking even the self-awareness of a honeybee), and she had no intention of doing that.

"You..." She couldn't find words. *So... So that's the way things really are. That's what love's like. Took me damn long enough to learn it. The sex is all he ever really wanted. It's all I'm good for.*

He groaned. He was tired... tired of dealing with her instabilities, her unpredictabilities... hell, he was tired of dealing with *another person*. He was ready for something safer, something—just one aspect of his life—where he was in control. He wasn't sure he even believed in the distinction between hollow and cognizant machines, no matter what the robopsychologists said. In Kim, he had the perfect woman, and what was wrong with that? What in the world was wrong with that? It didn't hurt anyone!

Well, it would hurt someone in the short run. But Indira'd get over it.

"I'm an artist," he said. "Okay? Kim's my magnum opus. She's all my dreams made manifest, in flesh and steel!"

"Yes I am!" Kim bubbled.

"You didn't *build* her! You made up a list of charac... charact'ristics," Indira caught herself slurring and cursed the alcohol, "and handed 'em off to *engineers* to build her... That's not art. That's telling the food machine what to put in your sandwich. You're dating a sandwich!"

"It's just like where *I* came from," he snarled, disgusted with her. "I was *born* deserving this. I deserve this!"

It took her a moment to realize he was talking about his genengineered origins. Surely he hadn't just compared himself to a nonsentient droid. Even a neurotic like him couldn't hate himself that much. But if he did, fine. "Yeah, you do," Indira said. "Oh don't expect me to feel *sorry* for *you* right now! Poor little unloved synth boy? Where'd you get the money? You're always broke! Wait... That's *why* you're always broke? You were saving up for *this?* All the fucking time we were dating!"

Indira addressed the android, still unsure whether it was sentient. "Anybody in there? In there to listen to this?" On cue, the machine turned away embarrassed, reached for Aleksei, and took his hand.

He looked at Indira sullenly. "Why don't *you* make a boyfriend. Huh, engineer? Make a robot that'll put up with your own crazy self."

Indira said, "You're pathetic."

"Not as pathetic as you, Indira." Aleksei said. He looked at Indira defiantly. When she insisted on still standing there instead of leaving, he added, "Get away from us, you psycho, all right? It's *over!*"

The world whirled.

Indira tried to think of a comeback, and instead she just shrieked. And then she ran from the bar. Out of the restaurant. Onto a fast slidewalk away from the civilian areas. Toward Engineering. For the rest of her life, Indira would question how drunk she had been that night, how much of her subsequent behavior could be blamed on simple alcohol.

As she remembered it, she'd become almost disassociative. Her thoughts came fast and ran together like spilled paint. She told herself that her higher brain functions had shut down and she was acting on pure animal instinct, but she knew that couldn't be true or she could scarcely be observing and commenting on the fact in her own mind, and she passed a control panel for the lights on 7th deck and opened it up and ripped out every connection and coughed up a big ball of phlegm and spat it into the controls and watched it spark and considered laughing hysterically but didn't bother and then moved down the corridor to see if she could find another panel she passed a light panel and tossed her triwrench through it and it went dark and produced a loud crack and then a long persistent whine that was irritating and somehow satisfying at the same time and she realized vaguely that she shouldn't stay here or the security bots would come *well let them come!* and she thought of how the repair nanites would already be working on the stuff she'd broken and she went over to the frame around the light panel, ripped it completely out of the wall (which stopped that godawful whining sound thank God) and hurled it across the room and muttered "Let the nanobugs fix that, fuck 'em!" and then suddenly ran at breakneck speed for an elevator and all the sounds she heard swirled together or did she just want them to swirl together God damned melodramaticism defines every fucking thing I do no sense of perspective at all Where's the God damned fucking elevator Here it is Control center 8 I said control center 8 you hellspawn little machine Nobody will be there right now What do I want to do when I get there God, I can just picture the whole God damned station blasting apart The pieces Oh God I can see the sunlight glinting off the little metal pieces against the stars and there's body parts floating by A hand? Oh Jesus God what am I thinking Calm down Hyperventilating Breathing too fast Calm down Calm down Damnation I don't wanna calm down My floor, huh? All right I'm here What do I want to do here "Hi! Gomez! It is Gomez, isn't it? Hi, I wasn't expecting to see you here! How are you?" Leave! God damn you, why do you have to be here right now?! Thank God he's here. God, I'm breathing so fast. Why's everything going to hell Why's everything everything going to hell He said he loved me God damn him! "Oh, just wandering, I guess. I'm off-shift."

She got through with no trouble. Everyone knew she was authorized, and no one took note of the expression on her face. Soon she was in a deserted section of Engineering.

She stared at the oxygen system. One quick adjustment, and it would be the end of everyone. All the oxygen-breathing life forms, anyway. Most of them, anyway. Probably couldn't evacuate fast enough. Especially if she nixed the sensors. She stared at it. Stared at it.

She curled up on the floor and tried not to think. Tried so so hard not to think.

She was soon asleep.

"What are you doing?" came a voice.

"I... I..." She opened her eyes. It was Rivka Perlman. Her boss. Indira's head ached.

Recollection came slowly. And horror with it.

Seconds later, she lay sobbing in her boss's arms and babbled out a summation of the past several hours' activities.

She was terrified of her actions, horrified. Scared, too, of what might come next as consequence. What had come over her? she wondered. She'd suffered what in antiquity had colloquially been called a nervous breakdown. It had been building a long time, ever since she'd left the Earth. Now, she could not trust herself. The station had survived her mania, but Indira herself felt destroyed.

Indira stopped her tale a long moment. The telling of it was extremely difficult for her. "I knew how everything on the station worked, and how to wreck it. Trash recyclers, power systems, even water filters. I managed to stop myself before I got to the air system, but... I'm horrified at how close I came to trashing it. No one was hurt, thank God, but I mean, people could have gotten *killed*. I'd gone completely psychotic. I absolutely should've done jail time. My boss pulled some strings for me to save me from legal action, but she recommended I get off the station, and of course she fired me. You don't ever want to see me angry, Paul. Trust me, you don't."

He didn't know what to make of all this. Paul said, "You stopped yourself from damaging the oxygen system. Surely that's the important thing."

She noticed his tentacle-arms tense. It always happened when he was upset, he'd get all stony and rigid. *So much for his being unreadable,* she mused, as she realized she'd known this about him for some time.

"You were drunk," he said. His own people had their own depressant substances, though none filled quite the cultural niche that alcohol did for Earthlings.

"Not that drunk," she said. Paul could hear her heart thudding as if she'd run a marathon. She said, "God. I couldn't trust myself again. That's why I returned to this... womb." Indira said, "I probably deserved it. That... mania. Brought it on myself. He and I had been living in sin."

Paul said, "Don't say that."

Indira said, "Why not? I'm sure you were thinking it."

Paul said, "Earthlings' sexual and romantic mores are completely outside my culture and my biology. When studying the Faith, I admit I didn't pay much attention to such matters because they seemed irrelevant to my situation."

"Hmp. Yeah, I can see that," she mumbled. "Here's a primer. Fornication equals bad. And so the Lord visited a madness upon Indira Fenstermacher."

Paul said, "I don't think you were mad."

"Oh I was livid," she said.

"That's not what I..."

"Okay, I was *raving,*" she said. "I'd *better* have been crazy. That would've been my only possible defense if I'd gone to court."

He said, "I'm glad your boss didn't do that to you."

Indira said quietly, "I'm not."

Paul said, "I understand."

Indira said, "You don't."

Paul said, after a pause, "I think I do. We *are* alike. I'll tell you my story. But first, what happened after that?"

She choked on the next words. "Pa invited me back here, and I tore his head off for humiliating me by offering it..."

"Tore his head...?"

"God, Paul, it's a metaphor. I yelled at him."

"Sorry."

"But I finally *did* come back, and I keep telling myself it's not just because there was no place else for me to go. I wanted to get back to something simple, to pull myself together, to figure out what to do next. Life doesn't get much more basic than a Mennonite farm." She shrugged, and muttered, "Someplace without any tech infrastructure for me to wreck when I get in a bad mood. And even so, all I figured I was likely to do was to sit here and fester.

"But you know something? God help me, part of me actually is coming to enjoy it. Part of me. It is very pretty here. And it's honest labor."

"It is lovely here," Paul said. "I was slow to see it. It's a very alien, exotic place for me, and I suppose that's the very opposite of what it means to you. And... the fact that people here peacefully cooperate in their labors... like my people, I suppose, but the folk here do it *by choice,* even though it's not necessarily in their natures, which makes it far more meaningful. I... I'm sorry, I interrupted you."

"That's all right," she said.

"Go ahead."

She cleared her throat. "It's nice here. People are nice, just kinda stiff. I have to admit, I was expecting to take some flak when I came back, for having left in the first place, but everybody's been pretty decent about it. Pa is... well, he's Pa. Least demonstrative guy you'll ever meet, but I can tell he's glad to have me back in the community.

"But... it can be really really dull, too. I was just starting to get properly discontented with it again. Thinking that I'd taken long enough to heal, that there's a big world... big solar system, big *universe* out there... And... Well, then I met you." She patted his thick gray hide. He clasped his tendrils together, unsure what to say. "And I haven't wanted to leave. Quite so much. You're my best friend, Paul," she said. "Thank you."

"You're welcome," he said uncertainly, but deeply moved. "I'm... glad that you're... not angry any more."

Indira said, "Ruthie welcomed me back. I haven't spent nearly enough time with her since then."

Paul said, "And the others didn't?"

Indira said, "Oh, sure they did. Probably all superficial."

Paul said, "I know little of insincerity and can offer few insights."

"Hrmph." She regarded him sidelong, not sure what to say to that. "Now you. Go. Top that. I dare you to top that. Story. Now."

After a long moment, Paul said, "I was responsible for the Battle of Adrastea."

She thought for a moment. "The who?"

"No. The Who was a British musical band credited with the invention of the 'rock opera.' What does that have to do with anything?" he asked.

"I can never tell when you're trying to make a joke. No, I'm just trying to remember, it sounds familiar... Oh, right! Freshman history, duh! Adrastea. I think I remember. Um... Yeah. It was a big scandal."

"I actually find it very reassuring that you're barely aware of the incident," he said quietly.

"It just means I was an engineering major and I thought the teacher for my required history class was dull," she said. "Wait, so that was... you? Personally?"

"I suppose I should start at the beginning." He stopped to consider where the beginning might be. "I'm fascinated by the fact that humans, at least under ideal conditions, treat their soldiers as heroes. Not as objects of contempt."

"Well of course we do!" Indira said.

"I thought you were raised a pacifist," he said.

"Well, *non-resistant,* which is a little different, somehow..."

"It means you're supposed to be even more pacifistic than the pacifists," Paul said.

She sighed. "I was raised not to curse, either. Everything within reason, Paul. I won't wage war myself, but if someone is willing to risk his life for my benefit, I'm not going to condemn that."

"What do you know about our Warrior caste?" he asked.

"Not much," Indira admitted. She felt like she was giving a school report. She cleared her throat. "You have three castes, or genders. The Matriarchs are your females, and they run things. The male Workers make up the bulk of the population. The Warriors are sterile, and they... well, they fight. It's what they're... for."

"Yes. A Worker like me can be trained to fight, but compared to a born Warrior, we're poor combatants. We're slow, instinctively nonviolent, and just generally bad at it. Our Warriors are deadly. Back in primitive times, on the Jan homeworld, they were vital to our survival against larger predators."

"Oh yeah, you said. Critters even bigger than you," she asked.

"Oh certainly. We're not descended from predators like humanity is. Our ancestors were *prey.* An adult great *hoon* could swallow me in one gulp. All our natural instincts, let alone our culture, are based on that. It's why we're compulsively honest. We had to cooperate all the time or we'd be dead. Humans like to compare our warrens to beehives. Well, it's a good comparison. And our homeworld was full of bears. The Warriors were our stings.

"As we've spread through space, the Warriors have successfully protected us against hostile civilizations you haven't met yet, like the Membrul, the Ucipagth, and the Hu-Lon. And a Matriarch can breed a lot of Warriors in a hurry, when there's a crisis."

He continued, "The problem is what to do with them once the fight is over. They're born killers, and they don't adapt well at all to civilian society. So, the Matriarchs breed only a minimum of them, usually. For combat, we use nonsentient robots, or alien mercenaries led by specially trained Workers when we can."

"You mean the Jannite Corps?" she asked, referring to the famed Foreign Legion of Outer Space.

"Yes. And we use Workers too, although, as I said, we're not very good in a fight. Before I was born, when Jannite vessels first reached your solar system, after years of exchanging long-range messages with mankind... naturally my ancestors hoped for a peaceful encounter, but they couldn't be sure what to expect. From what humans themselves had told us, Earth's history was a bloody one."

"I think part of that was deliberate bravado," Indira said, a little embarrassed on her species's behalf. "In case you turned out to be hostile, we had to make sure you knew we wouldn't be pushovers."

He bobbed his eyestalk, his imitation of a nod. "So, my ancestors figured they had to be prepared for a fight if one started. So, the ships carried a large contingent of Warriors, who had been born en route to Earth. Fortunately, they weren't needed. Captain Xaioming and Ambassador Dwight hit it off very well, and our peoples have been friends ever since. But this left the problem of what to do with all those Warriors."

"Well, wouldn't you *want* a standing army of some sort? Even in peacetime? You *can't* have... mothballed or retired or whatever... your whole military. That's crazy. I mean, I guess *you're* nonviolent like we are," and she gestured to indicate the town, "but I didn't think most Jan were. I mean... what'll you do if mankind wakes up evil one day and decides to kill you all and steal your tech and stuff?" She amended it, "Well, wakes up eviller."

"We do maintain a military, and there are Warriors permanently assigned to it. But... when my ancestors came here, I think they overestimated Earth's military might, because of that 'deliberate bravado,' as you called it. We really had no use for a standing army of that size, and it was decided that maintaining it in a highly visible fashion in Earth's own solar system could only antagonize Earth, when we wanted very badly to earn its trust."

"You were a handful of ships coming into an entire inhabited foreign *solar system*. You *couldn't* have *too many* soldiers."

"Indira... You know my people haven't shared all our technology, though we have shared most of what we use on a daily basis. We have not shared our weapons technology. It is the prevailing opinion among the Matriarchs that the combined might of your solar system's militaries could not successfully invade Callisto."

"Really!" said the pacifist woman, glaring at him. "I feel like my honor's been slighted."

"Mind you, I'm not saying they're *right.*"

"Of *course* not," she said.

"I'm not saying they're wrong, either," he said.

"Do you even know?" she asked.

"I'm not saying that either," he said.

*"Pbbbbth,"* she said.

"I don't know what that means," he said.

"Take a guess." She considered the problem. "So, what did you do with them?"

"They'd always lived apart from us, at the borders of our communities, even in ancient times. They protected us from *outside* threats. They had their own rituals, traditions, they often worshipped different gods. The differences were deep, neurological. They functioned better in loose societies, and were unable to learn the boring, repetitive trades required in the warren proper." *At least, that's what I was always told,* Paul thought. *Well, I witnessed the truth of it at Valhalla, didn't I?* "On Callisto, there's a crater canyon which your astronomers long ago named *Valhalla,* of all things. We set it aside as a reservation for the Warriors. We figured they could squabble and bump heads there as much as they wanted without hurting anyone."

Indira grunted. "The United States tried a reservation system with the Native Americans. If I remember my history, it was pretty God awful for them."

"Yes," Paul said. "I suspect that it's a decision Dwight and the other Matriarchs would not have made when they were older, and wiser, but an adult Matriarch is... simply too *large* for spaceflight, so they had to be young for the journey here. Pardon me, I'm not comfortable questioning the Matriarchs' wisdom."

"Pfft," Indira scoffed.

"I don't know what that means either."

*"Pbbbbbbtht!"* she said. Then, more seriously, she asked, "Do the Warriors have any say in any of this? Can they *vote?"* she asked.

"Even *Workers* don't vote," Paul said.

She'd known that, but, since it was a culture full of aliens, she hadn't given much thought to it. "Well... Fie on you and your socialist utopia! Fie on it!" she teased him, though it was only half teasing.

"I have *never* called it a utopia," he said, very gravely.

"Sorry," she said.

"You know, there are Jan colony worlds with legislatures. It's not an unknown concept among us," he said. "There, the Matriarch is more of a... chief executive, I suppose. But the system we've got here is... the traditional one."

"Well, some traditions are good. Others stink," she said. "If *they're* your *fighters,* and they feel they're mistreated, why haven't they rebelled?" The whole situation reminded her greatly of the Tesks, except that the Tesks freed themselves from servitude to Alfheim's Imperium. Not that life had been easy for them since then, but it was better than their previous slavery.

"They have a very strong inborn sense of hierarchy. As do we Workers, I suppose, though it is stronger among the Warriors. Certainly there have been Warrior rebellions, in Jannite history. But they are relatively rare."

"Loyal to the pack. Like dogs, or wolves," Indira said.

"Or bees," Paul said. "Anyway, by the time the Matriarchs *were* older... well, such things I suppose take on a life of their own in a bureaucracy as vast as ours. I was born years after all of this, when Dwight had matured and become fertile. And like you, I never fit in very well among my own kind. You were right, the day you met me. I have... I had a temper. A terrible temper. People told me I should have been born a Warrior."

"I'll have to take your word for that," Indira interrupted him. "I mean, sometimes you get frustrated easily, but I've never seen you *angry.*"

"Good," he said, quietly. "I'm glad you haven't. Because of my temperament, I was made one of the Administrators of Valhalla. They figured I could identify with the Warriors, so I would treat them well. It sounds logical, doesn't it? But there was one problem. I hated humans in my youth."

"You did?" she asked.

"Yes. It wasn't a well thought-out hatred, if there is such a thing. I suppose bigotries never are. A mix of fear and hatred. All Jan, and all humans, face something of an instinctive difficulty in coming to view members of the other race as equals; but my own instinctive bias was very great. The human form repulsed me to my core. Xenophobic horror.

"I was young, with anger I had to attach to something. And there were hideous little blob creatures whom we were taught to always treat with obsequious deference because we were guests in their solar system. The blobs' whole history was taken up with wars among themselves, they could never be trusted because they were liars, and they couldn't even speak properly without elaborate translator equipment. So I hated them. Yet my superiors, in their 'wisdom,' had essentially put me in charge of a fair-sized contingent of our military. Mothballed as it was."

"That's hard to believe," she said.

"You doubt my word?" he asked.

"Of course not," she said. "So you were in charge of, what, thousands of these guys?"

"I was one of nine governing Administrators. Our hierarchies are hard to explain to a human. It's rare in our society to have a single 'highest ranking' individual—rather, ranking is determined situationally. One post might be in charge of food supplies, another in charge of the police, another in charge of sports and recreation... all shifting around depending on what was happening at the moment. And even these posts are rarely filled by a single individual."

"It sounds redundantly redundant," Indira said.

"I'm not even explaining it in English very well. Suffice it that *we* can keep it all straight."

"Okey-doke."

"So, I was not *in charge* of the whole of Valhalla. No *one* individual was. But, by any meaningful description, I was fairly high ranking. I suppose I was pretty good at the organizational minutia of the job," he said, suspecting Bill at the Consulate would disagree. "Anyway..." He paused to collect his thoughts. "Well, generating a Jannite biosphere on Callisto was an ongoing process. At one point, our superiors told us we'd have to evacuate Valhalla so they could do some environmental engineering of the area. The prejudice against Warriors was so strong that rather than sending us to another part of Callisto, they sent us all the way to Adrastea, one of Jupiter's smaller moons."

The transport's bridge was ugly. Nearly everything was painted in a dull green like dirty malachite. Exposed coolant tubes snaked all over the bulkheads like bloated cliff worms who had had the misfortune to be painted the color of dirty malachite. There was no acoustic scalloping, and the echoes could easily cause vertigo to one who wasn't used to it. Illumination came from three broad sickly yellow-brown lighting stripes across the ceiling. The ship's Captain for this flight, Valhalla's Fifth Administrator, wondered whether the paint would look blue if the light weren't yellow.

He realized he was sulking. In his forties, The Fifth Administrator was still a fairly young Worker (Workers taking far longer to mature than Warriors). He resented this detail. Hardly unusual, as he was a Worker full of resentments. He hoped to prevent the Warriors under his command from seeing his petulant mood, but they were not fools and he was sure they could tell. They didn't want him to be there any more than he did.

The whole business of having a single individual in charge of the ship was a Warrior custom he could have done without.

The bridge crew of Warriors stood at their station podiums in a circle around his station, engrossed in their tasks. The one acting as Pilot informed him their vessel was prepared to settle into orbit about Adrastea. The Administrator acknowledged this and told him to proceed.

There was no real need for a pilot. The task of moving a few of the unemployed Warriors from one place to another could be done more efficiently by machine. But this gave the Warriors *something to do.* Something to keep them occupied. Perish forbid that ever they should feel bored or discontented! Keeping them occupied had been the sum total of his professional life since his graduation from Mining Corps. It had become that because the Matriarchs and their subordinates had felt that a sullen, recalcitrant lad like himself would relate well to the Warriors.

He did not. They scared the hell out of him.

He tried not to show it as they towered over him. He feared them and he held them in contempt, because they seemed like all his own worst faults magnified and given towering six-armed life. He disliked himself for being temperamental, and the Warriors were that failing incarnate. Their manner of speech was hideous, full of images of dead bodies and ichor, and he had to listen to it daily, at least when he was stuck in close contact with them like this. At least this flight had been pleasantly and unexpectedly calm, relatively free of deafening insults hurled between the Warriors or at him, and free of brawls.

Perhaps they wouldn't snipe at each other so much if they had more tasks to perform regularly. He often wondered that. There were probably myriad squabbles going on down in the ships' barracks, where the Warriors had nothing at all to do.

Most Warriors he'd met were a fatalistic lot and revered Survival as their patron, but the Administrator had heard one Warrior (who was filling the completely nominal post of Gunner on this little milk run) mention that he revered Survival's child Glory, the battle god. Although not a Gloryist himself, or a devout follower of any god, the Administrator sympathized with the concept. He certainly felt he needed some glory in his life. All the same, the Gunner intimidated the Administrator. All the Warriors were big, but he was huge.

He'd thought often enough of leaving his job. He was old enough now that he was free to do so. He knew it could be worse: there were Jannite societies where he would not have had that freedom. He would have been assigned a job when young and been trapped there, as things had been in ancient days. Few societies were like that any more, though, and he was free to leave. But where to go?

The Gunner announced that their ship was being scanned.

This news was so unexpected the Administrator wasn't sure he even understood. *"Inquiry repeat?"* he asked.

The Gunner's hulking form tensed in anger at the Administrator's stupidity, and the Administrator tried not to visibly recoil. Carefully, as if speaking to a dim child, the Gunner projected images of Adrastea, of humans, of missile batteries, of the Warriors' own ship vibrating as though being tremorsounded: they were being scanned by humans on Adrastea, with weapons. The ship was in imminent danger of attack.

Abrupt panic seized the Administrator. *Combat!* In this solar system where nothing ever happened? Well of course. The Earthlings were murderers, butchers. Why was he surprised? But still! The Administrator knew himself to be nothing but a glorified babysitter, and now his ship was in combat! It was surreal.

He didn't know what to... Wait, of course he knew, he reminded himself. The Administrator projected images of safety straps, and ordered everyone to their battle stations. Simple enough. But what n...?

Eager as a newborn given his first dish of gravel, the Gunner requested permission to fire the ship's bombard at the Earthlings on the worldlet below.

The Administrator hesitated. This was so far outside any experience he had ever...

The Gunner barked his request again, practically snarling an image of their bridge full of Jan corpses if the Administrator continued to hesitate. A few of the other Warriors gave low grumbles of agreement.

They could actually all die here, the Administrator thought. Fear birthed excitement at the thought that, for the first time in his life, something was actually *happening*.

He determined he would be up to this challenge, and show that self-important hoonkiller at the gunnery station what he was made of. The Administrator projected an image of the bombardment cannon and of an explosion. The order was given.

There was a barely perceptible thump as the rockets fired from the ship's ventral bombard. On the view display, they were white streaks against the black night, turning black against the glaring gray of the moon's surface. Jupiter was to their back, leaving Adrastea clearly lit. The Gunner announced that the instruments registered an explosion on the moon's surface, though from their orbit the Administrator could not see it.

There was a moment's pause, and then the Structural Integrity Officer announced that the humans had returned fire. Had in fact hit them. The humans had struck the transport ship with preposterously antiquated, Pre-Contact artillery lasers. The transport was only lightly armored (until now, the Administrator had thought it absurd that it was armored at all), but that minimal armor was more than adequate to withstand these few anemic flashlight beams. The humans' counterattack had done virtually no damage, and the crew hadn't felt a thing. The Administrator wouldn't have even known they'd been hit if not for Structural Integrity's report.

The Administrator felt a mix of confusion and satisfaction that his ship was winning so handily. He was about to give the order to fire another volley and secure their victory.

Victory... in a fight where his ship had fired the first shot.

Terrible misgivings suddenly formed in his mind.

He ordered a cease fire.

The Gunner inclined his apex toward the Administrator, such that the eyesphere atop the Warrior's body was aimed almost straight at the Administrator. The tripartite warmouth in his side opened slightly, providing a thin glimpse of row on row of gleaming, axe-like black fangs. The Gunner projected an image of raucous victory celebration, and then of human corpses. *"Glory!"* he said. *"Fury!"*

The Administrator repeated the cease fire order. He said their own ship had fired first. It would be viewed by the Matriarchs as an unjustified attack, and they were all now culpable.

The Gunner screamed a detailed image of a platoon of warriors fighting an enraged *hoon*. The picture was deafening in the enclosed bridge.

*"Non sequitur. Explain,"* the Administrator said.

The Gunner said that they must complete their task in wiping out the enemy, because a wounded and enraged enemy could be the deadliest of all. The humans still lived. He pleaded to be allowed to fire another missile volley.

The Administrator hesitated.

They were all knocked about in their straps as the hull cracked open with a tremendous bang followed by wind.

The Administrator would later learn that the Adrastean humans had fired the only relatively state-of-the-art weapon they had: a single, old, cloaked Thunderchild missile.

The screaming wind really lasted only a moment—and the Administrator had the briefest glimpse through the fissure in the bridge bulkhead of a gray sphere tumbling away from them to be replaced by racing white stars on black—before sealant foam closed the hull breach. The ship was spinning. Alarms blared, reporting more breaches below decks. Debris crashed and ricocheted against the interior bulkheads.

He could hear screams through the floor from elsewhere in the ship. As a rabbit screams only when mortally wounded, so it was with Jan.

Struggling to organize his thoughts, the Administrator shouted to the Pilot to stabilize the ship, and to the Gunner to fire the bombard. His voice carried mainly through the floor to which he was strapped, as the air was now very thin. The sickening spinning came to a stop through the Pilot's efforts, and the wreckage from the explosion soon floated freely. The wails from below continued, and he heard war cries mixed with them.

Structural Integrity reported the obvious fact that they could not survive another such hit, but the Gunner did not oblige with the cannon. The Administrator soon saw why. One of the Gunner's arms had been sheared clean off by a flying hull chunk, and he appeared unconscious. Muddy, fibrous clods of Janflesh and viscous ichor spilled away from the stump, as the arm itself floated tumbling lazily away from its owner.

Horrified, the Administrator unstrapped himself. He kicked away from his station and floated over to the Gunner's control podium. Floating above it, he stared at it helplessly for a moment and yelled, *"Query!"* with an image of the controls.

The Pilot called back an image of a large triangular control in the center—a blockish thing designed for a Warrior's claw, not a Worker's tendrils. The Administrator formed a fist and mashed it down.

This time, *eighteen* lines of missile exhaust were visible streaking toward Adrastea. This explosion was big enough to be visible from orbit, a lovely tiny blossom of smoke and light on the bleak gray surface.

It was all over. The whole incident had been absurdly brief. Whoever had been there was now very dead.

The process of the Administrator's arrest and return to Callisto was a blur. Not that he couldn't recall every detail with agonizing clarity if he so chose in later years, but he rarely chose.

The transport ship had set down on the far side of Adrastea from the attack. He remembered the rocky terrain, the strange closeness of the horizon, the low gravity. A quick count had revealed many injuries, but only five deaths out of the 243 aboard ship. *Only!* A relief ship arrived not long after, and police with it. Then he remembered a lot of rushing around, many questions, and himself feeling numb through the whole ordeal. There seemed to be great urgency to have him taken away by Jannite police before human investigators could reach the scene. He was loaded into a transport back to Callisto, where he would be held in the prison in Third Warren.

It turned out that there had been a colony of human homesteaders on Adrastea. Space hermits. There was no guessing for how many generations they'd been sitting on that tiny rock, happily inbreeding and keeping such a low profile that nobody knew they were there. They weren't hostile; but, being good and proper libertarian space hermits, they *were* armed.

The Administrator's actions had been completely unprovoked. All the humans had done was to scan his vessel as it passed. As captain, all responsibility for the atrocity fell on him. He was a murderer.

Among Earthmen, there was a common, naive notion that because the Jan were scrupulously honest and (the Workers, at least) were generally less violent than humans, that they were all model citizens. This was nonsense, and the Administrator was far from alone in the dank prison. Violent crime might be less common among the communally-minded "bee people" than among Earthlings, but it was hardly unknown. Alongside him now were every stripe of murderers and thugs and thieves and petty vandals. Just no liars.

He didn't know where they kept finding blunt instruments to smash into each other. It didn't matter how many times the guards took them away, new ones were always improvised. Living flesh cracked open, mortal fibers fraying out like spilled dinner asbestos, ichor dripping in slow, thick, muddy plops. Here he witnessed pointless barbarisms the like of which he'd never conceived. And the reason he'd not imagined them was that the Valhallan Warriors' violence among themselves, that he knew so well and had always considered brutal, was simply the release of tension. It was horseplay, not malice. The criminals here had malice to spare, against their jailers, against anyone within reach. No small measure of it was directed at *him,* and he had to avoid getting caught in the random fights, constantly and not always successfully, as his injuries came to attest, painful ugly cracks sealed with medical cement.

Worst was that he knew he *deservedly* walked among such as these, for he had a larger deathcount to his name than any of them. The Administrator wondered whether Earthlings could *possibly* be any fouler than this. Than himself.

His misery was a deadweight. He had little to do but think, remember, and regret (much later, when he learned English, he took note of the root of the word "penitentiary"). He could not believe he had done this thing. There was great temptation to blame his stupidity that day on circumstance, on his surprise, to convince himself that if the situation had been just a little different, he'd have been wiser—but circumstances weren't different, and he ultimately concluded there was no getting away from his culpability. The Gunner, his own subordinate, had given him an order, and he'd obeyed. And a lot of people—five of his own charges, and a large family of Earthling "people"—had died. There had been at least thirty humans, but the investigators weren't sure that they had found all the remains.

It bothered him that he hadn't seen the humans die. He hoped this wasn't bloodlust. But to kill so anonymously seemed vile. The Administrator envisioned what it must have been like on the ground for the humans. Alien monsters—him and his ship—raining fire on them out of the sky for no reason. The fire spreading effortlessly in the high oxygen atmosphere. Soft carboniferous bodies oxidizing like fuel. Or else, wall breaches spilling their precious air out into space, the wind maybe pulling humans with it to die in the void.

He believed he would die. The logical thing for his superiors to do was extradite him to the Earth savages, and they would kill him. He'd be lucky if they didn't torture him first. Slowly melt him down into molten sludge and magma. Or more likely, some unguessable torture specific to Earth. Something organic, biological. He pictured himself cooking and drowning in a pool of living organic slime, as hot, wet, fluid pseudopods slithered into his every orifice to shatter him from the inside out. Even in the battle—if the massacre he'd directed could be called a battle—he'd not felt such mortal dread.

All he was or should be was thrown in doubt, and he felt he had violated some primal rule of the universe. His eminent mother Dwight was a believer in the Supreme Matriarch and her offspring pantheon, one of the most popular of the Jannite faiths, but the Administrator had never been particularly pious. *"All events we experience are buffets in the backward-rushing gale of time."* Or some such.

Prisoners were provided reading materials. He picked one up more or less at random and was startled to realize it was a holographic Janscript translation of an Earth book. The Janscript floating above it gave the title "Different Book." He would later learn that the original Hebrew word for "holy" meant, literally, "different," as in "different from man or anything in his world;" and that Bible was simply an antiquarian synonym for "book."

At first, he was very unimpressed with it. It was told from a completely Earth-centric view, with Earth as the center of creation. He kept reading. Monotheism, that was mildly interesting. He found himself identifying with Adam and Eve a bit, when they fouled up. And still more with Cain, whose anger turned to murder, and who was sent to wander the Earth as punishment. He was surprised when he came to the reconciliation between Jacob and Esau, for Jacob appeared to have wronged Esau greatly. Overall he was struck by the completely natural individualism of the humans. The nomadic existence of the patriarchs, so basic and primal, was intriguing. His growing fascination with the alien culture kept him reading.

He would later learn that the sections of scripture which humans themselves usually found the least interesting were the ones that most resembled Jannite writing. Lots of lists. Lots and lots of lists. Rules, begats, descriptions. He had no problem with that at all.

There was a great deal of blood and savagery. Of course, that also served to make it feel honest, especially bearing in mind his preconceptions about mankind. It was compelling, reading this long, multigenerational history with a single central Figure. Assuming any of it to be true, the Administrator wasn't sure what to make of Him. It was difficult to get a clear idea of His character, even within the context of Earthling psychology (or, at least through the filter of Earthling interpretation and writing, if indeed He existed as a being transcendent of Man and Jan alike). Unsurprisingly, the Administrator likened Him to a Matriarch, as indeed most Jannite deities were depicted.

At times this Being's justice and punishments seemed harsh, bloody, merciless as only the most vicious of history's Matriarchs had been... while other times He and His prophets spoke of love, forgiveness, and compassion in a way that even his own far more communal race would do well to heed.

Yet despite the obvious contradictions, there was a sense of coherency to it, as of a single Being. And his impression of Him was one of goodness.

At first the Administrator only entertained the possibility of His existence as a way to understand the text. But as he read, he was slowly persuaded. He found his guilt over the wrong he had done to a group of humans fueled a desire to better understand what motivated these strange beings, whom he'd held in contempt and then stupidly slaughtered.

Eventually, it spoke of the God of the Hebrews being omniscient, omnipresent, and now open to all, not just Hebrews. If this were true, the Administrator reflected, it would mean He was aware of what he was thinking at this moment. And every other moment. Might as well address Him, then.

Yet doubtful that anyone was listening, Paul prayed silently.

Paul said, "It was the lowest point in my life, and I often ask myself if I would have grabbed hold of a tract on any religion just as eagerly. I don't think so, but that idea troubled me very much in the beginning. I appreciate the recognition of the individual found in the Hebraic faiths. It's... largely foreign to my people. Now, of course, the Greeks had that to an even greater extent, with their talk of *arete* and tradition of egalitarian debate. But they were polytheists, and even they gradually seemed to conclude that a heaven that was just like their own world, only bigger and full of more impressive petty scheming people, didn't provide many ultimate answers because it just begged the question of what lay beyond *that.*"

The ground rumbled with Paul's tremor-sigh. "Dwight took the blame for the massacre, which makes mockery of all our claims of racial honesty. The notion that one of the most brilliant beings in the Solar System could have been responsible for such a manifestly stupid disaster is absurd. Trust me, no one deserves blame for that horror except me."

"The... survivors' wounds were tended. The Gunner received a prosthetic arm. The surgeons could have made it look natural, but Warriors prize their scars, so he opted for a metallic one. My subordinate at Valhalla, who had taken the name Heimdall, and who of course had a penchant for mythological names, nicknamed the Gunner Nuada. After the Celtic war god with a silver hand." He said quietly, "I assume there was a funeral for the five who died."

He continued, somberly, "The homesteaders' family name was Steven. Innocents killed in a volley of projectiles, and their name was actually Steven. There's irony for you."

"Irony for...?" Indira was confused at first, but then got the reference. "Oh!" she said, then, "Steven is a common enough name," she said softly.

"A human missionary eventually helped me interpret some of what I read. His name was Kazuo. A very nice old man, and I had *many* questions. I haven't seen him in years. In reading those scriptures, I came to realize that I hadn't understood your people. You have your faults, just as mine do, but it's not as if you're not aware of them. In fact, in your penchant for senseless violence, I felt more in common with mankind than I did with my own people."

"Like Saul of Tarsus, who was guilty of the stoning of Saint Steven, but then went on to become Saint Paul," she finished for him.

"Yes," he said.

"How is it you weren't extradited?" she asked, fascinated but cautious of hurting old wounds.

"Dwight... my mother... is a mistress diplomat, and the most senior Matriarch in the Solar System. She tried to take ultimate responsibility for my actions without claiming to approve of them, and she further persuaded the human authorities that a circus trial, which my trial would surely have been, would benefit no one and only lead to more violence, possibly even war. She emphasized that we have our own justice system." He paused. "A justice system which, when you come down to it, is mostly just Matriarchs' fiat."

For years, he'd wondered precisely what byzantine politicking among the Matriarchs had gotten him off so scott free. Between telecommunications equipment, and simple globe-spanning tremorspeech below the range of Worker and Warrior hearing, the Matriarchs were in constant conversation, debate, and collusion over the daily fate of their people. These inter-Matriarchal communiques could carry vastly greater sums of information than the simple tremorspeech of Workers and Warriors, or the air-carried symbol-words of Earthling men. No doubt Dwight had consulted all of them. Then again, she had enough seniority that she might have forced the issue. But why?

"An Old Boys' Network," Indira said. "Or Old Girls' Network, rather. I'm glad she did, but I'm surprised your mother got you off the hook."

"You call this off the hook?!" he shouted. "Look at me! I live among the very monsters I hated. I've practically become one of them. I spend my days crushed by your atmosphere and your gravity, baked by your sun, cut off from my heritage..." He trailed off.

"You mean..." she hated to say it, "you're living on Earth as a punishment?" *Just a moment ago, he'd spoken of how he'd come to view Earth as beautiful.*

He hesitated before he spoke. "Self-imposed punishment, and I'm sorry for boasting of it just now. I had to repent, Indira. I'd been absolved of any official wrongdoing, but I *shouldn't* have been. I realized that the Warriors had prodded me into starting the fight because *I* had taught *them* to hate humans, and they were only *able* to do it because of my own hate. The responsibility was mine. The guilt for those pointless deaths ravaged me. Conscience was tearing my soul apart.

"I determined I must come to know and understand those I'd previously wanted to destroy. And in studying you and your culture... I found a monothestic faith centered around forgiveness. And that's how I felt. That I'd sinned not just against the Stevens, but against the very Mind and Soul behind all that is. Enough of the Law was imprinted on my heart for me to appreciate the hellishness of what I'd done, and the weight of it was destroying me.

"I suspect... maybe that's *why* Dwight didn't punish me. She knows her children. There had been no humans on my ship during the battle, of course, and most humans have trouble recognizing individual Jan anyway. So my anonymity on Earth was reasonably assured," he said.

"So... now I know a big secret?" she said.

"Your governments know who I am. I haven't made so massive a secret of it as all that. But it's not something I'm eager to talk about. I've often thought that I *should* be more open about it. I owe penance to your entire people."

"Mmnh..." she said, "I dunno. Around *here,* at least among the sincere and pious ones, you might be okay. But in the wider world? People are mean, and they like to see the guilty punished for the entertainment of it as much as anything."

"I've read about the Roman public executions in my religious studies," Paul said quietly.

"Well, there you go. Society has changed, but people haven't."

"Hasn't the Word of God *made* people better since Roman times? God's Law written on your hearts?"

"The world's hardly all Christian, and it would *not* be a paradise even if it were. I assure you of that. If you think Christians don't go for punishment as lurid entertainment, you should read up on something called the *auto de fe* in Spain. We made the Romans look *classy* by comparison."

"Hm."

"I mean, do you want me list our crimes? The Crusades, the Inquisition, pogroms, bookburnings..." she said.

"Mennonites never did any of those things," he pointed out.

She grimaced. *Okay, so he had a big life crisis, broke down, and maybe went a little loopy, and he found something to cling to, to tether him to reality. Well, there's no harm in that, I guess. Little weird, maybe, but who'm I to talk? And he says he's learning* individuality *among the Old Order Plain people? I wonder if he sees the irony in* that? "No. No we haven't," she said. "Look, I'm not mocking your faith. It's... ostensibly my faith, too. Just... keep your yap shut about this thing unless you *want* to get martyred. And that would be pretty darned inconsiderate to me. I'd miss you."

"Thank you," he said slowly, and with emphasis. "So now you know. Do you forgive me?" Paul asked.

She was very slow in answering. Finally, she said, "What have I got to forgive you for? I have no connection to that battle."

Paul was surprised by her answer. "You're human. I sinned against your entire species."

"But... Well, all right then, Paul. I forgive you, if that's what you want to hear. But all the time I've known you, you've dedicated so much of your life to penance and contrition that as far as I'm concerned, there's nothing to forgive. I said you're my best friend." She patted his huge gray arm with her tiny, soft, warm right hand.

A little awed, he said, "Thank you." After a time, he said, "When I came to Earth, I hated it. I went on hating it for a long time. And then... as you said... I met you." Paul said, "I live alone. That itself is a relatively foreign concept to my people. Some Jan religions have hermitic traditions, but it's considered a personal sacrifice."

Indira asked, "Do you get lonely?"

Paul said, "Yes, but I was lonely among the crowds of home, too." He laid a finger tendril lightly across her hand. "I am not lonely, right now."

She smiled in the darkness.

"I should get back," she finally said. "Get a little sleep before I go to work in the morning." They said their good-byes. Despite her tiredness, she ran home to keep warm in the night chill. She had removed her cap, and her dark locks trailed in the wind behind her, in the moonlight. It startled him how graceful the sight of her lithe form dancing across the grass was, and he wondered why he had never noticed it before.

He remained awake after she left, and he watched the sun rise. The birds began their morning chorus; and the hills, so green they hardly seemed real, danced and sang in the morning light. Beyond them, distant mountains of pale turquiose were limned in the gold and ruby of sunrise. How had he ever been blind to the beauty of this place? The rosy fingers of Earthly dawn would never carress Callisto. It didn't seem alien at all, any more. That fact unsettled him a little, but not much. All God's terrestrial creation seemed in harmony.

But what of extraterrestrial creation? The homey and rustic simplicity of a colony warren scarcely a generation old. The tunnels and the crowds and the crystal plants shimmering with rainbows in the light of Jupiter, and Jupiter itself filling the sky like the face of God, making it no wonder that the Romans had worshipped it, though to them it was only a dot. And also the endless bureaucracy; the deferential, unimaginative lockstep mentality; the tedium. He needed Callisto, and he needed to flee it. He keenly understood Indira's ambivalence about her home.

But *here,* now, in the afterglow of Indira's company, he felt fulfilled. Joyful. It was good.

# 5

Time passed. Thanksgiving and Christmas. The green mountains changed first to gold and then to glittering crystal, like an impossibly dense star-field come to Earth. The cold of winter was good. The impossible serene wonder of falling snow carpeting over all the visible world, the blessed chill of it on his skin, on his feet as he stomped crunching through it. For Christmas, Paul gave Indira some colorful crystals grown in the "rock garden" where he grew his food, and she gave him a small wooden horse, which her father had carved for her when she was a very young girl. Snow, and then spring. Indira and Paul's friendship grew closer. She purchased a deck of oversized playing cards, and she would spend time at Paul's house playing hasenpfeffer late into the night. Or sometimes they'd play Parcheesi, again with an oversized set. Were it someone else, her father would have taken issue with the matter, but of course, the Jan was not human. Jawaharlal said, "Anyone would think you two were courting." She laughed.

Jawaharlal pitied her; she did not realize that, and would have hated it if she did. She already believed he felt disappointed in her, and that was burden enough.

Paul and Indira became close in the following years. At first he'd supposed his happiness at their friendship to stem merely from a sense of validation—that he'd finally grasped Earthly things well enough to count a human as not merely an associate, but a friend. It was only later that it dawned on him that, as she had once said of him, she had in fact become *his* best friend. The best he'd ever had.

Unlike most humans, but like Jan, she was honest to the point of bluntness. And unlike most Jan, but like Paul, she had a temper. Talking to her felt the easiest and most natural thing in the world, and he looked forward to any time he might spend in her company.

Paul's writing career proved successful. He garnered a modest following as an essayist among Humans and Jan, acquiring a regular column in the venerable *Event* telemagazine about his Earth experiences and insights. While his prose style was frequently found wanting, readers seemed to believe he made up for it in substance. His perspective was unique and his insights struck many as poignant. And entirely apart from his writing career, there was always someone who wanted stonework done and was willing to pay for it. People had come to like Paul, in time. Indira used to tease him that the locals liked him better than they did her.

The atmosphere was cloudy and clammy, hardly unusual for central Pennsylvania. Rain might come on that evening, or the clouds might stay unchanged a week or more. The air felt damp and dank, and the Fenstermachers' sole dairy cow was very ill.

"She's all ferhoodled today," Jawaharlal said. "Not right in the head."

"I can see that!" said Dr. Tamsanga, the new local veterinarian, narrowly dodging a hoof kicked in his direction as he tried to get in close to the dairy cow.

"She's normally very gentle. Can you help her?" Jawaharlal's voice, typically stoic nearly to the point of monotone, betrayed his compassion for the animal, for Rachel had virtually been his late wife Ingrid's pet. Theirs was a produce farm, and Rachel was there for milk, not meat. Ingrid had loved animals, and she would watch the birds and squirrels and rabbits of Pennsylvania with childlike fascination quite beyond Jawaharlal's ken, but he had loved to watch her watching them. Ingrid had been raised an educated, sophisticated woman, but she'd abandoned the city for this rural world she loved. If only their daughter had shared her fascination with nature, he thought. But to young Indira, such things were intimately familiar and therefore infinitely uninteresting, and so she followed her mother's example by leaving the world of her youth for something completely different.

"First I will have to get close to her." Tamsanga spoke with a slight accent, betraying that English was his second language. He pulled out a portable psychontronic microwave projector, adjusted its controls, and pointed it at Rachel's head; the pleasure centers of the cow's brain were stimulated, and she quickly quietened. "There. That is the way. I must not use it for long until I have figured out the trouble. If her problem is neurological, too much of this might make it worse. But a short zap to quiet her down should not hurt anything." He quickly extracted a blood sample with his bioscanner wand and then examined the various readouts it gave him.

Several moments passed. A pinprick of water struck Jawaharlal's nose. So it would rain today after all. He watched the vet with concern.

"Hm," Tamsanga finally said.

"Eh?" Jawaharlal asked.

"Mm," the vet said.

"What?" Jawaharlal asked.

"Wait..." the vet said.

"Hrm," Jawaharlal said.

Rachel lowed morosely as the psychotron's doping wore off.

"Wow," the vet finally said.

"What?" Jawaharlal reiterated. Wow couldn't be good.

"Well. That is different," the veterinarian said.

"Hm?" Jawaharlal scowled. "How's it different?"

"She has an alien virus," the vet said.

"Alien!" Jawaharlal said. "How could that have happened? Now there's a Jan, lives up the road..."

The vet waved that off. "No, sir. Jan are organosilicates. They cannot be a vector for parasites that affect Earth life. This is classic *xenoxia Khrytonica*. A harmless symbiote in some Elavian animals... that is how it was discovered... but, ehm, unlike most alien germs, it can infect Earth life. And... well, um, I am embarrassed to say this, but the usual vector is alien drugs like lotos or kreg. Really, those drugs are varieties of *xenoxia*. That is why she is delerious. She is..." He was about to say *high,* but the implication that Mr. Fenstermacher's cow was under the influence of narcotics had already produced an expression of scandalized incredulity on the farmer's face. "Well, it is affecting her. I think that a human drug user probably caused this."

"That can't be," Jawaharlal said. "No one here would be mixed up with anything like that."

The vet shrugged. "Well, she must have been in close contact with someone. *Xenoxia* is not an airborne bug. Hmh. My best guess would be that she got it when she was being milked."

"Well, the only ones who milk her are me and my two farmhands," Jawaharlal said.

"Well," the vet said, shrugging again, "I do not want to, um, go pointing fingers, but you might want to talk with them."

Jawaharlal grunted, took off his hat for a moment, and ran a brown, bony hand through his hair in disgust. He couldn't believe such a thing, and yet now he'd be obliged to confront both of them about it.

"Did you figure out what's wrong with Rachel?" asked a young woman coming from the direction of the house as Jawaharlal replaced his hat. Tamsanga assumed her to be the farmer's daughter. She seemed very concerned.

"Doctor says it's a space disease," Jawaharlal said slowly as though the words didn't feel right in his mouth.

Indira was startled. "You don't mean *xenoxia?* That's crazy! No one around here would be using kreg."

The doctor turned to her, clearly surprised at her familiarity with such matters. He hadn't even mentioned the bug's name to her, but there were only a handful of "space diseases," and this was the most common. "Well, that is what we are trying to find out here," he said. She was an attractive woman, in an aquiline-nosed kind of way. A little big in the hips, perhaps, but it gave her nice curves. He could see black hair peeking beneath the bonnet. And he noticed how wide and how very deep brown her eyes were. He found himself smiling. "You know about this... ehm, type of thing?" he asked.

Jawaharlal eyed her. She rolled her eyes. *No, I never did drugs, Pa. Alcohol was quite enough.* "I used to live on Felice Station," she informed the doctor.

"Oh! That's interesting!" he said. He held out his hand. "I'm Tendai Tamsanga. I have just taken over Dr. Edo's veterinary practice."

"Oh, yeah, she said she was retiring," Indira said, shaking his hand. "I'm Indira. You've got an accent. Zimbabwe?"

He laughed. A very nice grin, white teeth in a dark face. Very high cheekbones. His beard marked him as a non-Mennonite, or at least belonging to a more liberal Mennonite conference than Lufthafen. Short, close-cropped, full of fifty skillion little black curls, it looked good on him. He was older than she was, maybe not by much, or maybe just well-preserved. She realized she was staring as he said, "I did not realize it was still that strong."

"Try using contractions. They're good for you.."

"I will," he said. He almost corrected himself to say *"I'll,"* but caught it in time. "Yes, I was born in the Capital, but I've lived in North America ten years now. I'm mostly Shona background, with some Nuer from my Sudanese grandfather—which is why I am so dark—one of my great grandmothers was Greek, and I have some Dutch family if you go back far enough." She seemed surprised at this last, and he clarified, "The *other* kind of Dutch. Not German."

"Oh! Netherlandsish. Hollandaise," she said, grinning.

He didn't quite get the joke, but he smiled back. "I went through Felice once, for a school trip to the Moon years ago. That was really my only time off-planet."

She shrugged. "Well, Felice barely counts as off-planet. I've never even been to the Moon. Where'd you go, Armstrong?"

He nodded. "Everybody told me that Armstrong was a tourist trap, but I had a good time."

She said, "When I was younger, I wanted to go take a trip to Mars. Best skiing in the Solar System, everybody said." He smiled. She cleared her throat. It had been an *awfully* long time since she'd done this dance with anybody.

"Are you talking about Olympus Mons?" he said. "I know the gravity is low, but um, I've heard that anybody who tries the slopes there is crazy," he laughed. He hoped he sounded sophisticated. Then again, this being where it was, perhaps she didn't like sophisticated. "Have you ever played zero gravity tennis?" he asked.

"That's the only kind I've ever played," she said.

"Really! Oh, I tried it on the ship to the Moon, and I got dizzy," he said.

"Eh-hem," Jawaharlal eh-hemed. "My cow."

"Oh, yes! Of course, I'm sorry." Dr. Tamsanga dropped into lecture mode and recited, "Typically, the human immune system can fight off *xenoxia,* but until it succeeds, you experience a euphoric, frequently hallucinogenic high. But fighting off the infection once does not immunize you, it just leaves your immune system weak for a while. So if you take another hit of it soon afterward, the high lasts longer because the infection lasts longer. Eventually, you can wind up in a delirium that lasts for days.

"Different animals can be more or less susceptible to it than people. I don't, mm, think there's been much research on cattle, but poor Rachel here is obviously taking it pretty hard. I should be able to clear this up without trouble, though. But even after she recovers, she is going to be in a bad mood for a while because she will experience withdrawal."

Indira whistled, and she petted Rachel, trying to calm her. "I can't believe we have a junkie cow. Is she... enjoying this?"

"I think she looks scared, don't you? She probably can't tell up from down right now," the vet said. "Here, I will prepare a solution of nano," he said. As always, the doctor was relieved that the local luddism traditionally did not extend to medical matters, and typically not to veterinary ones either.

"Nanites? Hmph, with nanites, you could turn her into a cocker spaniel," Jawaharlal said, wincing.

"That's a... pretty big exaggeration," the vet said. "Here..." He made several adjustments on his medwand and a couple of minutes later, it had produced a small tablet. "Now, if she will just swallow that..."

"I'll give it to her," Indira said. "She trusts me."

He had clearly mixed it with sugar, because Rachel swallowed it eagerly enough. "She should be over the infection by tomorrow," he said, "but she will probably be tired and grumpy for a day or so."

"Good, good," Jawaharlal said. Then he regarded them both. He was no dummy. "Daughter, I've other work to attend to. Look after this business," Jawaharlal said and turned and walked away.

"Yes, Pa," she ended up saying to his back.

"Thank you, Miss," the doctor said, and smiled brightly beneath his trim moustache. It would be a cliché to say that Tendai Tamsanga was tall, dark, and handsome, but it would also be literally true. His body looked lean and strong, his skin so deep a black it was almost blue. "What did you do for a living on Felice?" he asked.

"Oh, I'm a... I was a general engineer," she said.

"General? Like they have out on the space platforms? That's a pretty important job. What are you doing... here?"

She sighed. "I ask myself that every day. Actually, I run the Fix-It shop on 3rd and Maple."

"Um... Do they even have anything complicated around here to fix?" he asked.

"Not a blessed thing, no," she said.

"Do you ever get bored?" he asked.

"Do I ever *not?*" she asked. She smiled and braced herself as she felt her dark face flush beet red. *God! It's been so long since I've even tried...* "Would you like to come in for a slice of pie?" she blurted as suavely as it is possible to blurt.

"Um..." He hesitated. "No. Thank you. Your dad scares me. A little."

"Ah," she said. *"But I made it myself with fresh apples from our own trees." Should I say that? Will it sound desperate? Ah hell, he's already said no. Just walk away...* "Well, yes, he does do that," she said.

"I would like some coffee though," he said, hiding his nervousness. "I know there is a diner just down the way. My treat."

"Hochleitner's! Yeah, sure," she said as casually as she could. *Yes!*

She drove them in her church-approved matte black groundcar to Ruth Hochleitner's diner. Barney Estragon took their orders. He used to tell people he had taken the last name as a pun having to do with his being a "waiter," but since no one seemed to get the joke, he rarely mentioned it any more. A surprising number of genengineered and artificial beings were attracted to religious and luddite lifestyles, and there was a lot of talk among psychologists about why this was so. Perhaps it made them feel more human. Or perhaps it was that a being who knew himself inarguably to be a creation took solace in the notion that his clearly flawed creators were creations themselves. Like the near or remote ancestors of everyone in town, Barney had expressed a desire to escape the industrial civilization that spawned him, and Ruth had welcomed him.

He brought them their meals. Indira had a plate of sticky chicken with zucchini bread and apple cider, and Tendai had a ham sandwich and a Thurmadine Fizz.

Tendai said, "What do you think of President Ramalinga?"

Indira said, "He's a boob."

Tendai said, "Okay..."

Indira said, "This is nice. Nobody around here follows worldly affairs enough for me to commiserate about what a boob he is."

Tendai said, "Well, I grew up in the Capital. I follow politics out of habit."

Indira said, "You voted for him, didn't you?"

"Yes," Tendai said.

*"Sigh,"* she sighed. "Well, I won't hold that against you. It's its own punishment. How come you moved here? All roads lead to Zimbabwe, right?"

"Earth Capital is a noisy headache. And natural animals have always held more interest for me than genenged ones. Luddite farm country sounded good, and I wanted to get away from home. So, I studied at Teviotdale Farm at the University of Zimbabwe, and after I graduated I moved here and worked for a small veterinary practice out in Lancaster. Eventually I got word that Dr. Mary Edo was retiring, and I figured it was a chance to have my own practice."

The date went well. He appeared to be a genuinely nice guy—kind, as a vet should be, to man as well as beast, and he was indeed Mennonite (there having been a sizable Mennonite population in Africa since the late twentieth century), the converse of which might not necessarily have dissuaded her, but it certainly simplified matters.

For his part, Tendai could scarcely help being attracted to the farmer's daughter. She was small and shapely (as shapely as one can be in an Old Order dress), with a smooth almond complexion and the aforementioned nose. She reminded him of a tiny, nervous little bird like a timba. But far and away, her most striking feature was her eyes—deep and dark as space, fiery and magnetic like stars. They spoke of restlessness, life, danger, and of unspeakable loneliness. Even in Shona, let alone in English, Tendai was not a particularly eloquent man, and he could not have very adequately described just what he felt looking in those eyes—but as they talked, he knew that more than anything else, he wanted to hold her.

They spoke of this, that, and the other. Ruth came out at one point to say hi, and presumably to scope out the fellow Indira had come with. They finished their meal and shared a piece of rhubarb pie. The rain had started, so Tendai lifted his topcoat over their heads to shield them as they ran, and they both laughed as their shoes splashed on the wet pavement. She drove them back to her home, where he retrieved his car and went on his own way. Jawaharlal was busy, so she then returned to the diner to talk to Ruth about her new acquaintance.

Ruthie's eyes glittered as she said, "I like him. Don't let him get away."

"Thanks" she said, blushing. "You know, he is Mennonite, but he's not Old Order."

Ruth said, "The world would not end if you married someone not Old Order."

"Woah, woah now..." she said, a little angrily.

"Oh, you was thinkin' it yourself, and don't tell me you wasn't," Ruthie said.

While Indira had been out with Tendai, Jawaharlal finished the chore he'd been working on, and then went straight to the distasteful matter of speaking to the farmhands individually about the vet's diagnosis, in the living room of his house. Amos denied any knowledge of the matter, and Jawaharlal moved on to Thrym.

Thrym's catlike yellow eyes narrowed. "So. You found me out," he said softly.

Jawaharlal was so startled he found himself momentarily at a loss for words. "Oh?" he said.

"Yes. Clever of you. Bunch of pacifist farmers with a born killer. What'ja expect? Course he's a drug addict. Probably does it to control his... wild rages."

Jawaharlal's patience with this business was rather thin. "Why are you mocking me?"

Thrym shrugged. "'Cause I can't take pacifists seriously, I guess. Oh don't mistake me, Mr. Fenstermacher. You've been a good boss. But I'd been planning on clearing out anyway. I'll be... taking my leave now."

He left the house without saying another word, Jawaharlal gaping in surprise in his wake.

For all his anger, as he walked away, Thrym looked small and old and tired; still he refused Jawaharlal's entreaties for him to return and stalked into a cold rain that had begun while they spoke.

Thrym was a hard-bitten man who'd lived a hard life, and he came from a line of such dating back to when Alfheim's Imperium first bred the "Grotesques," shortened to "Tesks," their cannon fodder in the Genomic War. The Tesks' rebellion against their masters was one of the main reasons for—some would say the deciding factor in—humanity's victory. Yet man did not warmly welcome his former foes, and so, many generations later, the Tesks' lot was still a hard one. They took such work as they could get, usually involving violence because they were good at it. Military careers were common. Thrym had fought on humanity's side during the Android Uprising, long ago. He was weary of war and had intended to retire here—but now he'd chucked all of it, and he was far too proud to admit he was already starting to regret the decision.

A blessing (or perhaps a burden) for Tesks was that they were good at reading people, their heightened awareness of others' body language and mannerisms making a kind of extra empathic sense. There was much speculation as to why this was the case, as it had certainly not been any intent of Alfheim's genewrights, who had wanted simple dog soldiers. The most popular theory claimed it was an aspect of their augmented situational awareness, their strong eye and memory for visual details which were meant as a tactical advantage in battle; it was only natural that this awareness should include facial expressions and such. Or perhaps it was their animal-derived DNA—canine and many others—since beasts are of necessity born masters of nonverbal communication, and can often read a man's moods far better than can other men who must judge him by his words. Or, just perhaps, it was literally a Providential gift to a people who might otherwise be called utterly cursed; a peculiar knack that made almost everyone they encountered an open book to them.

Unfortunately, this was the main reason Thrym had taken an instant dislike to Paul. The creature was *unreadable,* which felt *wrong* on every level. It had made him lose his temper at Paul during that dinner, years ago. He'd felt like a fool afterward, and had come near to apologizing, though he never did. Then, still later, in light of new discoveries, he came to believe he'd let the alien off too easily. None of it mattered, now.

Jawaharlal Fenstermacher, on the other hand, he understood. When Thrym had started working for him, the farmer's wife had just died, and his daughter had left home and possibly the family faith. The guy was a walking wound, and it had hurt just to look at him. But Fenstermacher had responded to his pain in the way Thrym himself considered most admirable, with a stiff upper lip. He was a rock. A good soldier. A man Thrym was proud to work for. Maybe not a friend, as such (for Tesks are slow to give friendship), but a respected comrade.

Then the crazy daughter had come back. And he'd hired the Baumgartner kid, who just got dumber every passing day. And then came the daughter's tentacle monster boyfriend or whatever "Paul" was to her (he tried not to think about that too hard). *It was time to go,* he told himself. He'd be packed in an hour.

But for the life of him, he wasn't sure what he would do next.

Sol was setting and the stars were coming out, and Indira was up late with Paul, gazing at them. It was chilly, which she supposed he must be enjoying. She wore a black woolen coat her mother had made for her, ages ago. It was snug, but she was pleased that it still fit. On Sundays (the traditional visiting day), or on weekday evenings when her work at the shop was over, as was the case today, it was their habit that she and Paul would sit outside his home talking. These talks were usually about nothing of any great import, and they were very good talks.

"You seem nervous today," Paul said.

"I'm always nervous. Or melancholy. Nervous melancholy," she said.

"Well, you're not melancholy," he said.

"I like him," Indira said.

Paul sorted through all the possible meanings of "like" and concluded that she meant it romantically. This unsettled him. "Indeed?" he said.

"God, Paul, he makes my toes tingle!"

"I beg your pardon?"

It wasn't traditional to blab about courtship, but as she did with Ruth, Indira regarded Paul as family. "I didn't even know that actually happened. I thought it was just an expression. But they tingle! They actually tingle!" Indira said, gleefully.

"That could be a circulatory problem," Paul said. "Not that I'm speaking from personal experience, of course. Toes are beyond my ken."

She swatted his gray hide playfully. "And you say you don't have a sense of humor."

He owed his grasp of humor almost entirely to her. "So he makes you happy," Paul said blankly.

She shrugged, suddenly embarrassed. "The date went well," she said, more composedly. "He's very handsome. I feel like I've been living in a bubble for... how long's it been now? Six years? Sweet Lord. How'd it get to be six years?" She chuckled a little. "Can't believe how fast time passes now that I'm this age." She picked up a sweetgum ball from the ground with her right hand and spent a moment examining the seedpod's spiky intricacies like a Japanese teacup. She said, "Not meeting anybody new, not doing anything new. I live so bottled up in my head, I'm not sure I'd know what love is, anymore, anyway."

Paul took her left hand. "It's this," he said.

She chuckled and tossed away her sweet-gum ball and patted his tendril. "No, no, it's more than that."

"Well of course it's more than that," he said.

She eyed his black eyesphere, and her own eyes twinkled. "I'm talking about physical love."

"Oh. Sex," he said.

"Yes, I mean sex," she said, stifling a chortle.

"Well, as long as I know we're talking about sex," he said.

"Yes. A nice Mennonite talk about sex," she said.

"Have you ever had sex?" he asked.

She was silent, and then said, "Yes. With Aleksie."

"Oh," he said. *"Fornication equals bad,"* he remembered. "I have not. I'd like to go home to Callisto and have sex with a Matriarch one day."

"It's different for humans," she said. She'd heard of the Jannite mating ritual. It was bizarre. "With a crapload of other implications."

He felt uncomfortable with this discussion, and he wasn't sure why for some time afterward. "You do enjoy the liberty of swearing around me, don't you?" he asked, changing the subject.

"Hm?" she asked.

"'Crapload,'" he quoted.

"Yes. Compound word," she said. "I don't think I want to again. Like that, I mean."

"Out of wedlock?" Paul said. The whole business of "two becoming one flesh" fascinated him with its spiritual implications, but his discomfort with this conversation remained.

She grunted. "Pa has always wanted grand-kids," and she sighed with that worldweariness born of one's relatives. "I haven't dated much in the time you've known me, have I?"

"Not until recently," he said. "Why don't you?"

She shrugged languidly. "You may not have noticed, Paul, but I'm not pretty."

Paul wanted to tell her this was untrue, and indeed suspected it was untrue, but he did not trust his own ability to judge such a thing with no human instincts. "I don't think I can judge that," he conceded.

*"You're* a big help," she said.

"I am here for you, though," he said.

Tendai arrived to visit Paul one Sunday. Such visits among neighbors were the lifeblood of the community, but it was mildly unusual both because Tendai was a Mennonite but not a member of the Lufthafen Conference, and also because Paul did not receive as many guests as most townsfolk did. Tendai seemed a little hesitant. He told the mildly surprised Paul, "Hi. Indira tells me that you are her best friend. So, I thought it would be good if we could be friends."

Paul kept a small supply of human food on hand for guests. He retrieved a container of vegetable soup from his freezing back room, and warmed it on his hotplate for Tendai. They waited while it heated.

Paul was quiet. He had reached the point in his Earthling cultural acclimation that he could normally make a good first impression on people, but he couldn't think of anything to say to Tendai.

"I saw those silicon-based plants out there," Tendai said. "They are, hm, really something!"

"Yes. I suppose they are," Paul said. Silence.

"It looks like rain, today. That should help them, right?"

"No, but I did pick hardy crops that can endure regular dousings with dihydrogen oxide, so it won't harm them." *I've mastered sarcasm,* he mused. Actually, water resistant crops were common on Callisto, since there was a large amount of liquid water to be found beneath the surface. It made mining difficult. Underground, the place was really much wetter than the Jan would have preferred.

Tendai laughed at Paul's joke, at any event. Then there followed a period of small talk—"How big do Matriarchs really get?" "What was your trip to Earth like?" "How did you build this place?"—during which the soup finished heating, and Paul gave it to him, and Tendai complimented him on it even though he actually thought it was rather bland. He asked about the decor, and about the icecrawler shell collection. They were the same sort of questions everyone asked Paul, so he wasn't sure why they irritated him now. He tried not to show his irritation and was pretty sure he was successful, though Indira surely could have told. Tendai seemed to enjoy the visit, though. Paul did not get a bad impression of the man. Indira was right. He seemed nice.

Tendai told Paul, finally, "Meeting her was... good for me. I hate the, well, the whole thing of dating.

I was so glad to find someone." His name, in his native language, meant Thankful. Indira had mentioned that. *Appropriate,* Paul thought.

Paul felt resentful of the man. It was hard to say why.

Some months later, Paul and Indira spent a late afternoon together, on the broad lawn in front of Paul's property, near his "rock garden" of organisilicate plants. He'd been seeing less of her now, with Tendai in the picture. He didn't care for that.

He had installed a wooden porch swing of the sort that was common in the community, for when guests came, and Indira certainly used it the most. Yet today, by the garden, he held her in his outstretched arm like a tree limb, shading her with his other hand like an overhanging branch. His hand wasn't big enough to shade her completely, but he could shift it with the movement of the sun to keep her face in shade. Holding her and his shading arm in position was no effort for him. He had finally adapted to the gravity. *She weighs nothing,* he thought. *Even in this gravity, she weighs nothing.*

"And that one looks like a phase modulator," she said, pointing at the sky.

"If you say so," he said.

"Or maybe like a duck. You really can't see it?"

"I have 360 degree vision. Optical illusions that work for humans don't work for me. You know I can't make out drawings. Just holographs and sculptures."

"These aren't 2D like constellations. Clouds are puffy!"

"Even so," he said.

"Mm," she said.

"It delayed the invention of writing on the Jan homeworld. After all, your ancestors drew before they wrote, and mine never drew. So we had no hieroglyphics. Our writing derived from sculpture."

"Mm," she said, and shifted her weight languorously in his arm. She already knew everything he'd just said, but there was comfort in hearing it repeated. "You know something, Paul?" she said through half-lidded eyes as a dragonfly droned through her field of vision. "I'm content. Right now. It's not something I ever expected; at least, I hadn't in a long time. Least of all, *here.*"

Mouthless, Paul smiled inwardly for her. *But am I content?* he asked himself. Up till recently, he had been remarkably and uncharacteristically content, as she was now. He had honestly come to love his adopted home, even with all its environmental harshness. He loved the sights and smells of it (well, the smells were easy enough to love; the methane was pure ambrosia). He loved the friends he'd made. He loved *her.* It was only now when she had someone else, that he realized that he loved her so much it was an ache. An ache which had once felt *good.* Now there was Tendai. Paul was no longer first in her affections, but merely an increasingly distant second.

He'd first been attracted to her (if the term was applicable) by simple virtue of the fact that she'd shown no reaction to his appearance. No fear or revulsion, not even gaping curiosity, she'd simply accepted it. He knew that that was because of her time in the orbiting port of Felice, when she'd met many of his kind, but it still endeared her to him. And since then...

"Tendai says he loves me," she said.

He felt as though struck with a hammer. His arm shifted, and she almost lost her balance. She let out a cute little yelp, and he steadied his arm again. From what he understood of human courtship, the simple statement of those words was of enormous importance. Paul said, "He said that?"

"Mm-hm," she said. She was smiling, and her eyes were half-shut.

"How do you feel about him?" The question sounded very banal as he said it, he thought.

"I like him. I like him a lot," she said. "Every time he smiles at me, I just want to melt."

Visual cues for a mating response. Inwardly, Paul groaned. It had taken him years just to learn to decypher human facial expressions with any kind of adequacy, and he still preferred to supplement it by listening to a speaker's heartbeat to judge his or her mood. What she was talking about, the kind of instant, instinctive response to the most basic of stimuli for her people, that was denied him. He couldn't feel it himself, nor inspire such feelings in others.

She stretched out her arms to yawn, and he cradled her gently.

"He's... I just enjoy spending time with him," she said. "I mean, he's not as *smart* as Aleksie was, I suppose, but... Aleksie turned out to be a... Liberty to swear in front of you?"

"As always."

"...toaster-fucking asshat. Thanks."

"Of course."

"A guy has to have more than just brains. There's maturity, responsibility... And Tendai's so earnest, so incredibly sweet. Especially when he *smiles* at me, God... And those *shoulders!* And I guess... Yeah. Yes. I do."

"Do what?"

"Love him. He's the first *since* Aleksei, you know that? That was such a long time ago." She closed her eyes, though her brow was creased a little, as though in frustration. "And he loves me. I didn't think anyone ever would again. God, I need it."

"Everyone needs that," he said evenly as his soul crumbled. *I'm superfluous,* Paul thought.

He wanted to rail out at the universe, cry lamentation to God that it wasn't fair, but what was unfair about it? It was amazing that his little self-imposed exile had worked out as comfortably as it had; and back at its outset, comfort had been the *last* thing he'd wanted. So why shouldn't things curdle a bit now? It was overdue, and he'd allowed himself to become spoiled. Then he chided himself that surely only he could see the sort of life he'd chosen to live here as decadent.

He regarded her (though of course his 360° gaze had never left her) and the ache in his soul flared incandescent with love and the fear of loss of love. He gave no outward sign of any of it. It's easy to be stoic around humans when one lacks a face. He rocked her gently in his outstretched arm, and within himself, he wept.

They spoke of inconsequentialities for an hour. Finally, she failed to answer one of his questions, and he realized that she'd fallen asleep in his arm. Above, puffy phase modulating ducks drifted slowly across the ceiling of afternoon.

Tendai's hovercar pulled up after a while. He was off-shift (or, at least as off-shift as a country vet ever is) and had come for his daily visit. "Hey, big fellow," he addressed Paul quietly.

"Hey," Paul said without inflection. He took a quick sonar reading of Tendai's internal organs. How vulnerable his soft body would be to Paul's stony limbs. He had to quickly remind himself that morose delectation was a wicked thing. Did he hate the man? No, that was perhaps the worst part; he didn't. Were Tendai Tamsanga a bad man, it would be simple. But, in every respect other than his relationship with Indira, Paul liked him, or at least could find no reasonable fault with him.

*He's blameless, excepting that he is my rival. And I can't even hold that against him, because he doesn't know he is my rival. He is a good person, and he provides her with what I cannot.*

"She is beautiful when she is sleeping," Tendai whispered.

"Yes, she is," Paul said, and meant it.

Paul prayed that night. He did it standing, as always, for Jan cannot kneel. He usually went to his refrigerated back room for extended talks with the Lord, both because the heat outside it was a distraction, and for the added privacy; but tonight he entered into prayer as soon as he was in the door, and so he did it in his foyer.

Covetousness had by now replaced the deaths of the Stevens as the sin over which Paul spent the most time agonizing and for which he begged the Almighty's forgiveness and guidance.

Competing for her was out of the question. He wasn't human. Their concept of "romantic love" was fundamentally about *mating,* wasn't it? Something of which he was both incapable and completely undesirous. So why this burning jealousy? It *was* jealousy, not envy, for he felt he was losing something that had previously been his: the right to be foremost in her affections.

Did he love her? he wondered. It wasn't the first time he'd wondered this, but there was urgency to it, now. He didn't know what *love* was. How could he? He believed he knew what Christian love was. He cherished it. To love one another through the love of God. The communication of souls past the barriers of flesh and space. Removal of the masks placed on us by nature. Turning away from the shadows on Plato's cave wall to actually face one another. That kind of love, Paul understood.

But the love in the Song of Songs? He could know nothing of that. It was completely specific to the human experience, and the reading of that book only served to remind him how alien, how unknowable these beings were.

He agonized over his passion for her. He agonized over the *nature* of his passion for her. Was it *love?* It seemed the most ill-defined word in English. More sensible Earth languages like Greek had different words for the different types of love. He loved everything about her. Even her appearance, now. He knew full well that a man seeing her would see a dimension to her beauty that he would never comprehend; but to him, her form was one of amazing, alien beauty. The roundness, the smallness, the quickness of her; the darkness of her hair, the brownness of her skin—where years ago he'd found the human form repellant, he now perceived beauty in hers because it was *her* form; she was herself, unique among all mankind, unique in all the cosmos.

He wanted desperately to believe that even if sex were a useful *aid* toward spiritual union, that it was not an absolutely necessary one. After all, among promiscuous humans, it seemed to actually be a hindrace to that end; and for all their liasons, such people seemed terribly lonely. *Oh yes, Paul, and you speak from such experience, don't you?* he scolded himself. And then he analyzed his scolding: *Irony? I'm using sarcasm? Words in my mind, again. I scold myself in words. I analyze my scolding in words. Do I even know how to shut them off any more?*

It was while he was thus engaged in pious navel-gazing that Paul heard footsteps. He'd been so preoccupied that he hadn't even tremorfelt anyone's approach. The front door of his rural Mennonite home had, of course, been unlocked.

Being radially symmertical, he didn't need to turn to face the intruder when he entered. It was Amos. He wore no hat, which was unusual. He looked unsteady on his feet and was drenched in sweat, in all looking very ill. His unfocused eyes wore an expression Paul wasn't sure he recognized, since he saw relatively little of it in this calm little town. He'd seen human anger, of course. But not hate.

"Don't move," Amos said.

"What are you doing here?" Paul asked.

"You gotta ask?" Amos said, producing a small utility laser from his pocket. "I took some alien stuff. Got sick with alien germs. Ta Hell with aliens." He stopped for breath. "Thrym told me who y'are. I know whatcha did," Amos said.

Even in the terrestrial heat, Paul went ice cold. How had *Thrym* found out? It didn't matter. It probably hadn't even been hard for him. As Paul had told Indira, he'd never been able to bring himself to hide it very well. Any serious research into his background would have brought it to light. He supposed that up till now, he'd mostly counted on being too low-profile for anyone to bother. Then a likely answer came. *Of course. My essays. I'm slightly famous now, aren't I? I wonder how many other people have figured it out.* He wondered if the Earthling and/or Callistan governments were suppressing it. Was it vain to think so?

Paul recognized Amos's weapon as a stonecutter's laser. A farm implement. It was doubtless the only remotely gun-like item Amos owned, but Paul had to admit it was an excellent choice. A direct hit from a gun designed to fell human opponents might only injure him, but this would be quite lethal.

Paul was terrified.

"You're the one, killed that family. I remember that... Heard about it once...." Amos's voice kept changing volume, like he couldn't decide whether he wanted to shout or mumble, but it was actually because he couldn't hear himself reliably. "Y... You're a monster!" The kaleidoscope colors which had painted Amos's world for hours that felt like days now drifted into a deep indigo black, so that it felt like he and Paul were alone in an infernal void. It had *never* lasted this long before, and Amos wanted to pull out of it but couldn't.

Amos saw Paul's form distort and bend. Horns and a fanged mouth sprouted from his eyesphere, and his tentacles multiplied and stretched out toward him. Amos heroically drove them back, waving his laser threateningly. He wiped his hand across his brow to stop the sweat dripping salty and painful into his eyes. Had his hand always been plaid? He didn't think so. Damn alien's fault. "You keep back!" he screamed. "And stop doing that to my hand!"

Thoughts whirled through Paul's mind as Amos ranted. Paul marveled that, in his idiot youth, he had ever believed he could be a leader of soldiers (not that he'd chosen the job, of course)—Paul was too scared to even move, right now. *Some soldier. I can direct a massacre from orbit, and that's all.* When all was said and done, Paul thought, Amos was probably right.

Justice was overdue, and Paul suspected he should just accept it, but he was afraid. "Amos... This isn't our way," Paul said.

*"Our way?!"* Amos barked. "Don't you talk about 'our way'! You're not one of us! You're just a thing!" So many tentacles! Like a potato growing runners. Amos's stomach turned, and the walls boiled and turned a sickly orange.

Paul couldn't deny it. He knew himself a killer. *This is justice,* he thought. Then he thought, *No. Justice would be conviction by court. This is just murder. Just like I committed.*

Paul's long arms dropped heavy and limp down his sides, his fingers splayed on the ground. It was a pathetic sight. "Please don't kill me," he begged, very softly. "Please. Please don't kill me."

Amos, his addled mind previously so certain, wavered. The gun shook in his hand.

"Daughter, where've you been, I've looked e... Amos?"

Amos whirled and beheld Jawaharlal coming in the open door behind him.

Amos panicked and fired.

Paul had known humans were mostly liquid. Perceiving them with his sonar, it had always been manifest that they were sacks of pulsing water and jelly over a delicate stony frame. But to see that outer membrane pierced was indescribable. Red liquid life sprayed out of his friend's torso. Jawaharlal spasmed monstrously for no more than a second and then lay completely still.

The deaths Paul himself had caused long ago had been caused from orbit. Abstractions. He'd never seen human death before. He didn't scream. His people were prey by nature, and rabbits are loath to scream.

Indira was screaming. Paul hadn't noticed her arrival. He wasn't even sure how much time had passed. Nor had he noticed till it had happened that Amos was now gripped solidly in Paul's own fingers, two meters above the floor where his dropped laser lay.

Amos was nothing. A living, terrified bag of jelly in the Jan's hand. Were Paul merely to close his fingers, apply the slightest pressure, the murderer would burst like an overripe tomato in a vice.

*He's not nothing,* Paul reminded himself, seething. *He's a living soul. There is a soul in this quivering blob of meat. I am holding one of God's children in my hand.*

"What are you waiting for?!" came Indira's voice. *"Kill him!"*

"Please... Please don't kill me," Amos whimpered. His senses had actually settled down a little as he flooded with adrenaline, and he now perceived his predicament with a kind of crystal, hyper-clarity. He was terrified.

Paul considered just crushing his legs. It would keep him from running away. It could be mended easily enough at a hospital. And it would hurt him like hell. *"Put the fear of God into him." Isn't that the saying? But... Have I learned nothing?* "Revenge is the Lord's," Paul said. "Not ours." He paused. He realized he was shaking. "Indira, please call the police," he said.

She was kneeling by her father's body, her eyes like searchlights. She screamed.

"Please... please Indira, calm down." He wasn't convincing, since he was panicking too, but at least he could control his vocodor to make *it* sound calm. It still wasn't very convincing.

"What happened? Christ, what..." she pleaded.

"He's on kreg. And he found out about Adrastea," Paul said.

She stared blankly at Paul, taking a moment to see the connection. Then she rose.

She grabbed a bunch of icecrawler shells in their alcove, and began smashing them against the ground one by one.

"Why are you...?" Paul asked.

"Your fault!" she howled. "It's all your *faaaault...*"

She collapsed to her knees.

He reached out to her. She shivered at his cold touch. "Please. Please calm down," he said. Paul held her. He tried not to hold her too tightly. He knew his strength could injure or kill her if he were careless. And it was hard to control his movements because he himself was panicking—and, for lack of anything better to do with the murderer, he was still clutching him in his other hand. But he just kept repeating over and over, "Please calm down. Please calm down. Indira, please calm down. Please."

She reeled back her head and shrieked like the damned. The sound seemed to last for days. Then she collapsed against Paul's arm and wept, shaking.

Indira would have spent the time afterward in seclusion were it possible, but was instead inundated with sympathetic neighbors. Looking back long afterward, she conceded that isolation would likely have been more harmful to her, but at the time, the flood of pestering goodwill was a torment. Still, the mutual aid of her neighbors and cousins came.

They offered to care for the household and the farm, so she could visit extended family to share support and condolence. In fact, she'd had little to do with the farm's management since opening her shop several years ago, but it would certainly *need* tending now, so she was grateful for the aid (even if she was in no temper to properly express gratitude; they seemed to understand, for which she was doubly grateful). Jawaharlal had hired young Gid Chan to replace Thrym months ago. Now Jawaharlal was gone, Amos was in prison, and Gid was just a scrawny teen. Even if she'd been in any emotional shape to keep the farm running until it could be sold *(hideous* thought), she had her own obligations. So she was glad of the help.

The Fix-It Shop was closed for the duration. She gave Rachel to the Lajevardis, giving the cow a sad nuzzle and promising to visit. She worried about the animal's ability to cope with a new home, let alone new caregivers, as she was pushing twenty.

Paul and Tendai were there for her as well, of course. Indira did not repeat her accusations at Paul, but neither of them had forgotten them.

Amos's relatives were a picture of misery. Indira couldn't get them to stop apologizing to her. She appreciated it, but it seemed pointless, as *they'd* done nothing wrong. Nobody in town blamed the rest of the Baumgartner family except themselves. The anguish on his mother Leah's face would haunt Indira's dreams the rest of her life.

There was a part of Indira that wanted desperately to run, but getting away from the funeral wouldn't get her away from this new reality. The whole situation was a horrible impossibility that surrounded her on every side and just wouldn't end.

There was a sizeable turnout at the funeral, for Mennonite Communities were very supportive. Yet it seemed to Paul, as nearly as he could interpret, that few of the attendees had known Jawaharlal well. There were many extended family members, but none who had been close to him, which in such a community was remarkable. Paul wondered what, if anything other than natural inclination, had made Jawaharlal such a misanthrope. Since he had not kept a diary, Paul supposed nobody would ever know now, except God. With her mother dead these many years, it was no wonder Indira had been lonely living with her father.

*He was so quiet,* Indira thought. *There were times I wondered if he really did care. Oh, I guess he did.* Relations had been cool between her and Pa for years, and yet she'd always felt his presence. *You don't need to see your backbone to know it's there.* One person who knew all her innermost foibles, even if he didn't understand them, and who did not condemn her for them, at least not overtly.

She had never met a more closed man than her father. Intensely private. Simple farmer, never said a thing profound except country wisdom. But she'd never, ever considered him stupid. She had to wonder why not. She could almost hear his voice. Which was odd, since he spoke so little. She knew him so well she could practically run an entire conversation in her head with him. How was that? *I didn't know what went on in his head, but I knew what came out of it,* she supposed. Machines like that, where she couldn't guess what inner workings produced their output, made her want to take them apart and examine them. Not that he was all that predictable. He could surprise her sometimes.

Her leaving so soon after her mother's death had surely been terribly cruel to him.

At least she had come back for a while.

Now he was gone.

She tried to think of being reunited with him, with both her parents, in Heaven. There had been a time she'd never doubted such things. Did she doubt them now? she wondered. She looked around at the religious trappings of the place. To most of her friends on Felice, those who gave it any thought, faith had been synonymous with hypocrisy. She'd maintained her faith in God out there, in her own way, despite that. Now? She reached over her shoulder and pulled her shawl tighter, so she could feel the comforting pressure of the fabric against her arm. She wasn't really cold, in fact she knew the shawl would quickly make her too warm, but she needed that pressure, she needed to be held.

"So much we should have said." Indira said. "He didn't want me. He wanted a daughter, but not me." She said this purely from frustration and recognized even as she said it that it had no substance. She knew he had loved her.

Paul, not being a mind-reader, said, "That's not true."

"How would you know?" Indira said, although she herself hadn't believed her words. She was only venting.

He supposed he couldn't really know, but he said, "Well, you know I mean it. I can't lie. I'm sure he loved you. He always did."

She said nothing.

Paul said, "He didn't know how to show it."

"Hey," Tendai said. She jumped. She'd been so absorbed in her thoughts, she hadn't seen him approach. Tendai said, "Are you okay?"

"Oh Tendai," she said, and went to him. They hugged. Tendai held her tightly against his chest. Paul tried not to stiffen, for he was sure she would notice and ask what the problem was. She did notice, but assumed it was the obvious reason, his sorrow at the death of her father.

Ruthie came over and gave Indira a long hug. Barney offered his condolences. Paul recalled the robot once having expressed curiosity about what it must be like to have family. Ruth was probably the closest thing he had to it.

Since Paul had been one of Jawaharlal's friends, the preacher had requested he do the scripture reading, from Romans.

"If God is on our side, who is against us?" he recited. He couldn't read off a flat page very quickly, so he had memorized the passage. "He did not spare his own Son, but surrendered him for us all; and with this gift how can he fail to lavish upon us all he has to give?... Then what can separate us from the love of Christ? Can affliction or hardship? Can persecution, hunger, nakedness, peril, or the sword?... in spite of all, overwhelming victory is ours through him who loved us. For I am convinced that there is nothing in death or life, in the realm of spirits or superhuman powers, in the world as it is or the world as it shall be, in the forces of the universe, in heights or depths—nothing in all creation that can separate us from the love of God in Christ Jesus our Lord."

After the service at the red brick meeting-house, everyone departed in various black ground vehicles for the graveyard. The sky was mottled gray with clouds, the air moist. Some-where a crow made a loud comment, but otherwise it was very quiet.

Cemetery Hill rose gradually from the surrounding ground, such that elderly visitors did not have very much trouble walking up it, but from its summit once reached, much of the surrounding area could be seen: Eppleberg's green, brown, and gold fields punctuated by barns and farmhouses; Lofthaven Wood, now a fiery autumn copper; Lake Lofthaven shimmering behind the former's branches; the creek wending its way to the lake through the waterwheels of several farms down from its mountain source. Lofthaven proper, the town which had lent its name to these geographic features, had some time ago been politically absorbed by Lawrenceton (though it was still a distinct district), that city being visible in the distance, towering and decadent and beautiful and vain. On the horizon marched the purple Appalachians.

The unadorned pine coffin was removed from the black groundcar hearse, set upon two poles above the grave, straps wrapped round it, the poles removed, and the coffin lowered slowly into the ground. Some cousins whom Indira didn't know very well had acted as pallbearers.

To Indira's surprise, she spotted Thrym Scyllaschild among the mourners. He saw that she saw, and he acknowledged her. "Ma'am," he said, and doffed his hat.

She gestured him over to her. She moved to ensure they had some modicum of privacy in this public place, and said, getting straight to the point, "You've got a nerve, coming here. You're the one who told Amos," she began. When Amos had finally sobered up, he had reconfirmed, between pitiful wracking sobs, that he'd learned Paul's identity from Thrym Scyllaschild.

Despite her efforts to separate herself from the crowd of mourners, she saw that Tendai had come over to her, and Paul was trundling up as well. She didn't bother shooing them away.

Thrym had grudgingly skipped the funeral service of a man he'd respected specifically because he didn't want this confrontation to happen *there.* Now they were here in the cemetery. Thrym had worked at the farm long enough to know Jawaharlal's daughter's unholy temper, and he wasn't keen to indulge it, but there was no helping that. Thrym looked at her levelly. Tesks had slitted cat eyes, and could out-stare any other living thing. Thrym said, "When I started figuring maybe I'd leave, months before I did, I told the kid he ought to keep an eye on *him,*" he said, pointing at Paul with his thumb. "And I told him *why.*" Thrym stared hard at Paul's eyesphere, his eyes flashing an anger every bit as intense as Indira had shown toward Thrym seconds earlier. Then Thrym's gaze turned down. "Had no idea this'd come of it," he said calmly and directly.

"I'm surprised you didn't tell more people," Paul said softly. As Paul said this, he regarded Tendai, who was holding Indira's hand and watching the interaction. Tendai looked concerned, but not confused by any of it. *So Tendai knows, too. She told him about Adrastea, without asking me,* he thought. His feelings were mixed.

"I told someone," Thrym said, in response to Paul's comment. "My boss."

"Pa knew?" Indira said.

Thrym nodded. "Mm-hm. He was surprised, but then he just muttered something about forgiveness and offering sanctuary, and he didn't do anything. Wasn't sure who else to tell. Police? Report you to the government?" he asked Paul. "Feds already know who you are. Obvious they wanted it quiet. God forbid we offend our space benefactors. Could have gone to the *press,*" he said with distaste.

"You could have gone to *me,*" Indira practically hissed.

Thrym gazed at his late boss's daughter. He'd always felt there was a little too much more going on behind those eyes, more than could possibly be healthy. He'd always avoided her. "Yes, I could have gone to you," he told Indira. Then, changing the subject, he said, his voice now full of indignation, "Then he accuses me of using *narcotics.* I was disgusted. Pride got the better of me." He sighed. "Wanted to leave ever since I found out he didn't care the town was harboring a war criminal, but I'd stayed. *This* was the last straw."

"Why did you let us go on thinking *you* were the kreg user?" Indira demanded.

He gave her his level gaze again, but there was regret in there. "He shouldn't have accused me." He sighed. "Wasn't me, so the kid was on kreg. One more reason for me to leave. Figured the kreghead would get himself fired eventually. Never dreamed this'd happen. A good man's dead because of my actions." He bowed to Indira. "Miss Fenstermacher, I am sorry."

She stared at him.

"Good," she said, coldly.

Thrym accepted that as as much forgiveness as he was likely to get, just at the moment, and perhaps as much as he deserved. He looked up at Paul, and again there was fierceness in Thrym's eyes, and the expression was not entirely lost on the nonhumanoid alien. "What *are* you doing on Earth?" Thrym asked.

"Penance," Paul said.

Thrym was surprised. "You were *sentenced* to live in a hick town?"

"It's of my own volition. Somewhat to my own surprise, I've come to like it here."

"Hnh." Thrym sighed. He doffed his hat to Indira again. "Ma'am," he said, and he took his leave.

As Thrym walked away, she leaned against Tendai. "There there," Tendai said. He whispered it, little more than a grunt, really. While he certainly wanted to make her feel better, he wasn't sure how to do it except to hug her, which worked at least as well as any words would have, truthfully.

*That's all you've got to say to her?* Paul thought as they embraced. *"There there?"* But he watched her press against his body. Nonverbal communication. Soft flesh to soft flesh, and no words needed. *Is that any less valid a meeting of the minds than speech? Is the voice, or even the brain, any less a filter between souls than is skin? My skin is hard. God forgive me, for I hate Tendai right now.* Paul thanked the Almighty that the Mennonites disapproved of public kissing between men and women (though the Holy Kiss was a part of their worship practices). Merely seeing them together was painful. The concept of kissing intrigued him—not two truly becoming one flesh, as in the act of mating, but perhaps a small taste of it, he supposed. He regarded the tripartite lips in his own hands. Lips that could secrete acid strong enough to burn granite.

She was still hugging Tendai, but then she felt a sudden muscle spasm in her back and had to pull away for a moment. She'd hardly slept the past several nights. "Oh. I'm not young any more," she said, sniffling. She bent over backwards and listened to the bits of herself pop back into place. "Pa didn't have a single ancestor who was genetically engineered. Not one."

"Mm, yes, that is difficult," Tendai muttered uncomfortably, and nodded.

"Well, we are in Dutch County," Paul said. "Besides, I thought many Earthlings frowned on heavy genengineering."

"There are lots of things people frown on and do anyway," she said. "No, it's kind of rare for anybody to have a completely untinkered genome these days, going *all* the way back through their family tree. Mama didn't have any either. And she died young. So when I get old, I'm gonna get *old.* Old like in days of yore."

This thought disturbed Paul. Worker Jan lived longer than humans, though not enormously longer. He didn't want to watch Indira grow thin and paper-frail one day. By contrast, Jan got *heavier* as they aged, slowly petrifying, till one day they just couldn't move any more. It was a rather mean joke among Earthmen that a dead Jan was his own tombstone. He could imagine himself, ages from now, taking her brittle hand in his age-thickened stony tendril and accidentally smashing it. The thought terrified him.

Thanks largely to Arachne influence, longevity treatments were coming into their own again, after a long hiatus following the decade-long nightmare of the Genomic War. The interim during which such treatments were unfashionable had resulted in natural generational turnover, with the inevitable result that lessons learned from the war were forgotten. The Lufthafen Conference Mennonites were hardly the plainest of the Plain people, but that degree of biological tampering felt sufficiently like defying God's plan that they were exceedingly leery of it.

Thrym had meanwhile been standing by Jawaharlal's open grave, looking at the pine casket visible at the bottom. *Godspeed, boss.* The soldier in him badly wanted to give the body a salute, but he knew such a military gesture would be a huge faux pas here. As he looked, he overheard Indira talk to Paul and Tendai about her destiny to grow old, and he felt a sudden indignation and walked back to her.

Tesk empathy was an unintended genetic fluke. Surprisingly, disturbingly, it generally did not hinder them as soldiers, the career for which they'd been made; but to be a Tesk soldier was to kill without the luxury of dehumanizing one's enemy. They saw every drop of blood on their hands. Thrym had been a soldier many years. He believed he had no illusions about death. His own, or that of others.

"You out of your tree, woman? We're just putting your dad in the ground, and you're talking like this! To get old and *die* when you don't have to... that's *crazy!* I'm not as religious as all of you, but it's *sinful*, you ask me. You guys are all 'God this' and 'God that'. Well then, figure life is God's gift! I've had longevity treatments. You think I look old? I'm *older* than I look. Fought biodroids in the Uprising. I've seen death, seen humans and genengs and synths get their bodies blown apart. And there's *nothing* noble about it. You sound like the people who fought against penicillin."

Indira was shaking at his onslaught, though even she could not have said with which emotion. Finally, she told him very softly, "As much as I hate death, I dread the possibility that through technology, physical death may one day cease to be involuntary. I want to go to Heaven, and... I'm not sure I can get there by suicide." She was very quiet, and then appended it, "I'm not speaking for anybody else. Just for me."

Thrym was at an utter loss how to respond to that. He shook his head and said, "I don't know what I ever thought I was doing here." He glanced back at the grave, made his peace, and then walked away toward the small parking lot on the far side of the hilltop.

Thrym's words had stung her, Paul could see that. "What do you care what Thrym thinks? You never got along with him, right?"

She looked around at the crowd of mourners. In her entire life here, she'd never felt a part of them. Never felt that she was well-liked. Was never entirely sure she shared their philosophies. "I never got along with *anybody*. What am I doing here, Paul? Pa was the only thing really holding me here. With him gone, I can move on with my life. I can get the hell out of here."

"Now hold on," Paul said. "You've been through a terrible trauma. You should think this out when you're calmer."

"I beg your pardon?" she said, sharply.

"When you're calmer," he repeated. "Your Pa is dead, and Thrym was just being Thrym. None of that changes anything."

"I'm perfectly calm," she said. "Why don't you want me to leave here?"

"Well... I'd miss you," Paul said.

Tendai began, "Um, yes! And I too would m..." but Indira spoke first.

"Ah! So *that's* it. I'm your sole link to human civilization and Christianity and all that crap. *You* don't want me to go."

"No. I don't," Paul said softly.

"You selfish bastard," she said.

"Please stop," Paul said, seeing where this was headed. "You're going off on a tangent."

"What am I doing here!? You want me to stay here! You're the only one in town that does. The only fucking one! Everybody else here hates me!"

"Nobody hates you..." Paul said helplessly.

Tendai's eyes darted between the two of them as if watching a tennis match that had somehow degenerated into kickboxing. *Ah, he hasn't seen this yet!* Paul thought. *Watch and learn, little Earthman.*

"They do. I can see it in their eyes," she said. "Why do you want me to stay where people hate me?! So I can be your God damned pet, is that it?"

"Of course not," Paul said.

"It's not a matter of 'of course'! You fucking jackass!" Indira said.

"Um, hi?" Tendai said. "What's going on?"

"Paul's being an ass," she said.

*She's having a panic attack, and taking her anger at Thrym out on me,* Paul wanted to say, but he didn't want to embarrass her in front of her beau. "I hate it when you get like this."

Indira said, "Fuck that! My father's dead because of you!"

He froze at that. "I...." He believed she was completely right about that.

"Hey! It is, um, nobody's fault but Amos. And the police have him in jail. Right?" Tendai said.

She whirled on Tendai. "You...!" she started, and then stopped herself. She realized she hated herself for what she'd said to Paul, but she was too fearful of inviting rebuke to apologize. "Yeah." She turned back to the alien. "Well you were totally out of line, Paul. Totally."

"Okay," Paul said.

"It is not okay! Jesus!" Indira said.

"What do you want me to say?" Paul said.

"Nothing! Just stand there and be quiet! Do you think you can manage that?!"

Paul noticed Tendai's heartbeat had increased significantly. Clearly, he'd never seen her get upset like this before. *It can serve as a preview for him, then,* Paul thought grimly.

She kept simmering and occasionally boiling over with frustrated rage for the rest of the day. By the next day, she had calmed, and it was largely forgotten. Paul literally thanked God for that.

The thought of visiting a score of relatives she barely knew and who probably didn't like Pa that much practically gave Indira hives. Yet she did it, and the doing of it helped calm her. Thankfully, talking a lot was not obligatory on these visits. Simply offering one's presence was considered enough.

Tendai accompanied her on most of the trips, strengthening their bond. Paul badly *wanted* to come, and Indira would have gladly had him, but his size was prohibitive both for travel and for fitting into people's homes; and besides, the sight of an unfamiliar giant tentacled alien might have been unsettling for the relatives at their time of grief.

Amos Baumgartner had long since recovered from his high, and he'd pled guilty without any dispute. He was not a complicated man. Tears streaming down his cheeks, it seemed clear he would never forgive himself. He was wracked by guilt and muttered self-recriminations incessantly during the hearing. He told the police where to find his supplier, a lowlife who passed through town periodically on his way to Lawrenceton's junkies.

Indira's searing hatred of Amos was, despite herself, moderated by her keen awareness of how near she herself had once come to committing a far worse crime. She regarded him in the courtroom. His big form was curled over itself in anguish. *He was out of his head. Just like I was. Look at him, now.* It was possible that she would, in her grief, have failed to make the connection, had she not spent years as the close confidant of an alien obsessed with his own guilt.

Indira came to Paul's home that night. Except for the funeral, he hadn't seen much of her lately, with all the visiting.

"I wanted to apologize to you," she said.

"What?"

Her eyes looked hollow. "I just told Amos that I forgave him." She lowered her face. She couldn't look up. "I... I didn't put any flourish on it. I didn't say much more than those words. But it was the most Old Order... the hardest thing I've ever done."

"What did he say?" Paul said.

She sighed deeply. "Oh, he blubbered all over the place, like he's been doing." She closed her eyes and gritted her teeth. "He was stoned when he did it. I was only *drunk,* and I almost massacred half a city. It was either forgive him, or yell at him for being an underachiever," she joked. She was crying. She wept for a while, and then said, "Anyway... if I can... forgive *him*... and I suppose I've even forgiven *Thrym*, not that he's around now to tell... well, I suppose I could contact him, should contact him," she mumbled noncommittally, "...then I have to apologize for... blaming..." She gestured at him.

"No! You were *right,"* Paul said. "You were absolutely right. I should never have made even a half-hearted effort to keep my crime at Adrastea a secret." *And I am committing another sin against you,* he thought. *One which, were I to tell you of it, would confirm the sin rather than undo it. Ah, Indira....*

"Aw shit, Paul, *don't* do the self-condemning crap. I feel guilty, you feel guilty, shithead Amos feels guilty... You're naturalized Dutch yourself, you know everyone here feels guilty for something ninety percent of the waking day, and then we dream about guilt at night."

"I spoke to Bishop Lapp. I told him my sin," Paul said. *At least, I told him the one you know about, Indira.*

She regarded him. "What did he say?" she said softly.

He said, "Much what my mother told me long ago. That it was good that I am repentant, and that no worthwhile purpose would be served at this point by drawing attention to myself. It would only create *more* strife."

"He and your mom are both smart," she said.

"I suppose. I've often wished the Stevens had had some outside family or contacts to whom I could apologize. But they were an island unto themselves."

"Like Pa," she croaked.

"He had you," Paul said.

"Not half the time, he didn't," she said.

She leaned against his carapace, he draped an arm lightly across her back, and they were quiet.

# 6

Paul didn't learn of Tendai's proposal and her acceptance of it until after the fact. He said nothing as his soul imploded.

"With Pa gone, I need someone to give me away at my wedding, Paul. You're my best friend. Will you, please?"

"Of course I will," he said. He spoke nothing to her of his true feelings. He wondered whether such an omission constituted a lie. Mostly he just ached.

The ceremony was held outdoors. The service was very simple, compared to most Earthling wedding customs, but Paul had seen no others for comparison. She wore an uncomplicated blue dress, as was traditional in the Lufthafen Conference. Tendai's big extended family came from Zimbabwe—Indira thought they looked cold in the Pennsylvania climate, bright teeth chattering in smiling dark faces. Also in attendance were many relatives with whom Indira had recently reinitiated contact after her father's funeral, still mostly people she did not know well. Indira's younger female cousins made for cute little bridesmaids carrying flowers. Ruth and Barney were there as well, and Paul was glad for that. Reaction among the townsfolk had been favorable, if muted; on average, people were happy for her, but everyone knew Dr. Tamsanga was from a *liberal* branch of the Mennonite church.

Paul sang in the a capella choir, providing wordless low tones that no human could manage, though in fact he had to stretch his own range a good bit to make them audible. Almost every alien race capable of perceiving it liked Earthling music. General consensus among many peoples, especially the Jan with their acute hearing, was that if man were never to contribute anything else to the universe, music would be enough to earn him honor.

Paul maintained stoic composure throughout the wedding.

Indira and Tendai left for their "wedding trip," as honeymoons were called in that society.

And in subsequent years, Paul's inner life became a kind of purgatory.

Indira had fallen in love with a human and married. And that was good, Paul believed intellectually, since he himself could not be intimate with her. Yet it made him very sad. Envy was a sin. He knew that. "Thou shalt not covet thy neighbour's wife." The fact of their marriage cemented his feelings as sin.

He believed he understood now why his Biblical namesake had endorsed celibacy (although Saint Paul didn't *demand* celibacy of anyone, conceding that it was better to marry than to "burn" with lust). Most people, if asked, would say it was because carnality was a fleshly distraction from divine matters—and that was a perfectly reasonable answer, but Paul Dwightson suspected another reason. Romantic love was *exclusive* love. A gregarious person might have any number of close friends, but friendship was not love. Paul suspected that at least some degree of monogamy was hardwired into man, such that free love societies throughout history always eventually failed, torn apart by the jealousy and possessiveness that go hand in hand with eros. *But what is any of that to me?* Paul wondered. *I am not a man. Lust is beyond my ability to experience.*

Christ was once asked, if a widowed man remarried, and then he and his new wife died, which woman would be his wife in heaven? And Christ had answered that it was a naive question, because marriage was an institution for life on Earth. Paul personally took that to mean that in Heaven, everyone would love one another completely. That was Christian love as Paul understood it.

*All of this art and song and poetry on the subject of love. There has to be more to it than just two animals wanting to rut. Please God, let there be something more!*

"Lord, her temper," Tendai said, "I don't understand her, Paul. I really do not. I'm... I'm sure I haven't done anything wrong. Nothing important. I'm sure." They were in Paul's foyer, where Tendai had stopped by after attending to a mare having a difficult delivery down at Lajevardi's. His clothes were stained with mud, blood, and whatever fluids were to be found in a horse's uterus. He was very tired, and wanted to unwind before going home. He slumped in his chair and regarded the unearthly decor of Paul's foyer. "We were having a fight, when I got called away to attend to Carl and Eunice's horse. I've never been so glad to hear a mare was having trouble foaling."

"Is the horse all right?" Paul asked.

"Oh yes, fine. I had to anesthetize her, cut her open, and then seal the wound with protoplaster, but that's nothing major. Mother and colt are both fine." He wiped his hands across his face. "I don't want to go home tonight. Do you know that? But I have to." He leaned back in his chair and let his arms go limp. His head dangled back between his shoulders. "You're her best friend. Please tell me what I am supposed to do."

His friendship with Tendai was something Paul had not anticipated. He felt it was based, if not on deceit, at least on secrecy of his own feelings for Tendai's wife, and Jan disliked secrets. Yet what was the alternative? Shoo Mr. Tamsanga away, back to his apparently unhappy household? Besides, it did please Paul that he could be a friend to his rival, if only because it assuaged his guilt; but he was ashamed to feel schadenfreude at Tendai's suffering, as well. The husband had become grumpily morose this past year. His once easygoing eyes were sad and often creased in dark scowls. Paul pitied him even as he envied him.

"Love her," he answered Tendai's question.

Tendai threw up his hands. "How? She's impossible. I don't how to make her happy. Nothing I do is good enough. She gets mad at me for the most... stupid things. I'm *too neat,* and it bothers her! And I burp! I'm never *ever* supposed to burp. The way that I cut the crust off my bread before I make a sandwich! She has a huge problem with the way I eat bread. She tells me I'm a shmuck. To my face! English is my second language, and I had to look up what a shmuck is."

"Yiddish, originally," Paul said. He'd learned the word from her as well.

*Do I actually think she will leave me?* Tendai wondered. *Do I want her to leave me?... No. No! No to both.* He sighed deeply. "What can I say back to her? That I'm sorry? Even I don't believe me when I say that, because... I don't think I have done anything wrong. So she just stays mad. It's exhausting. I don't feel as tired from spending a night pulling a foal out of a horse. And my arms feel like they're going to fall off." Paul started to speak, but Tendai continued, quietly, "She told me once I'm too *safe.* And what am I supposed to say to that? She's all *passion* and cra..." He stopped himself saying "crap" and ended the sentence with an ellipsis.

"Clearly you *do* understand her, to have said what you just said, about her being passionate," Paul said.

"Oh, I'm just telling you what she tells me," Tendai said. "No, I don't understand it." Tendai said, *"You* understand though, right? What's going on in that head of hers."

Paul said, "No, I don't," and believed that he did not.

Tendai threw up his hands. "Well then... I don't know what. 'Cause she *says* you do. It's *damn* sure that *I* don't." Paul had no answer for that, and noted that Tendai had passed the point of self-censorship. Tendai continued, "She is right. You are easy to open up to. I see why she likes spending time with you. You're like her big brother."

Inwardly, Paul winced, but gave no indication. *He has no idea how I feel about her,* Paul thought. *Good.*

"Thank you for listening, Paul," he said, earnestly. That hurt worst of all.

Indira also would come to him with parallel complaints about Tendai, which was even more awkward. Again, he tried to be supportive and nothing else, and she appeared to be as unaware of his feelings as was Tendai.

"Early on, I asked if he loved me. He told me, 'If I think I might drop something, I hold it in my hands. But what I hold in my heart, I will die with.' And shit, I thought that was the most romantic thing I'd ever, *ever* heard. It turns out it's an old Shona saying, a *cliché*. He knows lots of them; he's a regular sack of African fortune cookies. I should've known, because he *never* talks all high-falutin' like that. No, not at all." Indira continued, "He's such an idiot. He just doesn't *think*. Not really think. Not insightfully. Not about anything. He's stupid, Paul. Oh, he knows more about veterinary medicine than I ever will, but..."

"You're being much too hard on him," Paul offered.

"Do you think?" she asked.

"Yes, I think often," he said.

"No, you dork," and she swatted him. "I mean do you think I'm being hard on him?" she said.

"Oh. Yes, I think that, too," he said.

"He's honest, he's hard-working... easy on the eyes. But, he takes his shirt off, and he's got a belly on him. You don't notice as long as the shirt's on, but it's gross..." Her voice softened. "I enjoy running my fingers through his hair at night," she almost whispered. "The feel of his ear in my fingers. Just being next to him."

Paul thought, *I am an utter bastard, listening to this. Granted that I'm not sure, ethically, what else I should or could do here, other than what I am doing, but I still feel like a bastard.* The whole thing was miserable for him. To his surprise, he found he wanted for Jannite company very badly at this time.

"He loves you," Paul said, and knew it was true.

# 7

"You had a question, Paul?" Indira Tamsanga asked as he stood outside her front door. It was a cool autumn afternoon, three years since the wedding, and the low sun filtered through dry multicolored leaves. Loose orange ones blew and brushed past Paul's eyestalk. Paul regarded their little house. Modest, but large enough for a family, eventually. Not perfectly in keeping with church mandates, but nearly so.

Paul had agonized over this. He had agonized, too, over whether he was being foolish because perhaps there was no sin to agonize over. But he felt there was one, and so he ached. None the less, he went ahead and asked his friend of many years, and he said it very casually, "Will you come with me to Mars?"

"To Jantown?" Indira asked.

"Yes. It's my mating season, and I've finally decided to act on it, so I need access to a Matriarch. And I don't really want to go there alone. I don't know anyone on Mars. I'd rather go back home to Callisto for this, but..." *but I couldn't ask you to travel all that way, and I wouldn't want to be away from you for that long,* "...it would take months, round trip, and getting away for that long isn't very practical," he said, and hoped she wouldn't question it. True, so far as it went, but the half truth made him ill. *Though it is just one more half truth on top of so many others. You'd think they'd be second nature to me by now.*

"I'd miss you too," she said, "You're my best friend." How frighteningly well she knew him!—And yet how poorly. To her, and to her husband, it seemed completely innocent, so she didn't take a great deal of convincing. And he supposed it *was* completely innocent, in every human sense. All he really wanted was to spend time with her. To have her near, while he did something very important which he was afraid would only add to his lifelong list of failures. There was no jealousy from Tendai. No more than if she'd gone on a trip with a female friend. *And why should there be? I'm not another man. I'm a thing.*

Preparations were made swiftly enough, and in under two weeks, Indira Tamsanga was packed and kissing Tendai good-bye for an extraterrestrial vacation, the Fix-It shop closed until her return. Paul had been concerned Tendai would want to come as well, and had fairly well reconciled himself to the inevitability of his presence, but Tendai said he didn't have anyone to cover his practice for that length of time and would remain. Perhaps they actually wanted some time away from each other, Paul wondered. That possibility made him feel far guiltier.

"Now you be careful out 'mongst them foreign tentacle monsters," Ruth told her before they left for Mars, giving the younger woman a hug.

"I will," Indira said.

From their airtaxi, Indira gazed out the window. It had been so long since she'd flown! She remembered now how exhilarating it had been the first time she had looked *down* on clouds, almost twenty years ago, and now she relived that feeling. It had been a very long time since she had seen the quiltwork of the agrarian landscape from the sky.

Then they came over the city of Lawrenceton, flying among towers of every description. She'd lived here in college, but had scarcely set foot in the city in many years. She'd never had a bad impression of Lawrenceton. Even when she'd been little, and it had been the inimical secular World-with-a-capital-W to ever be shunned, even then it had held a glittering Vanity Faire fascination for her. And it did glitter. All those windows, sparkling in the sun.

There were far worse cities in the world, she knew. The bleak socialist polises, or the cybertopias full of hollow simulated people. She supposed she preferred Felice's diversity, and the fact that she'd been nearer the firmament up there. But for a groundling town, Lawrenceton was a very pretty place.

The mark of a city that's stood for any length of time is a diversity of architectural styles from different eras. Down and to her right was a building like an ivory chesspiece, high and narrow like a spindle. To its left was a huge rectilinear block of nanoform jade, studded with square windows in a grid. Over there were shapes resembling beehives and spiralled narwhal horns, dating from the biotic architecture boom just before the Android Uprising. There was the Audrey Building, built as headquarters of what was once the most powerful corporation in the city, made from old fashioned steel, glass, and concrete. And there was Chow's Cathedral, built in the early twenty-first century, its round rose window sparkling in the sun.

And there... Spach Street Elevated Tubeway! She laughed. She'd driven Spach every day on her way to class, her senior year, after she'd moved off-campus. She flashed on a memory of taking a little red used hovercar up the elevated tubeway in the very early morning. Light pop music played in the car, there were no other vehicles in the structure, the simple joy of cruising through the transparent tube's curves and gentle twists as the sun shone in a pale blue sky, as the buildings flashed past shining blues and yellows and whites, the motor humming so soft most people wouldn't notice it. A totally inconsequential memory, it could have been any day that year, but it came with perfect clarity now. She smiled.

Her first days in the World, when that whole world had been amazing, intimidating. She'd seen countless things for which she hadn't even had names. It was her first time wearing pants! She chuckled at that. It hadn't been long till she'd bought a pair of very close-fitting ones. She thanked God that veesuits were already out of style by then—the stupid things had been the rage for a while, those metallic white jumpsuits with a silver V-shaped stripe on the chest. Seemed like *everyone* had been wearing them at one time.

She'd reinvented herself in those days. Yet how much of herself had she lost in doing so? After a decade of it, she'd practically *dissolved.* Then again, what had she lost by returning to Eppleberg? She shook her head. All her life experiences must somehow fit together. She believed a human being to be an additive sculpture, not a subtractive one, and that all her experiences could and must cohere into a whole.

Still the skyscrapers flitted past with their endless windows. No, *not* endless—finite, countable if one took the time—but very, very many. Windows with people behind them. So many creatures, all made in the image of God. She idly wondered why He wanted so many. It was His call, of course. And she wasn't going to complain about existing.

She mentioned these thoughts to Paul, and he listened, all the while thinking how amazing it was that this small entity should have become the most important person in the universe to him. And that she... *might* feel likewise about him, of all people? *Ah, if only.* And that people all over the world should find one another in like manner, and thus each person might gain significance and dignity, despite all man's sandlike multitude. Such is the miracle of love that God gave to humanity. As long as even one person, even an animal loves you for yourself, that is uniqueness, that is dignity. That is what he told her, albeit downplaying his feelings about her. She said it was a beautiful sentiment. He gave no sign that he was speaking of love in anything other than a general sense, and she'd no inkling that his words had a more specific significance for him.

She looked up at Paul—a being made in the image of God, at least as much as she herself might be, and yet all bound up in rock instead of meat. Now there was a good soul, no question. So very strange. So full of wonder, the universe was.

Next came the shuttle flight into orbit. After much inner deliberation, Indira had finally decided—no, insisted—that they take their outgoing flight from Felice Station, rather than from Phillips or one of the other, smaller orbiting ports. At Lawrenceton Spaceport, they boarded a shuttle and were soon inside the vast, slowly revolving cylinder.

She barely recognized Market Zone now. Most of the shops and restaurants from her day had either been replaced, or else had changed their decor drastically. Yet the overall architecture of the place was the same. The two of them wandered through. It had always been fun to people-watch in this nutty place, she thought. She'd forgotten how varied and cosmopolitan it was.

There went a minor Kyvadian lord in all his yellow and orange finery, flanked by a dozen golden security droids. He was probably overestimating his own desirability as a target, she mused. She wondered if he'd actually used something as soft and useless as real gold, fresh from a tokamak, to "armor" those robots. *Oh yeah, I'm sure* that's *what Eisatte had in mind when the Mars colonies won their independence,* she silently snarked. Silly as he might be, though, it was still weird seeing the Martian princeling's ostentation after years of Plain clothing (she tried to picture Barney with gold plate, and giggled).

Still, Eisatte's revolt had set a precedent for multiple governments in the Solar System, and she believed that was good. For while Mars's constantly mutating and frequently violent balkanization was hardly admirable, it's also true that in the brief time humans had had a single unopposed government centered on Earth, it had become gravely corrupt. She believed Earth's current loose federal government was kept relatively honest by the presence of other separate, competing systems out there like the Martians, Belters, and Venusians. Besides, the "global village" phenomenon really wasn't sustainable across interplanetary distances anyway.

Across the street, she saw a cybertopian synthman on some unguessable errand. He was still humanoid, unlike many such. The cybertopias had grown up long before she was born, when hollow AI's had still been popularly supposed to be conscious. The inhabitants had cyborged themselves repeatedly, until all their original flesh was gone. It was only afterward that it became apparent the tech they'd used to replace their brains was fundamentally inadequate.

The cybertopias were now ghost towns, full of mindless revenants who grew more eccentric and malfunctioning with every passing year as they drifted away from even any superficial resemblance to human drives or cares, machinery clanking and hissing away to no discernable purpose (not even expansion, thankfully). Many of these once-people were now sessile. It was theorized that in terms of computational ability, some of them must be quite formidable by now—but lacking purpose, motivations, wants, or even, in many cases, awareness of their surroundings, most of them amounted to vastly complex Rube Goldberg devices, but with less practical purpose than that. Still, there were a few synthmen like this who still behaved in a remotely human way. She wondered if he might have some glimmer of self-awareness, and what he might be up to.

"Look at those clones," she said, pointing at a large cluster of more-or-less identical guys (their hair and clothing varied, and a few needed to lose weight) sitting at an open-air restaurant. "Lord, if you had a face like that, would you clone yourself?" she said.

"If I had a face?" he said.

"Skip it," she said.

"Don't judge people," he teased her. "Naughty."

"Hmp!" she hmphed, grinning.

They passed a group of strikingly beautiful genengineered Elves, decked out in elaborate finery. She wondered what side they had been on in the Genomic War two hundred years ago. Of course, they could be younger than that. There was no telling, with Elves.

And there were Tesks, and cyborgs, and other examples of transhumanity.

"I guess I'm just being snarky because a crowd like this makes me feel vulnerable. Probably because of where I've spent the past several years, but... Am I a relic?" she asked him. "As a baseline human?"

"Beg pardon?"

"Do you think baseline humanity has a future?" she asked. It had been a very pertinent question in generations past, during the Genomic War and the Android Uprising; not so much, later; but now, in peacetime, perhaps due to the influence of Arachne culture, it seemed like a pressing question again.

Paul said, "I don't see why it shouldn't, for whatever my opinion may be worth. The universe is very big. Why shouldn't these people live their lives while you live yours?"

"Hm," she said. "If it wasn't illegal, in your society, would *you* make any drastic changes to your body? Or mind?"

He didn't answer right away.

"Felice to Paul," she teased.

"I don't think so," he then said very quickly. "Perhaps I say that only because I *am* so much a product of my society. And of yours. But I don't think so."

"I'm glad, I think." She patted his arm. "Do you think that makes us cowards?"

"Is it cowardice to choose the difficult path over the easy one?" he said.

"Dang you're a writer. Stop it," she said.

"Sorry," he said.

"Well, that's a good point, but what I meant was... is it cowardice to choose the familiar path over the scary new one? Is there anything actually wicked about what they've done?"

Paul gave his shoulderless almost-shrug. "Maybe not," he said, "but I just know it's not for me."

Her old flat had been near here. She wondered if it still was, and who might be living in it. She directed Paul through the network of slidewalks to her old apartment block. They were soon drifting past a tree-lined avenue with comfy-looking living quarter blocs rising toward the ceiling of the section. Yes, this place still felt like home. She realized that that awful final walk through Market Zone on her way to wreak havoc in Engineering years ago had cemented itself into her memory of Felice, but the city wasn't *all* obnoxious Market Zone, and most of it was a pretty nice place.

They didn't encounter anyone she knew. Even back then, she'd been too much of a work-addict to be very sociable. She realized now that she'd believed that that was part of what a boyfriend or husband was *for*— to provide society so one didn't have to seek it. She regretted not having provided herself enough time today to look for such friends as she *had* had back then, but she and Paul only had a few hours before their flight.

All in all, the sense of nostalgia seemed to outweigh the regret for the time being, and she was both surprised by that and grateful.

From Felice, they boarded a ship to Mars.

Jan took naturally to space travel. Their bodies could withstand enormous g-forces, and they could enter a torpor state at will. In this torpor they did not dream, though they might ruminate slowly, their slowed imaginations grown more vivid for lack of distraction.

Paul would have spent much of the trip in torpor if not for his wish to spend time with Indira. And toward that end, he enjoyed the journey tremendously. There was a theater on board, and they watched a number of live performances of plays, as well as music (music being the accomplishment for which man was best appreciated outside his own solar system). The plays fascinated Paul; fiction was a bizarre thing to a Jan, but to see fiction *performed,* people going through the motions of these emotional situations, feigning sincerity, was especially strange. He suspected that if the theater had been emptier, their heartbeats would have given them away as liars, but it was far too crowded for him to tell, had he not already known their words were scripted.

Apart from the various entertainments on board (for humans, Jan, Arachne, and what few other aliens might be found in the Solar System in those days), the two of them just enjoyed staring out the windows at the stars they had watched on Earth, now clear of the twinkling obstruction of the atmosphere. The stars sang their siren song. Indira and Paul told each other how much they'd both missed space, that they'd been too long away from the eternal ebon sea. God's country.

The exile spent too much time in light torpor. He knew that.

He never entered deep torpor, from which he could not have been easily roused. His current situation, out on the plains or in his burrow, was too precarious to allow that. No doubt the lack of proper, deep torpor was why he needed so much time in light torpor.

Yet another reason was that he *liked* to ruminate, to escape his bleak life, and that gave him every incentive to rest. In rumination, he imagined what Janworld must have been like in ancient times. Certainly, there had been wars since then—interplanetary and even interstellar wars—in which his kind had fought valiantly; but stories of Janworld's myth-shrouded ancient days held the most appeal for him. Stories of a fertile, stony world where Workers huddled fearfully in their warrens and in the Matriarchs, and the only thing standing 'twixt them and all the myriad beasts that would slay them were the Warriors.

He pictured his forebears on tunneled Janworld, living wild on the plains above the subterranean cities, or deep in remote burrows beyond the cities. Monsters, moving death incarnate, would dig through the ground or bound above its surface. If not hoons, then frost-linnorms or meltworms or breakers, or any of a score of wonderful nightmares now nearly forgotten. The battle is joined! Warriors fight and fall and are avenged. Flesh shatters on both sides. The enemy falls! Six-armed forms writhe in wild victory dances in remote cavern delves where no urbane cowering Workers dare tread. In the Great Times. Now dusty legend.

There had been wars, too, of course, when Jan had fought Jan, mainly over disagreements between Matriarchs. Petty disagreements, many of them, but no matter.

Glory acclaimed the valiance of those fights as well. Still later had the sky itself yielded foes to combat, with cannon and bomb and yet greater weapons. Always the Warriors heeded the call to aid their weak brethren, to trade their lives for them. Gladly had they done it.

But his own generation? Himself?

What did Glory think now of his people? They were become a pathetic lot. Yet not a pitiable one, for they deserved no pity. Nor did he himself deserve it, though he'd done as best he could in the wretched circumstances allotted him.

O, for cohorts in battle, with whom to swarm over some behemoth adversary! O, for an *adversary!* Risk of death alone made life worth living. He hated cowering in this desolation, but discovery would bring renewed imprisonment; and shame or even death were preferable to that. He fought nature, wrung his living from it. Too, hiding was an ongoing challenge. Such petty struggles would have to suffice him, though they never could.

His life now might be simpler had he excavated his home underground—such a stealthy nest would have made hiding far easier, let him relax his guard—but he preferred to avoid unnecessary burrowing. This was partly because the Matriarch might *hear* his digging and send investigators, partly because a set burrow would tie him to one location when it was necessary to avoid exposure by staying on the move, but mostly because mining was a task for Worker children in the Mining Corps and he was above such drudgery.

Meditating in torpor, he prayed to his gods but yet feared their taking notice of him. He was proud of his escape, but the noblest among a wretched people is still a wretch. He believed Glory sometimes trod the universe in corporeal form, bearing warpaint and carvings and embedded spikes. He feared that one day Glory would appear thus to him, and the god would find him hiding under a rock like vermin as he spent most of his days. In the unlikely event that this happened, he had determined he would tell Glory the story of his life (and it would need telling, for the string of mediocrities he called his life had surely been beneath the god's notice), and boldly demand of his patron just what else ought he to have done, given the time and place in which he'd been born? Perhaps such a preposterous display of mortal bravado just might earn him favor from the god of courage.

Emerging from under a boulder where he had sheltered himself, he stretched his good arms and his bad one, and regarded the horizon in all directions. Jantown and Ma'adim were visible from here. From a distance, he could see that something was happening in the city today. He was curious, and as he often did to alleviate his tedium, he determined that he would risk exposure to go observe it.

On Mars, Indira donned a full-body thermal atmospheric suit, much as Paul would have needed to visit the Earth's equator. Paul, for his part, moved more freely and easily than ever Indira had seen him to do, and she supposed it must be wonderfully liberating for him no longer to feel every little heat-generating movement as its own punishment. The gravity was far lighter than Earth's, as well.

The sunrise that morning over red hills had been spectacular, and no dust clouded the air that day, leaving the Martian sky a stunning blue. The Valles Marinaris was every bit the wonder she'd always heard it was. Most Earthlings commented that it dwarfed the Grand

Canyon. Indira had never seen the Grand Canyon, but could see that this was unbelievably immense, its distant walls stretching from one horizon to the other.

Here in this vast valley between far walls, she was surprised at how undeveloped the rocky terrain of the Jan's "city" was. There were *some* stone structures, most resembling giant stone igloos, and a few three-sided pyamids, but most of the visible municipality was empty space. She understood this was because most of Jantown lay beneath their feet, corridors and homes and bass relief-bedecked temples and enormous vaulted halls carved and eaten from deep stone, hidden from the sky that Earthmen considered *their* natural ceiling.

Here on the surface, rather than buildings, the most numerous and notable alien objects were the many silane *plants* scattered about in wild crystal shapes that put Paul's tiny "rock garden" to shame—weird glassene multicolored not-trees and not-shrubs, spectacular balls and spikes and curlicues that seemed the work of a mad glassblower, all of them shimmering and twinkling rainbows in the Martian sun. Some of the plants resembled giant insect wings—freestanding, crystalline and intricate, catching sunlight like panes of stained glass. Shiny white parabolic dishes like antique radio antennae slowly tracked the sun across the sky like sunflowers (though she guessed that on Callisto, they would have tracked Jupiter itself). Paths of Jannite glow-weeds acted as streetlights; glow weed was hardy stuff, selectively bred as a light source ages ago. "It's beautiful," she whispered. He was glad she thought so. To him, it was welcomingly familiar after all this time, but not what he'd call beautiful. Kind of a boondock, really.

In their youth, Matriarchs were not much larger than Workers like Paul, and at this size they would travel widely, experiencing as much of their surrounding world as possible (it was at this size that Paul's mother, Ambassador Dwight, had arrived on the first Jannite ship, and been greeted by Julius Xaioming at Pluto). Then, after many years, a Matriarch would find an appropriate place, literally plant herself, and begin growing into a structure the size of a small mountain, able to breed vast numbers of offspring, and grow wise and knowledgeable beyond human comprehension. As Indira understood it, a full-grown Matriarch like Dwight actually contained warren networks within her own body. A living hive. This one was still young, and had not yet reached those titanic dimensions which were her birthright.

Humans would not tolerate the "planting" of a Matriarch on Earth proper. But Mars's chronic political disunity had provided a solution—the Jan only needed one Martian nation's cooperation for a "planting," and Zvezdaruske had given it. Many humans still believed Ma'adim to be a security risk—that if the Jan ever developed imperialistic ambitions, they could use her presence on Mars to justify a territorial claim—but it was still generally conceded that if *any* Jan were going to live on Earth, there had to be at least one Matriarch within the inner solar system. The mating urge was a very basic biological need, and it would be a long hike for them out to Callisto.

Indira asked, "Hey, question: I thought after Captain Xiaoming accidentally named your first ambassador 'Dwight,' before realizing she was female, all the Matriarchs since then had made sure to take female human names. What kind of a name is 'Madame'? Makes her sound... well, vaguely indecent. Especially considering what you're here for."

"Ma'adim. It's the Arabic name for Mars. And it sounds considerably more feminine than 'Dwight,'" Paul said. "There actually is a place in the Tharsis Range called Maadim Vallis for the same reason, but it's not near here."

"Is she... nice?" Indira asked.

Paul shrugged his tentacle arms and said, "I've never met her. I've heard that she is. Actually, I'm glad you know enough to ask that question. Earthlings frequently seem to be of the mistaken notion—because they are so intelligent and, among my own kind at least, revered for their wisdom—that our Matriarchs are all of uniform personality. This is not the case. I have always found Ursula to be rather cold and imperious. Although I've never met her, I hear that young Ishtar is quite a firebrand. And though most Matriarchs are remembered favorably, our history certainly does record tyrants. Thankfully, Dwight, eldest of this solar system's Matriarchs, I have always found to be extremely kind and understanding. I am blessed to have a good relationship with my mother."

"I still think it's weird to be doing it with somebody you don't know at all," she said.

"It's different for us," he said.

She watched Paul trundle off to take his place. Her pressure suit felt peculiar. It had been forever since she'd worn one. At first she feared it was malfunctioning, because she was definitely cold, but she realized now that she was merely nervous for him. As she brushed past a round stone the size of a pumpkin, it and several of its fellow rocks of varying sizes suddenly extended trios of skinny chicken legs and scampered away. She let out a comical little yelp inside her helmet. She'd read about these things; they were called babayagas. Animals that served some function in the Jannite ecosystem. Looking up, she realized that several much larger round rocks were probably also babayagas. She wondered how the Jan kept them and the not-plants from spreading out over Mars. Perhaps the planet wasn't hospitable enough to them without a gardener's care? Or maybe the opposite was true, and gardeners worked to keep them *in*. She idly wondered if there were any icecrawlers nearby.

Dozens more Jan males arranged themselves in a broad circle around the Matriarch in the snowy waste. Seeing the bizarre spectacle, Indira was struck anew by how very alien the Jan were, that these were not just human beings in elaborate monster suits, but things born and bred in some dark corner of the sky totally removed from the realms of men; their minds not human minds, their thoughts not human thoughts. And what of their souls? How much of the Paul she knew was a mask, worn for her benefit? What inscrutable tentacled cogitations lay behind that mask? Then again, if it were a mask, it *was* a mask worn for her benefit. That seemed significant somehow. And reassuring.

The Matriarch Ma'adim was a living, conical hill some fifteen meters tall by thirty meters in diameter, with three arms reaching skyward like towers. One supported a frost-dusted black eyesphere, the other two terminated in tendrilled hands, their fingers pointed upward. Where a Jan Worker at rest normally coiled his two arms around the length of his eyestalk, the Matriach's three extremities stood freely upright. Indira wondered whether the hands were functional, as they must have been in Ma'adim's motile youth. It seemed unlikely, and she wondered if any queenship could be adequate compensation for paralysis. Perhaps the Matriarch saw things differently.

The ground hummed, and Indira supposed the males were tremorspeaking. Then she realized that she *could* hear an actual sound from the direction of Ma'adim—

vibrating up from the ground, through her legs, in her bones, like deaf Beethoven, hearing through his teeth. She laid her hand on Paul's side, and he was vibrating quietly.

Indira wondered what Ma'adim was saying to them all. *"Good luck, boys!" "On your marks, get set..." "Land o'Goshen, Ah'm so flattered!" "YOU ARE NOT WORTHY!" "Hey, sailors!"...* Heh. Nah. Matriarchs were supposed to be monstrously intelligent, cranking out epic poems and new mathematical theories as afterthoughts. So, whatever she was telling them, it was... well, probably very clever and touching, and alien beyond Indira's human ken. What she found remarkable was her impression, watching their reactions, that Ma'adim really was holding down individual conversations with each member of this multitude simultaneously.

The ground shook with a starting signal from Ma'adim, and almost as one, the assembled males surged toward their towering intended in a wave. The lusty Workers crashed one into another in their race to the center of their ring, and the ground trembled with the stony multitude's heavy tread.

She was surprised at how fast the revolving behemoths could run in this light gravity, she being used to Paul's slow pace. She would actually have had to jog to keep up with these guys.

When Paul had described this ritual to her, years ago, Indira had teased him about it and assumed an alien mating ritual would be repulsive. It was certainly strange, but disturbing for another reason. They were *hurting* each other. The Workers clubbed one another with their massive arms, or even slammed their eyespheres against each other like wrecking balls. It was like a rugby match from hell. At first she thought it contradicted all Paul's descriptions of Workers as inept combatants, but then it seemed to her that they were all visibly clumsy at it—yet none the less savagely eager, for all that.

Paul fought, swinging his tentacles like stone clubs and slamming them into his competitors' bodies. Earlier, he had expressed guarded optimism to her, because he figured that his time in Earth's gravity had made him physically far stronger than his fellows. However, as she now supposed should have been obvious to both of them, he'd also spent those years living among pacifists, teaching himself that all violence was anathema. The others knew roughly *how* to fight, targeting their opponents' arms and eyestalks rather than their torsos.

No sooner had she taken all this in, when her friend was among the first to fall. A much smaller Jan, who had no doubt been preparing for this event, reached out, wrapped both arms around Paul's apex where his limbs were based, and yanked. Almost in slow motion because of the gravity, Paul crashed into the permafrost like an overturned boulder. He was done. An upended Jan, in a plain with no handholds, wasn't much better able to right himself than a turtle.

The winners reached the center as Ma'adim opened her twenty-one ports, to which twenty-one winners ecstatically affixed themselves. The tenor of the communication vibrations in the ground through Indira's bones changed to a soothing bass, like a cello. Then all was quiet, and it was done. The next generation of Ma'adim's children was assured.

Paul had failed.

Indira said, "Hey! You're hurt! Let me see it..."
Paul said, "I'm *fine!*" he snapped. "I'm sorry."
They were aboard the automatically piloted skycar Paul had rented for this trip, headed for the spaceport at

Marsgrad. Titanic walls of red, gray, and brown stone, bigger than any Earthly mountain range, passed slowly by, far in the distance outside the windows. Indira said, "I don't mind. Really. Will you quit *rutsching?"* she said as he fidgeted. "You're like a big baby, you know that?" She felt him vibrate and recognized it as an subaudible grunt of frustration.

"I failed!" he said.

"Aww... You're my three-legged tentacle-muffin made of equal measures organosilate and angst. You were so brave," she cooed, applying cement to his wound.

"Yes, well..." Her presence made things far more bearable. "As your old songsmith said, I can't get no satisfaction."

"But you tried. You tried. Oh how you tried," she said.

His failure at the Matriarch ritual was deeply painful, physically as well as emotionally, but it had after all not been the real purpose of the trip. He'd had this chance to spend time with Indira. That was all he had really wanted, and he was similarly looking forward to the trip back. In retrospect, all his wrangling moral conflict over Indira's accompaniment of him here no longer seemed like so big of an issue, and Paul wondered why he'd built it up so much in his own mind.

Suddenly, the skycar's engine juddered loudly and then ceased. An alarm keened.

"What was...?" she began to ask.

And they were falling! Indira had been standing in order to tend to Paul, and so had not been strapped in. Paul shouted her name as she went tumbling and banging to the back of the cabin. The ground rushed up to meet them. Indira saw it coming through the windows and cried out. She could also see the craft's wings automatically distort as they frantically sought purchase in the negligible Martian air. A soft *chuff!* noise meant the braking jets had fired, slowing their descent. Then the ground came. The durable little craft banged and bashed along the terrain for hundreds of meters, but the ground here was mercifully flat. They skidded for quite a distance before finally stopping.

They were silent for a bit, surprised that the crash had not been worse. Then Paul unstrapped himself and went to her. She looked unhurt but very frightened, and her heart sounded like a triphammer. It occurred to him that if he had not been strapped in, and they'd both been flung to the back of the craft, he'd likely have crushed her. He thanked God that had not happened.

"Are you all right?" he asked.

*"No!!!* Well yeah, maybe," she said as she got up. She winced and cried out as soon as she put weight on her left leg. "Ahhhh!! My leg hurts." She said it high and quiet, like a little girl. She closed her eyes and steadied herself until she was standing more or less straight. "Are you okay?"

"I'm sore from the fight earlier, but the landing didn't hurt me," Paul said, full of worry for her. "Are you in a lot of pain?"

"Uhmm..." Her demeanor was calm, but her pulse was still like a rabbit's. He was grateful for her courage. She sounded almost normal again as she said, "No, I guess not. We'll have to go out and take a look," she said. "I... get to fix something. Yayyy. Feh."

"Can you walk?" he asked.

"Uhhh... Gonna find that out," she said. She downed a painkiller from the onboard medkit, and then grumblingly climbed back into the uncomfortable pressure suit.

They stepped out onto the permafrost and walked around to examine the craft, Indira limping awkwardly. The problem was instantly obvious: there was a large, round *hole* in the side of the thruster casing.

"What could have possibly caused that?" Paul asked.

Bracing herself against the hull so she could lift her bum leg, Indira examined the hole. The skin of the craft had been burned clean through, and a look inside showed internal systems melted and smoking along the path that the beam must have taken. Paul noticed as her heart sped up even more, and then she said in a low voice, "Paul, you were in the military. You know exactly what caused this."

He did, but he wasn't an engineer and had hoped some obscure mechanical failure might have punctured the hull. That was not the case. "An artillery laser?" Paul said. "Who would shoot us down?"

No sooner had he said this, but Paul noticed something and pointed. Indira turned and saw they were being approached by a figure she assumed to be a Jan, but the shape was wrong. It had no eyestalk, and too many arms. One arm was silver. It was far faster than any Jan she'd ever seen, whirling as it ran. A healthy human could still easily outrun it, especially in this gravity, but Indira's leg was injured. And why did she think she ought to be running...?

"My God..." Paul said softly. He scarcely ever took the Lord's name in vain.

"That's a Warrior, isn't it?" Indira asked, warily.

"It's Nuada," Paul said. With the metal arm, there was no mistaking him. What was his ship's Gunner from Adrastea doing *here?*

For a moment, Paul wondered if Nuada had died in one of the savage "sports" played in Valhalla. Maybe

Indira and Paul had both now died in the skycar crash, and Nuada's ghost had come to greet them. Even *that* seemed almost more likely than for Nuada to be here, in the middle of nowhere, on Mars.

The many-armed dervish was soon upon them, and Indira saw how much bigger he was than Paul; and unlike any stolid Worker she'd seen, the Warrior was full of movement—his whole body seemed more elastic than Paul's, and the six arms undulated like charmed cobras.

Nuada did not make the proper salutation gestures for a Warrior addressing a Worker, but gave a loud, terse greeting tone. *"Greeting!"* Nuada tremorspoke, and spoke Paul's birth name. *"Amazement! Amazement! Satisfaction."*

*"Greeting,"* Paul said and tremorspoke Nuada's true name, nervously. He asked what Nuada was doing on Mars.

The apparition answered that Heimdall, who had replaced Paul as Quinary Administrator at Valhalla, was a fool, and that escape had been surprisingly easy, once he had formulated a plan. Nuada had stowed away on a shuttle to a cargo ship bound for Mars, and then smuggled himself down to the surface with the cargo. It had been a marvelous challenge, almost worth the years of hardship that had necessitated it. Nuada had since lived on Mars, in hiding, for decades.

Paul responded that he'd had no inkling of any of this. He said he was startled and totally sympathetic to Nuada's ordeal, and that he admired his courage and initiative. Privately, it reminded him of tales he'd heard of the Pennsylvania Dutch assisting escaping American slaves in the days of the Underground Railroad, though he did not say so, as the Terran historical reference would mean nothing to Nuada.

This was not the reaction Nuada had expected from his old jailer. He naturally took the ex-Administrator's sincerity as a given. He took a quick moment to consider whether this reversal should affect his planned course of action, and then concluded that no, it should not.

Nuada said that earlier that day, he had watched the Jantown mating ritual from afar. He'd been astonished to see Paul there, he said. It was a remarkable coincidence.

*"Agreement,"* Paul said. Yet, he thought to himself, it was not so great a coincidence as it seemed. If any Warrior whom Paul had known in Valhalla were to manage such an escape, it would be Nuada. Mars was the most hospitable planet for Jan in the Solar System (Dwight and the colonists had settled Callisto because Mars was already a human-dominated world), so it was a logical place for him to go—and the wilderness outside Jantown, from which he could steal supplies, was the most logical spot *on* Mars.

Paul was appalled to realize the interned Warriors' circumstances were baneful enough to drive one of them to live as a fugitive, and ashamed that he'd turned so blind an eye to their plight and to his culpability for it. Beyond that, though, he was afraid. Jan were communal, Warriors no less than Workers. They generally did not fare well in isolation. Paul wondered about the current state of Nuada's mind. It was clearly he who had shot them down.

Nuada said the Warriors would have gladly endured any hardship for the Matriarchs and Workers. Any danger. Instead, they had gone fallow. Useless. Purposeless. And Paul had been their jailer. Their keeper. Yet, Paul's fortuitous stupidity had allowed Nuada that one passing instant of glory on Adrastea, one battle to cherish in his memory until death. Nuada projected an image of an idol of Glory—for to experience glory, as he had at Adrastea, was to be in the presence of his god. But then, his voice edged with fury, Nuada said he himself should have delivered the final blow! Killed the Earthling enemy. Instead, Paul had stopped him. That delay granted the humans a clear shot, he lost an arm, and then *his jailer* delivered the coup *himself*. Paul had stolen that one inestimably priceless crumb from a wretch starved since birth.

In self-imposed exile, Nuada said he had many times considered attacking the Workers at Jantown, wreaking havoc on the civilization that had destroyed his life. Yet always he'd stopped himself, believing at some instinctive base that there could be no honor in warring on those he'd been born to protect; even as he despised them, still he held them too dear for that. Yet there was *one* Worker he would gladly kill, one whose death would sate him. He projected an image of Paul as a corpse. Nuada concluded with a proxy English word he'd picked up which fit his purpose better than any Jannite term: "Revenge."

As he saw Paul stiffen, he added, almost incidentally, that the vile Earthling's death would cap off the day perfectly.

"No..." Paul's vocodor whispered, in English, mainly to himself.

"What?" Indira asked. "What's going o—"

"He's going to kill us," Paul said.

*"What?!"*

Paul saw no way to prevent it. Even if their faith hadn't prohibited them from physically resisting Nuada, neither he, nor still less Indira, stood any chance against him in a fight. Nor was there any hope of the normally speedy little human outrunning Nuada with her injury.

The old Warrior approached them, revolving slowly, his metal talon glinting in the sun. Paul saw irony in having survived Amos Baumgartner's attempt to kill him as vengeance for the Stevens's deaths, only for Nuada to kill him now for not *sharing* the supposed glory of their murder.

He was frightened in a way he had never felt before. At Adrastea he had panicked, but it hadn't been fear of death or even of killing, but fear of his incompetence, of his ignorance of what he was supposed to do. Then in Amos's attack, surreal as it had been in its unexpectedness and as horrid as was its conclusion, even then he had only feared for himself, because he hadn't known Jawaharlal was in danger until it was too late. But now...

Paul *begged* Nuada to spare Indira.

Nuada countered that killing humans was the very reason he'd been born. He said he'd waited so *long*. He projected an image of thick ichor and thin blood, splattered on snow. At least Paul assumed the thin liquid was supposed to be human blood. Nuada had never seen any.

Then Paul begged his Maker. *God, please spare her! Wasn't her father enough? Please Lord, let no one else die on account of my sins! Please don't let this happen! Please!!*

There came a new sound, in the distance.

Indira heard it through the soles of her feet and up into her bones, just as she had heard Ma'adim's speech; but this did not feel like tremorspeech, and it was far louder. In fact, it was so loud that she'd have sworn she very faintly heard it through the practically nonexistent *air*.

Paul knew what it was.

His already awful fear turned to unmitigated horror.

A white shape, streaked with stripes of gray, undulated over the snow. It was so big that at first Indira mistook it for one of the famous Martian dust storms. Yet this was solid, a living white form that surged across the wastes, implacable as a glacier. Through the spray of frost, she could finally make out that it resembled a vast ivory caterpillar. The thing named itself and the world drowned in a repetition of the noise she'd heard a moment earlier. It vibrated through her skeleton, through her skull, through her soul: *HOOOOOOOOONNNNNNNNNN*

Barely noticeable over the roar, Nuada was screaming as well—in frustration at his crime's interruption, Paul knew, rather than in fear. It took a lot to make a Jan scream.

"What the hell is it?" Indira screamed, though the answer was clear enough.

So frightened by the appearance of his people's most ancient enemy he could barely speak, Paul finally said, "The colony's *hoon,* Ares."

Indira remembered Paul saying, long ago, *hoons* had an almost totemic significance to Jan, and their colony worlds always kept a small breeding population of them. On their way here, he'd even mentioned that Martian Jantown kept one. She simply hadn't expected to meet it.

Ares had the trilateral symmetry common to Jannite life, but the walking legs on the right and left were far more developed than the dorsal ones pressed against its back; the dorsals were aids for burrowing, not running. The tapered white head sported strange whorls and angles, with three huge, round, black eyes. The overall effect rather resembled a three-way reflection of an Earthly horse or cow skull.

"The crash... must have attracted it," Paul said. Every fiber of instinct in his body screamed at him to dive into the nearest warren tunnel or die. There were no tunnels here. He was a lamb before a lion in an open field.

Indira was carbon-based. She would not be edible to it. It would be too stupid to know that. Instincts that would have served it well on Janworld would say any creature that moved was potential food.

Indira had scarcely reacted yet. The bizarreness of it all served as a barrier to any immediate emotional response. The analytic part of her mind worked quickly, while the emotional part, which might ultimately paralyze her, had yet to catch up. *The monster is free-range. That's what the babayagas are for,* she realized. *Food for this thing.*

Nuada cursed himself for not bringing the laser with which he'd downed the skycar, as he'd intended to kill Paul with his claws. He cursed himself that he had so little knowledge of tactics for this situation because he'd spent his life as a pet of the state instead of a soldier. He made ready to run, reasoning he might get away if the *hoon* were delayed by eating the slow-moving Worker and the Earthling. If Nuada could find cover, he had a very slim chance...

And then he realized. He was *aghast* that running had been his first impulse. Now he felt only eager anticipation. He stepped toward the creature, and the very living reason for any Warrior's existence bore ravening down on him.

With every ounce of his strength, Nuada *dove* away as the creature's massive, tripartite-jawed face crashed into the icy ground where he had stood. The hellmouth visage rose and swiveled to see him, but by then Nuada had moved round to its flank. It was heavily armored, and Nuada knew his counterattack to be futile, but he didn't care. As long as there was valor in it! He smashed his claws—his natural ones *and* the metal one—against the monster's hide.

The metal hook actually pierced it! The chiseled gash seeped black muddy ichor.

He was ecstatic that he would not die a murderer. Instead, he'd die *protecting a Worker from an attacking hoon*. It was the very *definition* of honorable battle. He would die like the legendary warren defenders of ancient days. He hammered furiously, joyously at the monster, breaking its flesh as...

Ares's pyramidal face fissioned lengthwise into three titanic clawlike jaws which closed on Nuada with a sickening crunch. Indira screamed in her helmet.

Joyful, Ares lifted its death's head into the deep blue evening Martian sky. Clots of moist gravel, all that remained of Nuada, dripped from its mouth as it chewed merrily, its other prey momentarily forgotten.

Paul had never seen someone eaten before. Where Jawaharlal's death was horrible in its alien strangeness, this was beyond imagining. It didn't look as if masticating would delay the monster long. "We're going to die," Paul said. He said it matter of factly. Neither he, nor Indira in her present condition, could outrun this thing. Even hiding in the car was probably futile, for it had no armor, and would provide no more protection than the crunchy shell on a bonbon. "I deserve this, but you don't," he said.

"Don't talk that way." Indira felt oddly calm, staring death in face. Even having just screamed, she felt calm, and she perceived the universe to move slowly, as though through fluid. *Of course. I'm in space. The waters above the waters.* And very much to her own amazement, she consciously realized she could still *think*. She knew she should be afraid. She could feel the fear above her, a hanging anvil held by a fraying strand of adrenaline, but for this moment, the strand held. Her thoughts raced ahead of the events around her at hyperspeed, and for once, the racing thoughts had *focus*.

She ran round to the side of the car. Paul assumed, quite reasonably, that she was hiding, though he didn't expect it would avail her anything.

For Ares's part, it had just had its first taste of its natural food. It was very good! Ares had wanted to catch one of these little things for an *awfully* long time. Now here was another one! And a different little... thing. It would see what that tasted like, too. Ares gave a deafening roar into the ground to paralyze its prey, and the sound of its bellow shook the terrain like a bomb blast.

Even as Indira moved, she could feel her bones shaking, not from fear but just from the sound the monster was generating. Yet her fear had passed beyond fear now, and so she could function. She had scrambled around to the side of the car and removed its outer paneling.

She heard a voice in her radio. It was Paul. "Indira!"

"What?"

*"I love you!"* he said. "I've *always* loved you! I can't die without telling you. Christ, I love you so much! I'm so jealous of Tendai, it's killing me!"

Paul's secret fell from him like the burden off the back of Bunyan's hero. He'd said it. He was free. She knew. Nothing else mattered. Nothing.

Except what she might say. She said nothing. Why didn't she respond?

The monster now faced him like a cat staring down a mouse. Paul knew he was done for.

"Eat fire!" Indira screamed, and Paul saw through his rear vision that she'd pulled a small thruster fuel pack from the wrecked skycar. The sort of thing an engineer would think to do. She hurled it with all her might. It struck the monster's upper jaw. Paul had never known she was so strong. Only later would he realize she'd been aided by the low Martian gravity.

The bank exploded in blinding flame. The ground shook as the *hoon* wailed its agony. Ares crashed onto its back and writhed fantastically, a dragon in its death throes. Flame seared down the thing's waterless throat, and then there was a second, smaller eruption as the fire reached Ares's liquid oxygen bladder and incinerated it from the inside out. Then it lay still, its charred white face smoking in the thin Martian air.

They stared at it.

"Ma'adim's pet..." Indira gasped. To which she then appended, "God. Oh. Oh my... *Fuck...*"

"You... killed a *hoon*... singlehandedly, without a proper weapon..." Paul said. "Great God. Indira, that's the stuff of my people's legends. You're a hero!"

She turned to face him, her face clearly visible through her thermal mask but still unreadable to him. She seemed to him some celestial warrior, an avenging angel, or perhaps a demon, limned in the flickering light of the *hoon's* smoldering form.

"You *love* me?" she said as wisps of dust rose within her mind from where the anvil had now fallen, hard.

"Oh. That," Paul said. He had worried that she might quail at the sight of the *hoon's* death. Looking back on this moment long afterward, he supposed that he ought to have known better. Only moments ago she'd shown great bravery because there had been no time for fear. Now that the danger was past, and her mind was acknowledging what had happened, *now* she was panicking. And she *always* expressed fear as anger.

"What... the *hell*... do you mean you love me?!" she said.

Where he had just feared for his life, the guilt of years of adulterous longing hit his soul like a flail. He moaned.

She felt the tremor of his moan in the ground. "Quit whimpering, I'm not done! Damn you for tricking me like this!" she said.

"What? I didn't trick..."

Panic seized Indira at Paul's words. The panic grew. And with it, the rage of a frightened beast. "The last honest guy in town! The one person I trusted implicitly! Fuck you, you stupid rock!" she screamed. "God damn you to hell! I hate you I hate you I HATE YOU!"

"You're not even making sense..." he said.

*"I'm* not making sense?!" *What were we to each other?* she wondered. *What have we ever been? What in hell has ever been going on in that stone brain of his?*

"I'm sorry..." he said.

*"Bas!* Oh shut up. Just fucking... God damn you..." Sobs wracked her and she fell to her knees. "God damn you." Indira demanded, "How could you lie to me about this?!"

Paul said, "I spoke the truth."

Indira said, "You lied before! Why... And how could you be telling the truth now? Why are you saying this?! It's... damn you!"

*What have I done?* He suddenly wanted to get away from there. "We need to radio for help."

"You were my friend!" She screamed, "All these years, you were my *one friend!*"

"Is it so different?"

"Shut up!" she said.

"No, maybe I actually don't know if it's different. Is it...? No, damn it! I *love* you! I do. The secret's gone, and I can't... I won't lie about it."

"Oh, so you *can* lie, eh? Well that's fucking amazing now, isn't it?"

"Yes," he said. "I think I understand human thought well enough now that I could lie if I wanted. That's the truth. But I don't want to. I haven't lied to you, then or now. I love you. I love you."

"Stop it!"

"God, I'm hurting you..."

"Hurting me?! Yew fucking.... Ohhh..."

She punched his body with all her strength. It hurt like she'd hit a wall. She was afraid she'd broken her fingers. She wept. "Just shut up," she said.

"You know there's no way I could have guessed this would happen..."

*"SHUT UP!* Just shut up."

Paul said, "I hate it when you get like this."

Indira said, "Fuck that! My father's dead because of you!"

Paul said, "What does that have to do with anything?"

Indira said, "You're not even denying it!"

Paul said, "You want me to deny it? Yes, *people die because of me!* The Stevens are dead. Your father is dead. Nuada is dead. You wanted me to kill his murderer, and you gave me hell when I wouldn't do it. I thought you were going to die, and I thank God that it didn't happen!"

Indira said, "Don't go going off on one of your big religious kicks that has nothing to do with anything!"

Paul said, "God has to do with everything!"

Indira said, "You do not love me!"

Paul said, "I do, damn you! I love you! And you love me!"

This produced an incoherent shriek. "You take that *back!*" she snarled.

"What?! It's... It's a simple statement of *fact* is what it is! You're a married woman. I never wanted to tell you, because of that. Let alone the obvious... problem."

"Damn right it's obvious! You're a fucking space monster and you think that I'd..."

"Please stop," he said.

"I will not stop! You brought this *all* on yourself! And you're going to stand there on your three stumpy legs and take it! Well?! Don't clam up on me *now*. Say something!" she yelled.

"I'm sorry," he said.

"Damn right. You're the sorriest fucker in the universe," she said.

"If not 'I'm sorry,' then what do you want me to say? What?" he asked.

"Just go to hell," she said.

"I don't want to do that," he said.

"Then go the hell back to your happy little communist utopia you came from."

"Please stop calling it that."

"Why'd you leave that to come live here with us monkeys, huh? You came here voluntarily. What'd you see in religion here, huh?"

"Christ taught that God is love. That sounded good to me."

"Uh-huh. Well, you do not love me. You don't know what the fuck love is. And I sure as *damn* hell do *NOT* love you."

"Okay," he said.

"What's that supposed to mean?" she said.

Blank silence for a moment, as he tried to guess what she meant. "Well, if I remember my etymology, it originally meant 'Old Kinderhook'..."

"This is not funny!" she said.

"I'm not laughing," he said.

"Oh yes you are. You haven't even got a mouth, but you're laughing. You think this whole thing is hysterical," she said.

"No. I can't laugh, but I know when something's funny," he said.

"Again with the jokes!" she said.

"What joke?" he said.

"God.... *damn* you," she said.

"What do you want me to do?" he said. "I asked that before, I think. To take the words back? I'm not going to do that. *I'm not going to lie!* Even for you. I spoke the truth. And I'm sorry I did. I'm sorry I said anything when I *thought we were both about to die!*"

Struggling to maintain composure, Paul lumbered into the craft and radioed for help. He barely heard himself as he relayed what had happened to them to an incredulous human operator; at least a Jan wouldn't have doubted the particulars, he thought. But help was on its way. He climbed back out of the craft. She sat on the tundra, her back braced against the skycar, her bad leg stretched out before her. He asked if she were going to come inside to remove the suit and she ignored him.

Then they had to wait. That was truly hell.

The Martian wind blew, fast yet lighter than a feather. He knew she could not sense it. The sun set behind red mountains. An aurora shimmered into existence overhead. They looked up at it.

Maybe... Maybe she was just upset because of what had just happened. Maybe that was all it was. Hell, they'd almost been killed by some nut out of his past, and then almost eaten by a caterpillar monster. Paul had to admit, in her place, he'd be annoyed too.

"We get auroras all the time, back home," Paul said. "I haven't seen one in a long, long time." He paused. "I'm glad you got to see one with me."

"Go to hell."

On the trip back to Earth, she didn't sleep for two days. *Thank God I don't know where the ship's oxygen system is located,* she thought. The emergency workers on the ambulance from Zvezdaruske had fixed her leg, and it didn't hurt much now, but it hurt a little. She massaged it as she thought.

*What did he mean by it? What did he mean?* she asked herself again and again, becoming more frustrated and confused each time. *He can't... he actually* can't *love me. The whole thing is... I don't know.* She tried to analyze her feelings but couldn't make head or tail of them. She projected onto him every possible motivation she could imagine for his words—none of these guesses were at all flattering, neither did they seem likely. And the possibility that he had spoken the simple truth... terrified her for reasons she could not delineate.

*Why... now?* she thought, and was startled by the thought, and disturbed by it. She pondered its meaning and, with effort, dismissed it.

She refused to see him. She paced abound her cabin on her tender leg. Then she wandered all over the ship, from one idiot entertainment to another. She had flashbacks of that drunken night on Felice, and so didn't touch a drop of alcohol. A sleazy-looking guy offered her something stronger and illegal; the mood she was in, she could have mauled him *(A night in the brig would just punctuate it all, wouldn't it?* she thought), but she just spun and walked quickly away.

She thought of the incident with the *hoon*. She was, flatly, impressed with herself. She thought back to that time with the hydro-correlator core on Felice, when her life had been in danger, and she hadn't given a damn, and afterward had worried why she had not been worried. She still believed that had been a death wish. This was different. This was significantly different. It was a *courage* she wanted to foster.

By her second day, she was mildly surprised she hadn't bumped into Paul. A part of her would have welcomed it, knew it might even *be* her motivation for wandering, as it would save her the awkwardness of actively going to see him.

Paul did not wander the ship. He languished in most pathetic fashion. After several unsuccessful attempts to speak with her, he had resigned himself to the manner in which his people usually spent spaceflight, in deep torpor.

Hibernating Jan do not dream, in the hallucinatory sense, but they do think, slowly and meditatively and undirectedly. As he slept, Paul thought over the whole of history that he knew—Jannite, human, and other— and it all seemed a long stream of woe with intermittent blips of illusory happiness and hope. He longed for the

Second Coming, because this fallen world had lasted far too long.

Everything seemed hopeless. His faith faltered.

*So Saul of Tarsus was horrified by what he'd done and suffered a nervous breakdown. Maybe an epileptic seizure or hallucination that he saw as a bright light on the road to Damascus. There's nothing necessarily supernatural about that, is there? And yet, the story* must *be true! Why oh, the* horror *of weak faith and indecision! Angst, angst, angst! If you go through enough hand-wringing, worry, and guilt on the thing, then that will make it true... Not just true, but profound to boot, right? Oh God, "Paul," you really have become human. You've gained all their idiot foibles for your very own. Congratulations. Even love. "Love!" Of all the ill-defined words in English! Love. May God save all other intelligent life from the madness of human courtship rituals.*

Thus he slept.

*Then* she came to see him.

After verifying that he hadn't dropped the temperature and air pressure to something beyond human endurance, she entered his cabin, noting that he hadn't blocked her palmprint from allowing her entry. "Paul? I wanted to... *Asleep?!?*" She gaped at him. His arms were braided around his upright eyestalk. He looked like a Parcheesi piece. Blind and immobile.

She tried various different methods for waking him, including shouting and striking him with blunt objects, but Paul had entered deepest torpor and would not be roused.

She fantasized what she could do to him in this state—these thoughts ranging from sledgehammering him to painting graffiti on him—but she left him be, and their conflict remained unresolved.

Her parting word was, *"COWARD!"*

The longer he remained silent and unresponsive on the return from Mars, the angrier she grew.

Tendai asked him over the audiophone (in keeping with Mennonite practice, Paul did not keep a visiphone in his home), "Did something happen between you two? She hasn't said, but I can tell. She's so mad, it's making her physically sick. She's puked into the toilet twice. She won't tell me what happened. I've tried to get her to talk to *you* to straighten it out, but all she keeps saying is that 'On the spaceship was the time for that.' It makes no sense at all."

Paul looked around his home's foyer. He looked at the rack with his remaining icecrawler shells. It was years since the others had been broken. He spoke into the air for the mic to pick up, "I'm not human," Paul said. "I'd be the last to know." *That's a lie, isn't it?* he thought. *No, I really don't understand her reaction to… Oh, I don't know any more.*

"What in hell happened?" Tendai asked.

Paul was silent, and then said, "I can't tell you."

"Well that's just terrific. I *wasn't* mad at you, but now I have to know. What in hell did you to do to my wife?!"

*I wronged him as much as I did her. Say something. You're committing a sin as long as you say nothing! Confess! Anything he imagines will be worse than the truth. Say something!*

A voice echoed through Paul's mind screaming the word "coward."

"I have to go," Paul said, and hung up.

He took a walk through town. There was Hochleitner's Diner. Here was Mitchell's Bakery. Maple Street. Oak Street. Lapp's Farm. Chan's Farm. Stodt's Farm. Rolling waves of unripe wheat. Pigs. Cattle. The pleasant aroma of the cattle. He would miss that. He would miss all of it.

People waved as he passed. He was a town fixture. He would be missed. That was good to know. Actually, he worried that among most people, he would be missed in the way that an old tree is missed after it has fallen, rather than missed as a friend. Or perhaps that was merely petty self-pity.

Paul had long since joined the local Mennonite fellowship, but he would explain to the elders that his conversion had finally made him keenly aware of unfinished moral obligations back home which he could no longer ignore with a clean conscience. His editor would also be displeased at his departure. No more outsider's-keen-insights into the human experience would be coming from him back on Callisto.

He told himself that what he had in mind was not cowardice (a vice he now recognized he had always had and had refused to acknowledge) because he would, in fact, be taking on a responsibility that he'd long known he should take up. If it meant leaving here, so be it. If it meant leaving her, so be it.

He entered his home. He considered calling from the foyer, but then decided he wanted to be as calm as possible for this, so he headed to the comforting frigidity of the back room. Then he phoned her.

"Why are you calling me?" her disembodied voice demanded.

"What do you mean 'why?'" he said. "We... need to talk."

"When we needed to talk, you spent the whole trip back sulking," she said.

"Hibernating," he said.

"Same thing!"

"You mean you wanted to talk? We can talk now," he said. "I thought you should know. I'm going back to Callisto. To Valhalla. Nuada had a point. It's a miserable place, and I know it intimately. I have to take responsibility for fixing it. Call it a part of my penance, if you want."

"What?" Indira said. She was stunned. It was so unexpected. "That was years ago. You're being an idiot!"

"This is an important, moral responsibility that I've ignored for too long. Maybe it's that my people don't have a strong enough belief in personal responsibility. We're a race of bureaucrats. But I think I've grown up here, on Earth. I can't... I shouldn't run away from my problems."

Dead silence followed that, followed by, "What in the *flying hell!* But... why am I mad about this? Why? For God's sake, run away to your fucking little moon and play with your murderers and giant caterpillars. Like I give a fuck." She took a deep breath and said, *"You shouldn't let guilt dictate everything you do!"*

"Guilt is just the voice of conscience," he said. "Would you rather that I be a wicked person?"

"I want you... to be a happy person," she said. "God, Paul, you have *never been happy!* Not in the entire time I've known you."

"That isn't true," he said.

"It is true! You'd die before you'd let yourself enjoy life even a *little."*

He imagined that she was there before him. He pantomimed reaching out and cradling her face gently in one finger—a bit of personal fiction that his literalism once wouldn't have permitted him. He said as gently as the artificial voice through his vocodor was able, "There has never been a day since you became my friend that I have not been happy. Even in my deepest sorrows, your face is there, in my mind. It is my light. I am happy."

There was a long moment of utter silence, and then a quiet moan which then began to turn into a shriek of confused frustration but then cut itself off. Then she spoke, her voice black with fury, "I repeat: Why are you calling me? If you're going to go, go. Go to hell for all I care. Get the fuck off my planet! Just go, Paul."

His knees buckled under him. Paul said, "I've been thinking for years that I should go back. I just didn't, because… you were… Nuada was right. My people have done something very wicked. I did… There has to be a better way. I've become something of an outsider, and I think that gives me a degree of objectivity about the Warri…" He trailed off. Even he didn't care what he was saying.

*"So go already!!"* Indira shouted.

He was quiet for a long time. "You take care," he said.

She said nothing at first, and then said, quietly and very incongruously, "You take care, too."

He hung up.

# 8

"I have to get out of here," she muttered. "There's nowhere for me to go, but I have to get out anyway." She'd muttered this mantra to herself for years. But this time, she repeated the sentiment to Tendai. "We're leaving," she told him.

"We are?" he said.

"Yes," she said.

Confused and exasperated, Tendai said to her, "Have you considered that *I* don't want to leave?"

Indira said, "I want to travel. More than I did in my youth. I want to see the world. Worlds!"

Tendai said, "What's changed your mind? What happened up there?" He had experience with her moods, and had developed what he regarded as a Job-like patience with them. "I like it here," he said. "I need a reason."

*There's too many memories here,* she thought, and then said, "You know perfectly well how long I've wanted to escape here."

"I d...?"

"I will not stifle here any longer," she said. "Let's leave. And then I want children. I want my life to move forward! I want to escape. I want to go buy useless, extravagant multicolored crap that no one in their sane mind could possibly need. What are the popular thneeds these days?"

"The popular... what?" Tendai said.

"It's a word! A literary reference. Why in hell don't you know words? He knows words. Why in fifty flaming hells can't you know words?"

"Stop it! Damn it," he said. "I'm not budging an inch till you calm the hell down."

She glared at him like a solar flare, and he faltered. She regarded him.

*I will be with this man every day. I will.*

And she ran up to him and embraced him. "I'm sorry," she said.

"Um, okay," he said. Such apologies were rare, and he wasn't going to reject one.

"Are you my friend, Tendai? Are you my friend?" she muttered, barely audible.

"Wh... I love you," he said.

"That's not what I asked. Are you my friend?"

"Well, yeah. Of course."

"Thank you." She pressed her face into his chest.

That night, she fingered her cap. Her *kapp*. It represented her heritage, through three generations of Jhumpafalas, twenty-seven generations of Fenstermachers, and countless Lapps, Koepplers, Changs, Steins... her father's heritage. It also represented her relationship to God. *I'm not rejecting You,* she prayed to her Lord. *I'm not. I do love You. But I am rejecting... all this. For now. All right?* She tasted blood where she had bitten her lip. She removed the cap. She had entertained an image of hurling it dramatically across the room. Instead she set it gently on an endtable. She went to look for a box.

And soon, like Paul, Indira and Tendai were on their way out of town.

Time passed, as per God's usual practice with the universe, and Indira and Tendai adventured together.

After leaving town, they used a sizable chunk of their savings (Indira still had most of her earnings from her General Engineer days, life in Eppleberg never having required her to dip much into them, apart from the ill-fated trip to Mars with Paul) to pay for travel. Tendai wasn't much for sightseeing, but he didn't begrudge her this because she seemed more tolerant of his supposed shortcomings than she'd been in a long while.

They toured the Solar System. They flew through the tumbling icy serenity of Saturn's Rings—once through the vast Cassini Division, then again through the far narrower Keeler Gap. They watched the ice geysers of the moon Enceladus continually spraying one of the vast "minor" ringlets into existence. They flew in the savagery of Jupiter's Red Spot, mightiest of maelstroms, the tempest to swallow worlds—and then, in a quieter part of that planet of skies, glided and beheld a golden heaven in which moons bobbed above clouds the size of continents. They hit a few of the countless tourist and historical spots in the Asteroid Belt: the museum at Piratesnest, Kip's Inn, Webra's Snare, the rose greenhouse at Expury, and they attended a worship service at God's Rock.

She'd been wary of returning to Mars, but decided that as long as they skipped Jantown, it was foolish to avoid a whole planet. They saw natural wonders like

Olympus Mons and the Iron Cliffs, and historical sites like the House of Belcanda, the Phillips Memorial at Romulus, and the bloody-historied Court of Kings in Kyvadia.

Returning to Earth, they spent a month with Tendai's relatives at Earth Capital in Zimbabwe. She found the heat oppressive and thought of what Paul must have endured in Pennsylvania (she winced at the memory). Tendai surprised her with his skill with the mbira "thumb piano," the traditional Shona instrument. He insisted he wasn't very good, but she found its xylophonic tones quite soothing and said as much, as his brother Kudakwashe joined in on hosho rattle. They hit the Zimbabwean tourist spots: the vast nature preserves where lions, giraffes, crocodiles and other schoolbook animals played, foraged, and ate each other in harmony. They toured the stone city of Great Zimbabwe and its sister cities from the Mutapa Empire, the golden age of Tendai's ancestors. At Harare they visited Heroes' Acre, the monument to those who fell in Zimbabwe's battle for independence from European occupation, and then viewed another somber memorial to the multitudes who died from the AIDS plague not long after, and those who'd died under the vile 21$^{st}$ century tyrant Mugabe.

After these travels (and grievous injury to their savings, Tendai lamented), they ultimately settled in Lawrenceton—so near her home town, yet a universe away from it. She would rarely visit Eppleberg in subsequent years, despite its nearness. Tendai found veterinary work helping the small pets (both natural and genenged) common to urban and suburban environments. It bored him, but the money was good, and he made do. For her. She knew it was a sacrifice and was grateful for it.

She was determined she would find some happy medium between the stifling sanity of home and the soul-diffusing inanity of the outside world. *I've associated the outside too much with Aleksei and his idiot friends I ran with. Wonder what Octo is up to these days? Gah! There's more to the world than that. Got to be. There's a whole universe out there, full of different people and different cultures, and I'll... find a way to stay myself through it all, this time. Not lose myself in it. And I'll have Tendai to help. He's got faults, but lack of stability ain't one of 'em.*

Dropping out of the engineering scene years before had of course been a terrible career move, even if it had been the right choice at that time. Re-entering the workforce as a space station's full all-purpose engineer was impossible, so she decided to specialize on life support tech, which had been the lion's share of her old job anyway. That field had advanced greatly, and despite having followed the technical journals over the years, she was badly out of the loop. She devoted herself to catching up, which required several semesters back at her alma mater, Rinstillor U. During this time the couple was dependent on Tendai's income.

While there, she availed herself of the services of the folks in the school's psychology department, and finally made a concerted effort to control her panic attacks. With help, she tempered her emotional extremes, even as her resumed career pursuits granted her an outlet for her passions. Tendai grew more adept at dealing with her vicissitudes and more accepting of them, which helped temper them yet further. There remained times the overstimulation of modern life brought back the old stress, fear, and anger, when she dreaded she would come undone as she had at Felice—but such times grew milder and rarer.

To compete professionally these days would be harder than when she'd been young, not only because life support systems had advanced—but thanks to Arachne influence on man's attitudes, today's youth was itself undergoing metamorphosis, with genetic modifications and bionic implants out the wazoo (up to and including bionic wazoos). While many such augmented folk did perfectly well for themselves, others were burdened with medical and psychological problems attendant to such procedures, and the whole phenomenon raised a specter of how this might affect Earthling culture as a whole in years to come—the Genomic War having long ago set dire precedent for conflict between augments and non-augments, and between different groups *of* augments. She hoped to God everybody could get along this time. At any event, the new generation was daunting competition—stronger, faster, longer-lived—yet she welcomed the challenge and determined to meet it.

And, rather to her own surprise, she *did* meet it. Absorbing her classes like a long-dry sponge, her capacity and eagerness to learn undiminished from her youth, her skills grew beyond what they'd been at Felice. Rural exile had strengthened her character; she now had *focus.* Not young in a world of artificially extended youth, she *felt* young. No, better than that. She felt like an adult.

She purchased a pocket omnibox the size of a bar of soap to help with her work—a nonsentient "hollow" A.I. that was useful for reference, with a wide variety of tiny repair tools swissarmied into its side panels. The mechanical part wasn't too different from one of Tendai's medwands, containing a few different specialized nanoforges and a variety of macroscopic tools. She disliked relying on the gizmo's brain for much; it felt like cheating, like using a calculator for an arithmetic test. But she knew how to use it to best effect, and it was, after all, her own skill directing it.

She completed the classes and re-entered the workforce. The long hiatus having crippled her resume, she restarted as a low-level maintenance tech at a ground-based facility owned by Alphonse-Bonaparte. Her aptitude for the work was evident, and her responsibilities grew steadily. Inside a year, she was doing minor assistance for design teams, shuttling frequently to and from orbital installations, and was a full member of those teams not long after. She was promoted to senior tech, and finally landed a better-paying job at Banashiwa. While there, she designed an improved meson pump for power distributor systems, which had applications well beyond life support. Years after her death, her design was incorporated into drive cylinders in spacecraft propulsion systems, and in that capacity, Tamsanga pumps are still in use today.

During this time, she attended a church and maintained her faith, but inevitably after having left the religious community of her youth essentially in a fit of pique, she sometimes felt a distance from God that discomfited her. Not a separation from Him, not by any means—she still felt His presence in her life, and was grateful for it, and tried to keep His commandments—but she did wonder about the danger of wasting too much time chasing the wind, as Solomon had described secular matters in Ecclesiastes. She remembered that by the time she'd left Felice, Aleksie's betrayal had been the last straw, but the Vanity Faire quality of wider human civilization had been on the verge of crushing her soul and mind by that point already.

She felt guilt in re-embracing technology. Even driving an aircar felt odd. For the longest time she was unable to download nano-specs for textiles and other simple products to her specialized forgeprinters without horrible guilt. This passed. Still...

*"Life is good." Isn't that what I used to say to myself on Felice? It frigging well wasn't true then. Is it true now?* She felt a reluctance to enjoy this life she'd anticipated and orchestrated. *And I accused Paul of never allowing himself to be happy,* she mused (and again felt pain and anger at the memory of him). Here she was flirting with the impious notion that the world and its experiences, even the purely sensual ones, had value. Did they? Clearly, deep down, she must believe that they did, or else what was she doing out here?

*Here I am in the world, again. Part of the universe, again. Why should this life be any less meaningful, or more meaningful, than the one I left?... Because it's full of meaningless distractions, that's why,* she thought. *But are they just distractions? Is God's handiwork not to be found in them? Provided that I avoid those things that are patently sinful?*

The world now felt novel as it hadn't since her freshman year—yet she *knew* from experience the novelty *would* wane once she'd been out here long enough. Familiarity breeds contempt, and all exoticism becomes mundane in time. Perhaps the secret, which the Plain people knew, was to find God's wonder *in* the mundane. She could see undeniable truth in that.

But did that mean no pleasure should ever be taken from novelty as novelty? Surely God's wonder lay not *only* in the mundane. The exotic and the familiar were one, and both bore their Creator's signature. The attentive can find wonder in everything. But she must not let the glare of the novel wash out the mundane.

As she'd hoped, Tendai's constancy helped make the chaotic outside world bearable, and they grew closer. Closer still when the duties of parenthood came. They had a daughter and a son, within a year of each other. The daughter was given the (needlessly long, Indira thought) Zimbabwean name Kugarakunzwana, meaning "To live together is to find peace," but they usually called her by her middle name, Ruth. The boy was named for her father. Ruth was dark-skinned and round-cheeked and always smiling. Jawaharlal was lighter-skinned and tall, and he lived up to his name, being far more moody and introverted than his sister; but he was a good student, and she didn't doubt he would go far. They usually called him Jay.

At each child's birth, she loved them overwhelmingly and instantly, more than she'd believed she could love. The sensation of nursing was a perfection of intimacy. At the same time, she was terribly afraid of proving a bad mother, and worried on some level that perhaps her intense love for the children might be just an overcompensation for some latent resentment about having to care for them. The fear was nonsensical, but it was the sort of self-doubt that had always defined her life, and it would in fact be odd if she weren't feeling wild uncertainties at such an emotional time. The fear passed, while her love for them endured.

She would always treasure the memory of Tendai cradling them in his arms and singing to them.

Motherhood inevitably cut into her career, but she had been prosperous up to that point, and the work that she still did paid very well. It was a great help that the couple had purchased a nonsentient maidbot years earlier, which Indira always kept in good working order.

She told the children stories at night, sometimes of dragons and knights, or of maharajahs and rakshasas (which her grandmother of the curried ham pies had quietly and somewhat surreptitiously told her); and other times she would tell them Bible stories like David and Goliath; and still other times she would tell them stories of her own life. Ruthie was quite taken with the stories of the alien creature Paul and often said that she wished she could meet him. At those times, Indira would say that she wished Ruthie could meet him as well. And then after the children had gone to sleep she would weep softly. Tendai would come and ask what the matter was, and she would tell him it was because the children were so beautiful, and that was true enough.

And yet it was during this time, surrounded by love, that she came, finally and truly rather than merely properly, to love Tendai.

Meanwhile, the rest of the universe went about its daily business. The Arachne made themselves at home in the Oort and Kuiper. Ramalinga made another run at the Presidency but was beaten out by Mosley, followed in later years by Rogers, Mtombeni, Herschel, Gusakov, and Yenfei. The smaller Martian nations made wars on each other and changed their border outlines and names repeatedly. There were pirate raids in the Belt. Crashboink became a popular music style, then vanished, then resurfaced as nostalgic kitsch.

Diplomats were finally launched toward Faldor, the diplomatic meeting-world for civilizations in Sol's area of space. Their ship would not arrive in Indira's lifetime, but at that speed, the passengers would experience only a few years of travel time and arrive scarcely older than when they'd left. She envied them a bit. Maybe Paul had had the right idea, getting completely away from his origins. It held some appeal to get away not just from her home town, but from humanspace entirely.

No, the family she'd made was in humanspace. She would remain within the Solar System, mainly on Earth.

She smiled quietly at the state of her life right now. Yet, at times, she feared she smiled *too* quietly—worried that, in reigning in her feelings, she'd retreated too much from *any* strong feeling, joys and pains alike. In building up safeguards on her emotions, she often found it took too long for them to register now, and she would meet crises with a blank numbness that only gradually gave way to solid human feeling. Perhaps this is what her father had felt. She feared the sense that all the pleasant mellowness of her later years was just a wall forged to contain that old, old voice of shrieking panic still flickering somewhere within her.

But again, this self-doubt was the height of normalcy for her, and *its* absence might itself have been cause for concern for her identity.

Indira had a good life and was grateful for it. She supposed in the final analysis it had been a fairly unremarkable one, but she was surprisingly content with it. Surely, from an Old Order standpoint, that was a good thing.

The children grew. Ruth became a minister, Jawaharlal a robopsychologist. Both found work off-planet, but still within the Solar System. Neither of the children married or had children, which saddened Indira. She wanted grandchildren. It might happen yet, she supposed.

Neither child ever really understood their mother's vague and rarely voiced longing for the countryside, although Ruthie had an inkling.

# 9

First Warren was Callisto's capital, located at the southern end of the Gipul Catena crater chain. Dwight herself was its centerpiece, as most warren cities were built around Matriarchs. Overlapping domes covered the city surface like bubbles, punctuated here and there by cones and spires, while honeycomb tunnels delved deep in the Callistan stone and ice below. Paul had been born here. In the center of it all was his towering parent. She'd grown visibly since he'd last been here.

He was home.

Indira was gone from his life. He felt dead when he dwelled on that. He'd hoped that leaving would cauterize the wound. He made an effort to concentrate on his surroundings instead.

The cavern metropolis was not exactly as he remembered it, for this world was being engineered at an environmental level. Wild silicon-based flora were now common, and he could hear fauna digging about below his feet, shoring and stablizing the stone and ice.

An artificial river of oxygen, heated to keep it liquid, now flowed majestically through the middle of the surface city. Mountains in the distance bore glittering glassy foliage.

Despite these changes, he attributed his feeling of disrecognition chiefly to dishonest nostalgia. One might not deceive others and yet still deceive oneself. Had he been nostalgic? He wondered why. He'd had little love for the place and still less for his fellows when last he'd lived here. He supposed he'd conjured an idealized vision of Callisto in his tedious years at the Consulate, and that vision had crystallized during his first months in Eppleberg when he'd been adjusting to that place, when home's familiarities had seemed very much worth missing. Now he was back.

He liked the weather, at least. It was actually *chilly*. He couldn't even remember the last time he'd felt real cold, but he was sure he'd readapt quickly. The ease of movement afforded by the absence of Earth's crushing air envelope was marvelous. The air was cool, dry, thin, and inviting. And yet thicker than he remembered!—the environmental work was progressing.

Thin air and light gravity made him feel delightfully free—indeed, compared to those Jan who had lived all their lives in weak Callistan gravity, Paul was now a Samson. Stars shone brightly, without the annoying "twinkling" of which humans seemed so fond. Drinkable oxygen lay in pools, and no gaseous oxygen burned his flesh. He felt the comforting press of firm tunnel walls upon him, instead of the omnipresent pressure of Earth's stifling, broiling atmosphere.

In many ways, it *did* feel good to be home. This reminded him he might be a naturalized Earthling, but he was no human. He was ambivalent about that. On one hand, it renewed his sense of personal identity, at least the elder part of it, and yet it left him concerned for the newer parts of himself. He didn't envy man his physical weakness or smallness or deceitfulness or brutality—though he might envy his speed and agility a little, as a man envies those qualities in a rabbit—and he sensed perhaps his attempt to assimilate among them had been futile. Maybe he'd been a fool.

No, that wasn't true, he decided. They'd accepted him. Eppleberg was *home,* if not his first home. He'd succeeded beyond any reasonable expectation he might have had at his pious experiment's outset. Here, not Earth, was exile. *"I left because of a broken heart,"* she'd said, years ago. *"How mundane an answer is that?"*

Her voice in his mind created a horrible longing.

He concentrated on the sky.

Jupiter, vast and red like a supernatural eyesphere, was a half-forgotten friend. He supposed he'd always unconsciously associated its cyclopean visage with the divine, even when he'd had a far less settled notion of divinity. That eye made him feel less alone.

Although he felt very alone on Callisto.

His fellow Workers bothered him. More now than when they'd irritated him in his youth. He reprimanded himself for what he now regarded as prideful snobbery. After so long away, they seemed simultaneously very rude (or at least blunt), and yet sickeningly cooperative.

Many insulted him, and these were not personal insults meant to offend—they once wouldn't have bothered him in the least—but they stung now, for he was unused to them. When he first returned, they told him he reeked of Earthlings and demanded he clean himself off. The accusation was without malice and literally true. Earth was full of odors, not all pleasant, and he'd collected many on his person. But he was accustomed to tact, and despite himself resented such treatment. He'd been *polite* among the humans for so long, it was now habitual.

Yet even as the Workers were rude, they were also submissive and unassertive. These were, after all, the people who had originally stuck him with the job of babysitting sociopaths because he was so temperamental that they didn't know what else to do with him.

They didn't react to things as humans did. That which might make a human laugh, cry, or shudder elicited little reaction, or sometimes even an opposite reaction to an Earthling's. On a deep, instinctive, gut level, the Jan's reactions felt right to him; but the instinct was so long out of practice, so suppressed in favor of human behaviors, it also felt nearly foreign to him. Every time he interacted with Callistans, he was reminded that the basic hardware of their minds, and of his own mind, were different than that of anyone he'd called friend in years.

As well as accepting his countrymen, he also had trouble being accepted by them, for his mannerisms, tastes, and outlook were now alien. He was an eccentric who made people uneasy. His peers found him circuitous in his manner, pointlessly reticent and indirect in everything he said and did. He missed "small talk," at least good small talk. He didn't even like *crowds* any more.

Prior to his Terrestrial sojourn, his memories were concrete images. Since then, they were interwoven with words, abstract symbols. It was frightening to come home and find that everything had become strange without its having changed that significantly at all. He was a stranger not in a strange land, but in his home.

The colonists had not been a homogenous group when they first came to Callisto; but, grouped together in foreign territory, it was perhaps inevitable that they had become a single culture. That wasn't even a bad thing, necessarily, but it made it difficult for someone to comfortably be different among them. Paul believed there was strength in unity, but weakness in homogeneity. The Jan needed balance between cooperation and individualism, just as Earthmen did. That was common sense, and he supposed most Jan knew it on some level even if they gave no thought to it, but his own recent experiences had focused the idea for him.

Finally, there were the times he encountered people who knew of his role in Adrastea, and most of these ruthlessly condemned him. He wished he had old friends here to whom he might turn for comfort from his disgrace, but he did not, not close ones, not after all this time. He realized that even though it had not been his reason for fleeing to Earth, by doing so he had until now avoided the public scorn his actions warranted. He knew he should embrace this humiliation as his proper due, but in fact it served as just one more incentive to get away from the public and get on with the purpose for which he'd come.

"Sociopaths," he'd called them in the privacy of his thoughts. A slander against the very people he'd ostensibly returned here to help (not that a non-verbal people had a concept of name-calling). Partly out of sincere conscience, but mostly to distract himself from the pain of separation from Indira, he threw himself into his task.

He thought of terrified, brown-nosing Tommy, back at the Consulate. Why had it had to be that way? Maybe they could have been friends, had circumstances been different.

He now regretted that he hadn't spent more of his time on Earth studying the myriad "civil rights" struggles in that world's' history. He knew the Exodus story of course, and he had become familiar with the persecution of the Amish and Mennonite Anabaptists in Europe; but now he needed to study the works of people like Anthony, Gandhi, King, and Stephenson, and their respective eras.

The Warriors' situation differed from those Earthly precedents in the Warriors' *sterility*. There were no future generations to safeguard from abuse. Even the biological androids whom Stephenson had helped after the Uprising had continued to reproduce themselves artificially. By contrast, the Valhallan dilemma would last only as long as this unusually large population of Warriors lived. That they needed dignity *despite* this fact was a concept requiring a respect for individuals not common to Jan. An individual was defined by his place and obligations. Those who *had* no purpose or duties were nonentities.

Were the situation to endure beyond this generation, then threat of eventual revolt would have made its untenability clear to the powers-that-be. But there were no throngs of angry young Warriors. Only old and terribly bitter ones.

Paul supposed there was an attitude that, since they would die off of old age, the problem they represented was self-terminating. He had shared this view, he realized. It never took much to make him appalled at himself, but this did it anew. His time with a far more individualistic people than his own (and the Mennonites would have laughed at being so described, but he meant humanity as a whole) had made the injustice clear to him.

His old colleague Heimdall, his successor at Valhalla, admitted Paul to the reservation. Heimdall supposed his predecessor's visit to be motivated by nostalgia, and Paul did not correct him (and he wondered if he would have let the misconception slide prior to his time on Earth).

Superficially, Valhalla had changed, just as First Warren had. After all, the whole reason for the Adrastea trip had been to evacuate the place for environmental engineering. Paul admitted that it looked more hospitable than he remembered it. Once barren, it was now lush with silane plants. Icecrawlers scurried merrily amongst three-pronged glassy hatrack trees. It was a far prettier prison than when he'd left it. This was not for the Warriors' benefit, he believed, but for the home-steaders who would come once the Warriors were dead and gone.

Yet Valhalla's essence was unchanged. Beings born for battle played incessant, savage games, made vicious by their chronic discontent at their idleness. As an Administrator, it had been his constant struggle to prevent fatalities, and he suspected there had been those above him who welcomed such deaths as incremental reductions in the problem's scope.

He'd never gotten to know any of the Warriors individually then (that seemed remarkable to him now in retrospect, but then again, he'd had few if any close Worker friends then, either). He must now try to correct that. He was wary walking among them. They were dangerous and had ample reason to hate a former Administrator. He wondered if Nuada's hatred was unique.

Only in its intensity, he discovered, as he was initially greeted with tremendous distrust and antipathy. Paul felt renewed identification with his namesake, who had presented himself to the Apostles he'd persecuted to beg their forgiveness. Yet Paul Dwightson's penitence surprised and ultimately pleased the Warriors. They were baffled by it, but as a Jan, his sincerity was not questioned.

To Heimdall's bafflement, Paul took up residence in Valhalla. He spent his days with the Warriors, and familiarized himself with their culture, one utterly foreign to the pacifist ways he had learned these past years. Psychological differences aside, he could never keep up with them physically, to participate in the endless sieges and mock battles and wrestling and brawls that made up their days. He felt more alone among them than he had among the Earthlings or the Workers.

They were organized in groups with leaders (only one leader to each group and a minimum of subordinates, not the Worker way of doing things at all), and it was clear to Paul that he would be dealing primarily with these leaders. He was amazed at the raw hate many of them felt for the Workers and Matriarchs. Yet he saw the openness of these insults against his caste as a gesture of their trust in him personally (as contrasted with obsequious Tommy at the Consulate all those years ago, who had been desperately afraid of angering him in any way), for they normally hid this hatred. Valhalla had fostered an attitude of secrecy, though not true alien deceit.

He'd learned a Warrior liberation movement existed among the Workers, but the Valhallan exiles were too far out of sight and mind to arouse much public sympathy. This group greeted Paul enthusiastically, believing a former Valhallan Administrator could add considerable weight to their cause. He feared he would be made a spectacle (an unpleasant prospect for a Mennonite) or that he might disgrace the movement because of his crimes at Adrastea. But the movement's directors successfully "spun" his presence there to the cause's best advantage. This quasi-dishonesty dolefully amused him, but at least it was in a good cause.

He was dismayed at the scant support the movement received from that minority of Warriors who *were* active in the Callistan military. He believed they felt their positions threatened by a sudden possible influx of inactive Warriors, and they felt a snobby superiority to them in any case. While there were individual exceptions, most of the military Warriors contributed nothing to the cause. Still, Paul concluded this might be for the best; if the hardline Matriarchs came to feel *threatened* by the Warriors, as protests from within the military might be viewed, a resultant crackdown might make things far worse. On the other hand, maybe some genuine fear *would* have compelled them into swifter compliance with the Warriors' demands. *On Earth, would King have been as effective without X out there playing "bad cop" to his good?* Paul wondered. The thought made him uneasy.

Though the opinions of common Workers were important (for it was their society the Warriors would be entering if this struggle succeeded), it was swaying the Matriarchs' opinions that was vital. Paul had never imagined his society's leaders to be so obstinate. *And Indira thought her people were bound by tradition!* he thought, with a pang. The Matriarch Ishtar, born on Callisto, whom he'd once described to Indira as a "firebrand" for her contro-versial opinions, had turned out to be no radical, but the stubbornest of the bunch.

It seemed to him that he was more inclined to take individual initiative than most Callistans in the organization, having been away from Jannite bureaucracy for so long. Following King's example, Paul quietly suggested and then helped the movement to organize a peace march on Seventh Warren, Ishtar's city, utilizing a small portion of the Valhallan population. With bureaucratic acumen gained from his years at the Consulate, he was able to not only obtain the necessary permits, but so maniuplate them that the Warriors could not be barred from making such a demonstration, no matter how Ishtar might fume, unless she chose to disregard the law entirely. He impressed upon the Warriors the necessity that they behave absolutely peaceably, no matter what hostility they might encounter.

Workers gazed at them in dread astonishment, while Worker police stood at the ready and glowered uneasily, for any large mass of Warriors *looked* like an army, regardless of its intent. As for the Warriors, many had never seen a city warren before. They were brave, but none were young, and many were afraid as they entered the beautiful jade and onyx-inlaid gate of Seventh Warren to file through its tunnels and ornamented piazzas. Vehicles the like of which they'd never seen floated, rolled, walked, and tunnelled all around them. Everywhere stood dwarfish Workers, gawking at them.

Having crossed the underground city, they finally marched upward through Central Colonnade to face Ishtar on the surface, so the Matriarch must see her petitioners with her naked eye. That great lady reacted as an Earthling might when met by a legion of angry, barking chihuahuas, and called them absurd to the point of indignity. A Warrior leader echoed back, *"Indignity!"* and launched into a series of images of harsh, miserable daily life in Valhalla, which all the surrounding Worker crowds could also hear. Paul was impressed and gratified at how loudly the Warrior could shout.

Paul was also surprised at how unthreatened Ishtar claimed to be, for though no violence was intended, a swarm of Warriors was far from an innocuous sight, and even a chihuahua legion has teeth. He suspected that, treated as royalty all her life, she'd never properly *felt* fear, nor knew when sensibly *to* feel it. He wondered how common that failing might be among the Matriarchy.

Had this confrontation been only with Ishtar, whom Paul now saw had a heart as hard as Pharoah's, it would have been futile; but Ishtar was transmitting the conversation through ground-waves to other, distant Matriarchs, who themselves acted as booster stations to relay the message all around the Callistan globe. Paul was certain she now regretted having done so.

Although he was present during all of this, Paul made no public statements and kept a low profile during the demonstration—partly from a Plain desire to avoid making a spectacle, partly because he felt the Warriors needed to prove their competency to Ishtar and so must state their own case unaided, but mainly because he felt certain she would respond to anything he said by bringing up his role in the Adrastean atrocity, and thus condemn the Warriors by association.

He was pleased that Dwight, his mother, proved the most reasonable of the Matriarchs. She was the first to come around to the Warriors' cause, and her help proved to be invaluable.

At first all of this was a welcome distraction from his pain of separation from Indira; though the struggle was fulfilling in itself, for he believed in what he was doing. It was bizarre to think, if they were successful, what a debt the Warrior caste of this solar system would owe to the attempted murderer, Nuada. That thought, too, made Paul deeply uncomfortable.

It took years, but the Warriors of Valhalla were set at liberty. They were granted a right to self-government (albeit still under the ultimate authority of the Matriarchs), and Valhalla was made a democratic province, a Jannite rarity.

Things were still far from perfect. There was concern that, now given an inch, the Warriors might well rise up in organized revolt seeking vengeance. However, Nuada's example notwithstanding, this did not happen.

Many Workers never adjusted to the change, and prejudices endured, though they were no longer legally enforced. Many Warriors, too, found they still preferred the company of their own kind—or even of humans.

Not that Earthlingkind reacted very gracefully to the sudden change in the Jan's visible population. Few had had any dealings with Warriors, or under-stood the circumstances the Valhallans were now escaping. Some believed the Warriors' sudden visibility meant the Jan were gearing up their military, and this created diplomatic problems that needed smoothing. In time though, the Warriors were permitted to enlist in human militaries, and soon Earth, the Martian nations, and many of the asteroid colonies boasted Jan Warrior units among their forces. These "foreign legions" for Warriors who wanted to escape the society which had mistreated them paralleled the Jan's own Earthling forces, the Jannite Corps. Of all the types of Earthlings they encountered, the Warriors got on best with the Tesks, whose background was so similar, having been bred for war and then unwanted afterward.

Looking back, Paul felt he ought to have recognized much sooner that this cause would become his destiny. He believed it mad presumption to try to secondguess what God intended for him, but he *suspected* this was it, and at any event, he now had a sense of purpose he had always lacked.

Sometimes it was almost enough to make him forget her. Almost.

Indira haunted Paul's memory. For years. And if time blurred that memory, it became beautiful and expressionist for the blurring.

He prayed for guidance. Christian groups on Callisto were few (most being centered at Earthling facilities, with primarily human congregations), but they existed, and he attended services at most at one time or another over ensuing decades. Paul was startled how ornately decorated some of them were and at how complicated their liturgies were compared to what he was used to; and he was frequently confused and confounded by doctrinal differences he encountered, some inconsequential, some very troubling, and some bizarre.

He had thought of writing a book at some point, based on his experiences with Indira. But he wouldn't think of embarrassing her, and he was more than a little afraid of looking like a fool himself. "The Jan who fell in love." It was absurd. No, no. His people were allowed to keep secrets, and it seemed wisest that this one stay buried deep. "Buried." Another metaphor. Inside himself, he chuckled ruefully to think he would never, ever be cured of the infection of human language. Even that was a metaphor, he thought.

He wondered if she hated him. Still hated him. Even to be hated would be to still live in her thoughts.

Years passed. He lived his life, and somewhere, he knew, she lived hers.

# 10

The sky was white with cloud, as Pennsylvania skies often are, when Tendai Tamsanga took his daily constitutional in the woods. He usually disliked cloudy days, but the sky matched the landscape that had been left after the snow last night, and the effect was pleasant. The only sound was of snow crunching under his boots. It was very still.

He often wondered why he didn't miss the home of his youth more. He remembered he'd felt frozen to his bones his first winter here. He chuckled at a memory. *"What am I doing here?" Isn't that was she always used to ask?* He sighed. He knew she was ambivalent about this place, but he was very glad they'd returned to Eppleberg for their retirements. It wasn't an arbitrary decision that he'd chosen this place as his home years ago. He liked it, and he had missed it. He wished they had returned when he was still practicing. Still, he was sure the local livestock was in capable hands now. The new vet's name was... Cooper? Yes, Cooper.

A cardinal flew above him, a bit of red in the white-gray sky. *Nice.*

He wandered among trees. He supposed that he could just as easily have driven out to these same woods from the city, when they were still living there, to take a walk like this. He wondered why he hadn't. Still, it was better now to be living close to them.

He had few serious complaints at this point in his life. His wants had always been simple. Meaningful work, a loving wife and children, a secure home, health. It was good to be back where folks understood that. He took a deep breath of cold air.

Their life together was and had been a good one. Yet, she had a secret place in her soul she wouldn't let him into. He'd always known that. He didn't begrudge it her, either.

In his younger days, he'd had a temper of sorts. But the tempests of her pique had long since blown his own temper out like a candle. He was consequently an even more sedate man than he'd been before marrying her. He wondered sometimes if that meant she'd broken him. Like a horse. He tended to see things in animal metaphors. Yet in turn, her own temper seemed to have quieted down in parallel to his own. Her fire was still there, but less fierce now.

He admitted he had become quiet and stuffy in old age. "My Hobbit," she sometimes called him with a smile, for his being such a stay-at-home quiet man. It had originated as a pun on his being a creature of "habit." He'd never read Tolkein, but he knew of the book. *And it's not fair! She's much shorter than me!* he thought with amusement. So what if he was hobbitish? Compared to her, who wouldn't be?

He remembered that he'd tried to sound adventurous and worldly when they'd first met. He wondered why he had. Perhaps there had been a bit more truth to the image, back then. Well, it had worked, and they'd been married almost forty years now. The ruby anniversary was coming up, he reminded himself. He'd looked it up, and fortieth was ruby.

Being married felt completely natural now. It had felt that way for a while in the very beginning, but then things had soured, and then they'd improved again after that long vacation. Or he thought that was how it had gone; there were several intervening decades now of memory fuzz. At any event, things had been bad for a long while, and then they'd come right again.

Though Tendai had the well-preserved look of his mildly genengineered ancestry, he was older than Indira; but with her less hardy biological makeup, they seemed to be aging at about the same rate now. At least, he told himself that they were. She seemed frail these days, and he worried about her.

Certainly, he felt healthy. His hair had gone wooly white, his face had ample wrinkles, he was far thinner than once he'd been. He felt good, anyhow.

He ought to fix the living room window, he remembered. The sill was made of pine, and it had begun to rot. Still, he supposed he would replace it with wood again.

He stretched. He was in a good mood.

He stepped forward and began to tread up a small incline that he ought not have done. His foot slipped on a patch of ice.

He gave a cry as he fell, and the ground hit him much harder than he felt it had any business doing. His head struck a tree root, and his vision started to fail before he felt any pain. In his profession, he'd seen the death of living things many times. He recognized his last seconds. These thoughts occurred in only the briefest moment of his remaining awareness.

His last earthly thought was of Indira.

Edith Klein lived down the lane. Fitting her surname, she was a small woman, and Indira had never known her well, apart from the fact that Edith had been generously inflicting huge unwieldy baskets of zucchinis on them every summer since they'd moved back. This tiny figure now ran up the street, knocked loudly on Indira's door, and frantically told Indira that her husband Boaz had discovered Tendai in the woods. Indira had been at home reading and considering what she and Tendai would have for dinner. The world stopped. The news was such a non sequitur that it took her a full minute to compose a reaction, which consisted of the word, "What?"

After a few more moments, she was aware she'd begun screaming.

The sound surprised her almost as much as the news, for she hadn't had much occasion to scream about anything in a long time. It hurt her throat.

Edith looked frightened; Indira knew she'd never been one to scream by half measures. Eventually she quieted down and stared out a window at the white sky. Her eyes swam in the blank light.

"Tendai..."

The shocking enormity of it.

"My God." She wasn't sure if she was saying it as a prayer or as profanity.

Her anchor was gone. The world pitched and tossed beneath her as it once had.

She was abandoned. Awkward. Ancient. Alone.
*Tendai, you're...? How...?*

*I wasn't supposed to outlive you. I'm not genenged at all. I wasn't supposed to outlive anybody.*

Neighbors and cousins came to console her. She didn't mind their visits as she had at Pa's death long ago. At least not as much. She needed the comfort very badly. As with her father's sudden death, decades earlier, she found herself thrust suddenly into a bizarre and awful new reality.

The kids returned home and threw their arms round their mother in their grief. Jawaharlal tried not to show his pain, and she wished he hadn't felt the need to hide it *(The kid's a shrink,* she thought. *Sort of. Robopsychologist. Don't robots get depressed? He should know better.),* but she put such behavior down to heredity from his namesake and let it be; Jay would grieve in private. Ruth's behavior was more balanced, but she clearly saw it as her job to be the strong ecclesiastical backbone for her mother—which to Indira seemed foolish, as it was clearly *her* job to be the strong backbone for her daughter, and anything else was wrongheaded. Nonetheless, the children's presence right then was invaluable to her.

They stayed for a time.

Then finally they returned to their own lives and left the planet again.

And Indira was alone with her memory.

Beside her in bed.

Sailing Jupiter.

Cutting the stupid crust off his bread.

Tending to four-year old Jay when he'd scraped his forehead so badly falling off his trike.

The horrid times he would try to *clean up* her workshop.

Weird idioms she heard so often she finally adopted them herself.

The rich, deep sound of his voice.

*I didn't get to say good-bye. Oh God. Tendai, I'm sorry I didn't say good-bye.* She said "I love you," to the empty air and trusted God to forward the message. *I didn't say it to you nearly enough. I gave you all kinds of shit. Truckloads of it. Lord, you were patient.*

Hysteria did not return. Though many tears came, she had not been hysterical since the first moment of shock had passed. She was surprised and grateful for that.

The sense of non sequitur remained, though.

She tried to remember what it had ever been like to be alone.

One day, when the matter of the Warriors' lot in life was finally concluding because that original contingent of Warriors was passing away of old age, Paul received a missive from Barney Estragon.

Paul had kept an irregular correspondence with several people from Eppleberg, though that had dwindled over time, either through neglect on his part or their part, or as he had outlived the correspondents. Yet ageless Barney Estragon always kept in touch, even when Paul himself was negligent. The robot was a bit of a gossip, really, and enjoyed communicating by letter, adding Paul to a long contact list that he kept. Barney had informed him when Ruth Hochtleitner married Eunice Lajevardi's widower Elmer, and Paul had sent congratulations. Both Ruth and Elmer died not long after.

In these letters Paul had learned the reason for Barney's simple, nigh-monosyllabic speech patterns which belied his intelligence. Barney had been made as a small child's toy, a tiny talking duck for a rich man's son, back when the full implications of sapient machines were not well understood. He had told the boy stories (and he still enjoyed fiction today). To avoid being deactivated after the child was grown, Barney had fled, and he'd lived in the nooks and crannies of civilization. At ten centimeters tall, he was literally vermin. By the time the Velveteen Act was passed granting rights to conscious robots, he had gone mad. That was well over a century ago. He had recovered by now, and had had a man-sized body built for himself (he'd chosen a visibly mechanical one, rather than an android). He changed his last name periodically, depending on his mood and circumstances, but he kept the name Barney, which the child had given him. For he still loved that child, who had once been his whole world, a child who had long ago died of old age.

Paul had great respect for Barney's endurance. Still, there was no denying that his gradeschool-primer speech patterns could make for dull reading, no matter the subject. Hence, he didn't read Barney's newest transmission immediately, and the letter sat in his visiphone for days before he got around to it.

When he finally did open it and learned of Tendai's death, he was stunned. Barney had earlier mentioned that he'd been surprised and pleased when the couple had returned to Eppleberg for their mutual retirement a few years earlier.

Tendai had simply tripped and fallen, and the body not discovered until it was too late. Barney, not human himself, had commented to Paul that, as human deaths went, "a quick one does not sound too bad.".

Paul mourned Tendai, although he'd never known the man well nor considered him much more than a rival, and so his grief felt a little forced and mechanical—for which he was ashamed because he knew Tendai had considered him at least a passing friend. He couldn't imagine the pain Indira must be going through. He obsessively scrutinized his psyche for any venal trace of pleasure at his rival's passing, for if he found any such emotion in himself, he could not forgive himself for it.

Paul had pined for Indira daily. Leaving Earth hadn't solved that. On the contrary, it had crystallized the totality of his experience on humanity's world in the memory of her face. Of her wit, her sarcasm, her laughter, the supple dancing grace of her every movement. If she were as one dead to him, that "death" had only transformed her into an unattainable Beatrice.

He'd gone through a long period of profound anger at her. And why not? Her treatment of him hadn't been fair, had it? He'd told the truth! Why should he be punished for telling the truth? A truth he should have told years earlier. Anyway, his anger ultimately never lasted. And under the circumstances, she was effectively dead to him. What use in getting angry at a phantom?

He wondered if, just perhaps, she had loved him, too. It would explain the intensity of her reaction. Or maybe he had simply repulsed her. And how could he not? Just *look* at him. For all their flowery poetry on the subject, the humans kidded themselves that love was more than what Freud and Darwin had said it was. Lied to themselves. Oh, humans were good at that. In his own case, it had been an honest mistake. He had *believed* the poets, the philosophers and idealists. He'd been a dupe, a chump, a sucker. Fair enough.

But still.

For the first time in decades, he considered contacting her. He decided that now, doing it right after her husband's death, would be monstrously insensitive.

Besides, he was not even really sure he wanted to do it at all. To risk getting hurt again.

So he did nothing, after all.

Five years after this, he received word—again from Barney—that she was in poor health. Her words of decades earlier came back to haunt him. "So when I get old, I'm gonna get *old*. Old like in days of yore." He cursed himself for being a procrastinating fool. He formed a plan.

He approached Dwight as he would a cathedral—and not unreasonably, as Dwight dwarfed many cathedrals. The comparison of her arms and eyestalk to steeples seemed inescapable, in his current mood. Older than Ma'adim, Dwight had also planted herself and grown in a lower gravity, and she now dwarfed her Marsbound peer.

About her base, gardens of crystal silica plants prismed the sunlight into countless rainbows. They were really quite spectacular. The plants in Jantown had been nice, he supposed, but why hadn't they planted *these* there, he wondered. These put them to shame, and Indira would have loved them, way back when. In fact, the lighting effects were too far into the ultraviolet to be visible to humans, and the plants would have looked drab to them, which was why they were not planted on Mars, but Paul did not know that.

Dwight's body was itself an extension of First Warren, full of tunnels, rooms, even offices. Paul walked into one of the many entrances and followed signs to the nearest private audience chamber, where he might speak with her. It was a small room, cool, dark, comfortable.

Paul rarely talked to his mother. The small handful of Matriarchs in the entire Solar System had thousands of young and were constantly busy. Yet on the rare occasions that he had sought her out, she had always made time for him, although he also always knew she was conducting numerous other unrelated tasks and conversations simultaneously.

Even now, he wondered whether Dwight had been fully aware of the injustices against the Valhallan Warriors. The prospect bothered him. He supposed she must have been, which meant either that she had not fully understood the nuances of the situation, or else that she had somehow justified it to herself. She was not perfect. She was mortal as he.

Paul performed a full genuflection arm gesture with quadruple eyestalk nod, the second nod very low, and sang a deep greeting tone. His mother acknowledged, and then Paul spoke to her in tremorspeech, projecting sonar images. The images were rapid, confused, and charged with emotion. Images of Eppleberg and of Indira as they'd been decades ago. Images of the horror and humiliation of Adrastea. Images of Nuada and Ares, of Indira's bravery that saved their lives and of her rage that had ruined his life. Emotion pictures of frustration, loneliness, impotence, and guilt. And then, as all these old memories were dredged up from him, despite himself, he began speaking in proxy English for the first time in several years (for how else to discuss the matter without the word "love?"). In his thoughts, indeed, he had never stopped using it. "I am changed, Mother. The very structure of my thoughts has changed. I think verbally, symbolically, algebraically. It's not natural, and I cannot shut it off. I can't make the words in my head stop."

Dwight said, in proxy-English, "It's all right. Use words, Paul."

Paul projected, *"Inquiry?"*

"You need to sort your thoughts," she said, "and human words, in their finiteness, are good for that. Words and wordish thinking are what separates Earth's men from Earth's animals. In their own eyes, it makes men greater than the animals. And I suppose it does. But it limits them, even as it elevates them."

"Yet, words have been a problem for me," Paul said. It felt so strange to speak words to another Jan, let alone to her. "I don't feel like one of my own people any more. My very thoughts are filled not with images, but with words. I returned home to escape all of that, and yet..." He trailed off.

"Nonsense. If I understand you rightly, you returned here because this Earthling rejected you. You came also out of a sense of moral obligation to the Warriors, of course, for which you are to be highly commended."

"Not so highly as had that been my primary reason for coming."

"Be that as it may," Dwight said. "But you have said nothing that indicates antipathy against humans or their culture, such as you had in your youth. In many ways, I suspect you feel that you are one of them. As for this Indira... You loved her for her soul. There's no shame in that, surely."

"Of course there is," he said. "She was married."

"But the physical difference makes such considerations absurd, does it not? Surely your love could not have constituted anything beyond friendship," she said.

"I felt... *I feel...* what I feel," Paul said.

"I assume you tell me all this as preamble to something more?" Dwight said. "For if you have come simply to speak on the matter for the sake of speaking, that is blameless, but it is remarkably human."

"I am getting to my purpose," Paul said.

"Yes?" she said.

"I have an idea," Paul said, very uncertainly. "It is the reason I have come to you, now. I want to be sure that it is, in fact, *legal.* Permitted by Matriarch precepts."

"Intrigue intrigues me," Dwight said, indulging in an English pun. "What is your scandalous plan?"

He told her.

She waited a moment before she answered, "It does violate the spirit, if not the substance, of our mores," she said.

"Not the substance?" Paul said hopefully.

"You are speaking of a remote, rather than of transformation. That is neither unreasonable nor unprecedented, in certain circumstances. We Matriarchs even use remotes upon occasion to compensate for our immobility. Yet *your* reasons for wanting one—let alone, a non-Jannite *exotic* one—are personal, and do not serve any higher public interest."

"Then, am I being refused?" Paul asked, trying as a human would to hide his dread of the answer. He had clung to this plan as possibly his only chance at happiness.

"Yet however," she continued, "your situation is unusual. In regards to humanity specifically, it is unprecedented. I might disallow this if I believed your particular situation were likely to become common in our society as a result—indeed, the fact that this has happened within a single generation of our people's contact with man raises a very real likelihood that it will reoccur—but for now, out of compassion, I will gamble that your situation will prove rare in the long run. I therefore give you special dispensation to do this thing, with the public caveat that any future such requests by Workers are to be reviewed by Matriarchs on a case by case basis, and that the requirements for permission shall become more stringent as and if such requests become more common. Yes," and she spoke his Jannite name, and then followed with his Earthling one, "'Paul,' I permit you to do this," Dwight said, "if it is so important to you."

"It is enormously important," Paul said softly, gratitude flooding him. "Thank you, Mother, very much. Do you think my idea will work?"

In a tone of voice perfectly evocative of a shrug of confessed ignorance, Dwight said, "Years ago, I read your Earthling essays with as much curiosity as anyone. I walked among humans in my motile youth, and learned much of their culture in that time, but their courtship practices always seemed byzantine to me, and apparently even to themselves. Without having met Indira Fenstermacher Tamsanga, I would not venture to guess what will happen. I'm a giant sessile cone, and you're asking me about human courtship. How could I know? However, if you could provide *me* with a description afterward, I would appreciate it."

"I shall," Paul said uncertainly, worried that if things went poorly, transcribing the events might be very painful.

After having put all his Callistan affairs in order, Paul took a flight to Pluto, resting in deep torpor through most of the trip. Arriving there and looking out a window, the planetoid was invisible except as a silhouette of black against the stars, for the attenuated light of distant Sol did not illumine Pluto's surface. Light came only from the Arachne structure itself, very dimly visible as a dot of brightness on the tiny world. On the far side of Pluto from this was a small human frontier city called Persephone. The Arachne city was called Mykki.

Like most Arachne architecture, the bulk of Mykki had been woven by their many-legged servitor biots, the Weavers (artificial servants were common among the Arachne, the Weavers being among the most basic of these to their society). The city appeared made of multihued spun glass, reinforcing the spider metaphor for which the humans had named them, but it displayed no central planning at all. Even a human city that grows slowly over time will still show more sense of symmetry and logic than were to be found here. Great asymmetrical lumps made of fibers rose from the planetoid's surface, some of them the size of low, rounded mountains, all full of strange ghostly lights. Toward this eerie and oddly beautiful irregular shape Paul's shuttlecraft descended.

Debarking in a broad field beside a hollow glass hill, he was unexpectedly greeted by an old friend, though Paul did not recognize him. It was a pink bionic spider the size of a small horse.

"Paul! I *heard* you were coming, but I didn't believe it!" the spider transmitted in English, clearly delighted.

"I don't think I've had the pleasure?" Paul said. He had brought his vocodor, which he would need to speak to any Arachne who was not equipped to understand tremorspeech, and it transmitted for him now in the Plutonian vaccuum.

"Thrym! I'm Thrym Scyllaschild!" the spider said.

"Thrym?" Paul said. "You're... an Arachne now?"

"Sho' nuff," he said. The cotton candy pink spider face was smiling like a child's toy. "I always said I wanted to take everything biotech could offer to make me live longer and happier. And look at me now!"

"It's been over forty years," Paul said. Then he added, "You're a pink bug."

"And you're a walking boulder with three snakes growing out of it," Thrym pointed out glibly and without a trace of malice.

"I come by it naturally," Paul said, conceding the pointlessness of morphological prejudice (from himself of all people) and scolding himself for it. Thrym laughed at Paul's answer. "You're... cheerful," Paul said in some amazement.

"A-yup!" Thrym said.

"'A-yup'?" Paul echoed in inquiry.

"I decided I wanted to be cheerful, so I had my brain reworked. Now I'm *always* happy and I love *everyone!* How does that sound?"

Paul's sense of human politeness had waned over the many years, and he did not stop the honest answer that came to mind. "Unearned, cheap, and soulless."

Thrym answered, "I *love* rude people! And if I ever get tired of this, I can make myself sad, too! But who would ever want to be sad? Actually, I can't get tired of it. I started to get tired of it once, so I had my brain reworked so now I *can't* get tired of it. Ever!" He let out a squeal that sounded at once childlike, orgasmic, and vaguely exhausted.

"I'm happy that you're happy," Paul said.

"I'm happy to *be* happy," Thrym said, "I think." He then said, a little more quietly, "How are things on Earth?"

"I haven't been there in a long time. I'm hoping to go back, soon."

"Is Callisto boring?" Thrym asked. "I've heard it's boring."

"I suppose it is," Paul conceded. "Eppleberg was hardly exciting, either, but I miss it."

"I'll go back to visit Earth, some day," Thrym said. "I'll need to change my body all around again. This one can't take the gravity. I... remember the sun shining on the hills. I've got perfect memory now, so I remember it perfectly. And it's like... I want to miss it, but I'm just not built to miss anything any more. Not much, anyway. Maybe I can have my brain reworked to miss things."

"Then you'd be sad," Paul said.

"Hey yeah!" Thrym laughed, a little desperately. "That's no good! I almost made myself sad! Thanks Paul."

"You're welcome," Paul said.

"And there'll always be *time* to go back. I don't get old. I can't die any more!" Thrym said.

"You will eventually," Paul said. "Everyone dies eventually. It will just take a lot longer for you, is all. The universe itself is mortal."

"Really?" Thrym said. "Well I love death. And I love life too! I love everything! I think. Really nice seeing you again!" Spider-Thrym then trundled away.

A little startled that the conversation appeared to be over already, but not sure what else he would have to say, Paul waved a good-bye tentacle to Thrym; and, now feeling more than ever as though he were about to prostrate himself before Moloch, he left to meet the Arachne technician.

"Oh!" Paul suddenly remembered something, and called to Thrym's receding form, "Indira told me... Years ago... she said she forgave you!"

The spider answered, "For what?"

Paul said, "Never mind."

The surgeon called himself "Doctor Cricket." The reason became clear when Paul saw him. Most Arachne favored multilegged arthropod shapes for ease of movement in low or null gravity (hence their race's name), and the doctor looked like an oversized grasshopper.

The grasshopper addressed him in Jannite tremor-speech. *"Inquiry your desires body change into what happy to do it happy to do it stupid Jan seen the light finally finally body modification make you happy..."*

"Stop!" Paul said. "You're... you're doing that very badly. It's shrill and incoherent."

"That's too bad," the bionicist said in surprisingly good English. "I know the sonoprojector I'm using is good. I suppose I haven't properly synchronized it to my new brain matrix. Shit shit. Of course, I don't do much business with Jan. You're all sticks-in-the-mud. You're rocks, and you like being rocks. Why not try something different? I could make you a bird or a horse or a twenty-armed golden god or an endtable. It's fun! Don't you ever want to have fun?"

Paul thought, *You'd carve out great chunks of my brain and nervous system, rewire them, redistribute them across this new body, replacing parts of it as you felt necessary. How much of this new, reshaped "Paul" would actually be me? How much of "Thrym" out there was ever the Thrym I knew?—Enough to feel a sliver of regret, apparently.* Paul reminded himself that this doctor had come highly recommended, let alone that

Paul had traveled far out of his way to reach him. "I'm here, aren't I?" Paul said.

"Yes, you are here. What do you want to be?"

"I want..." He hesitated. "Look, I don't want you to modify my real body. What I want is a remote."

"You have three new messages," Indira's telecom informed her when she stepped inside from her garden. Dusting soil off herself with thin hands, she checked them. One was from the venerable Hormel company, asking if she were interested in vat-growing the company's newest varieties of spiced ham (she figured they probably still had this house's address from the previous owner, a small vat-meat farmer). One was from her daughter Ruth, asking after her health. And the third was from Paul.

Her mouth opened and stayed that way.

She was dumbfounded, and she staggered a little. She stood frozen the better part of a minute as though her nervous system had crashed, while her mind tried to assimilate this news. When his image appeared on the visiphone screen, she felt a sudden urge to hide behind furniture. He was bulkier with age, his movements stiffer, but still clearly himself.

He'd taken off and said good-bye so *long* ago. After all this time, it was like getting a message from beyond the grave.

She didn't know what to make of it. It had been an impossibly long time. In the beginning, after he'd left and then she'd left, she'd had to struggle viciously to keep from thinking, brooding about him. Then the necessary effort had gradually diminished. Then she'd realized it *was* diminishing, and that had made her sad, and she'd found herself remembering him after all, and the memories then were less painful. She avoided the memory of their parting, though. When she did recall it, it was as to caress an old, poorly healed wound.

She felt the old panic, the old raving anxieties finding their way back to the forefront of her mind, just because this was so unexpected. Yet she calmed down.

*Paul. God....*

Paul did not receive Indira's answer for over a month, and he took that silence to *be* an answer, since he hadn't really expected one. Then a reply message came over the visiphone. *She has a visiphone,* he thought to himself.

She looked... so *old* now. That would have to have been the case, of course, and yet it still caught him off-guard. Her hair was white, her skin loose and wrinkled, her body very thin. But it was still her. A half-forgotten ache of joy surged in him—mixed with terror that he had no idea what she would say. Her clothes looked strange, and he recalled that human clothing customs changed rapidly in most of their cultures. Hers were modest, but hardly traditional. *She's wearing modern clothes,* he thought. *Not wearing her cap.*

She looked determined and angry, which in her youth he knew would have meant she was very frightened. He couldn't imagine that he had somehow scared her, but he hoped to God that he had not. This amazon who had taken down a giant monster to save both their lives, all those years ago. He hadn't imagined she would have the courage for this.

"Hello, Paul. I was very surprised when I got your letter." It was strange seeing her this way; not only because she was older, but because a visiphone transmission gave no sense of her heartbeat or her breathing or the rushing blood in her veins. That had always been an essential part of how he gauged human feelings. He tried now to interpret her expression and body language, and grew frustrated; he was out of practice. A simple written letter might have been better. He tried to put such thoughts out of his mind and just concentrate on her words.

"It's been... a very long time. Yes, I would like to see you. I'm living in Eppleberg again. Not in Pa's place, I sold that a long time back. I have a half-house. The other half belongs to Eleanor Stolzfus. Remember her? With the buck teeth? She's aged better than me. Probably got some genengineering back in her family tree somewhere. But if the genesmiths can still crank out someone with a mouth like that, I say the hell with 'em, I'll take my wrinkles." She paused. "I've missed you. I'm glad you wrote." Another pause.

He felt as though he could hear her heartbeat accelerating from nervousness. He supposed he could read body language better than he'd thought; or perhaps it was his imagination.

"I don't... really know what to... Look, just.... If you can make it here on, um... June 4. That's a Saturday. We can meet by Lake Lofthaven. My old fishing spot. All right?" She wasn't smiling, although she tried to force it a few times. She looked frightened. But she'd asked him to come. So of course he would come.

*It hasn't changed.* He thought that perhaps he should not have been surprised, since this was a community of people who had long ago turned changelessness into an art, but he was still amazed at their success at it. The town was perfectly recognizable, and the nearby forest doubly so.

The gravity was rough going. It wasn't that his strength had diminished that much in the time since he'd left—healthy, well-fed Jan didn't shed body mass with age as humans did, quite the reverse—but he'd stiffened with age. He felt old, massive, stiff, with Earth's mass pulling his bulk down toward its center. He knew he probably had at least a few decades left before death from petrifaction—longer, if he spent time in torpor or in extreme cold—but he had demanded a lot of his body over the years. His time in this heat had probably accelerated his metabolism, and he knew that it would likely end up shortening his life in the long run. He could feel his fibers fusing, his ichor hardening. And the air was like a vice.

But inside himself, he was laughing at his discomforts. God, he had missed all of it.

He heard a robin's call for the first time in decades. Distinguishing subtleties of sound came very naturally to him, and years ago, he had quickly learned to identify all the different bird and insect sounds of the area.

They'd agreed to meet at the lakeshore where they'd first met, decades ago. The willow against which she'd lain that day was gone, but the spot was otherwise largely unchanged. Neon blue dragonflies buzzed about the water's surface, and wildflowers still bloomed.

She was very late. He called her on his comm, growing concerned, and she didn't pick up. He vaguely remembered a term he'd heard used during his long-ago tenure on Earth, *"stood up."*

Then he heard a human approaching through the trees, and there she was. "Hello, Paul," she said.

Though wearing different clothes (still modern ones), she looked as she had looked on the visiphone message. He had imagined her in this state years before, when he feared that if his massive hand even touched her in this condition, she would break like a hollow eggshell. He feared that now.

For her part, the feelings of the moment threatened to overwhelm her, as they did when she was young. It was a pain which, in her largely successful long quest for self-control, she realized she had almost missed. She felt fire behind her eyes, and it was good. "God, Paul," she said. She laid her long, thin hands on his carapace—it was rough but not very hard, like old sweetgum bark—and laid her face against his side.

The feel of her soft warmth against his body was so familiar. Her flesh felt looser, thinner, but it was still her. It had been so terribly long. God in Heaven, he'd missed her. They stayed like that, wordless, for several minutes.

"Do you hate me?" he asked.

"Oh, you idiot. I don't hate you," she said, quietly. She pushed herself up, away from him, and brushed white hair out of her eyes.

"Well, back then you said that... Were you lying?" he said.

She cocked an eyebrow and looked at him in a mixture of fear and incredulity. Then she blurted, "Yes, Paul! Jesus...."

There was a pause. "That is a very important thing to have lied about," he finally said.

"Oh shut up! Damn! God. Look at me, you twit. No, I'm not angry at you. Well, I am, but not that much." She brushed silver hair from her eyes and sniffled. "God I'm old. I'm mad at myself. At the universe. Pissed off is my natural state. You.... *know* that. You know me."

"Yes, I do," he said. "How... how are you?" he asked. The most banal of all questions. But he *had* missed small talk.

"Oh... okay, I guess," she gave the most banal of all answers.

"I've missed you." He wanted to go on at length, but he was afraid, and nothing came to him. "So much," he finally said.

She looked at his eyesphere. In her creased face, her eyes were moist. "And I have missed you." She was quiet and then she said, "God, I've missed you, Paul. You were always the only one I could talk to. You were the constant in my life. The one constant. And then out of the blue, you... I mean..." She braced herself. "What the hell, Paul? Why did you tell me *then?* Not sooner? Not when..." She gave a dry swallow. "When did you get the notion in your fool granite mind that I was a patient woman?" she said, very quietly.

"I..." He was dumbfounded. "I have something to show you," he said. Gently, ever so gently so as not to hurt her, he stepped away from her. He gestured behind himself.

A handsome old man stood there, gray-haired and gray-eyed. He was clad in traditional Plain clothes, complete with hat. And then he spoke with Paul's vocodor's voice. "It's... me. Sort of," the man said. "This is a remote-controlled android body. With a full vicarious reality hook-up. I perceive the world through it, and I feel everything it feels."

She wasn't entirely sure what to make of this. "Oh... Lord..." she said.

Paul's new body approached her, and placed his arms around her. She didn't resist. After a moment, she hugged back. She felt the body's warmth. And he experienced hers.

Alien sensations and impulses flooded Paul. The feel of her caress against his own soft human flesh. Her hands against his back, her chest and face against his chest. He shook, trembled. His blood raced. And emotion! For the first time, the human experience became a *wordless* thing, as thoughts he could never have conceived or described in words assaulted his mind.

He was now made of soft, moist sponge. So was she, and her softness pressed down *into* his soft, *yielding* outer surface, and his temperature flared and a tingling suffused him and it felt... good.... and hideously alien, simultaneously. The simultaneity of the goodness and the hideousness intensified both. Foreign, strange, overwhelming.

His old nightmare images from his prison cell of how Earthlings might punish him, almost forgotten after all these decades, of his very body being drowned and penetrated by soft alien organic slime and losing himself in it, now returned with a vengeance.

It was too much. He recoiled from her.

He ran from his own real body, which stood near them. He ran on two legs, in a straight line without spinning. He ran without looking back (he couldn't see behind himself!). His eyes (plural!) stung him and his unidirectional vision blurred. Black sheets closed over them and reopened, and he felt hot trails of liquid on his face. He heard a weird, horrid yowling and realized it was coming from his own mouth.

He severed the V.R. link, felt just a second of his human body pitching downward, and suddenly he was beside her again. She was small again, he was himself again, and he was trembling, and the ground trembled with him.

"I... I'm sorry," he said.

"You know my history," she said, her tone hard, and difficult to read, and dangerous for that. She was shaking as well. "And you think I'm a *robophiliac?!* You... You idiot! How could you?!" And yet the truth was she herself had for a moment considered it, she knew. *I hugged the machine back,* she thought, with tremendous unease. She strove to calm herself. Her feelings were very confused.

"I'm... I'm sorry." His knees buckled under him. It was too much. This was too cruel. He started to back away from her. He suddenly wanted eyelids to close again.

"Don't you walk away from me!"

"I'm... I'm so sorry," Paul said, in agony. She would offer no forgiveness for this. "I'm so sorry. So... humiliated. All these years, Indira. I thought... always truly believed... I loved you."

She reached out and laid a hand against him. She said softly, "Of course you do. You always have."

And she wrapped her frail arms across him. She could see he was in pain, but there was an absurdity to the situation that she found almost laughable. A sad laugh. That Paul of all people had wanted to impose this kind of overcomplication on himself (perhaps it was consistent, though; after all, a Mennonite town on Earth had always been an overcomplication for him, nothing "simple" at all). But it was for her that he'd done it. That was important.

Indira said, "You know... my history. You know what I think of robophilia."

"Oh," he said. *Her first boyfriend, of course. Whatzisname... Aleksie.* "But I... I thought...."

"I am not touching that thing again," she said, and then added softly, "Why? Did you want to...?" she trailed off.

"No. I don't suppose I did." After a moment, he said, "All these years have gone by."

"Actually, your timing is pretty good," she said. She gestured at her withered frame. "I'm not up to much of a physical relationship these days, anyway."

They sat and talked late into the night, in front of her home. She sipped coffee as he sipped sand in a light solvent.

"I've had a good life, Paul. These past years. Things worked out between me and Tendai." Her eyes turned sad at the mention of her departed husband and friend. "Lord, I still can't believe he's gone," she said softly. "He and I were going through a pretty bad patch when you left," Indira said.

"I'm sorry if I was exacerbating that," Paul said.

"Don't flatter yourself," Indira said (a little too quickly? he wondered. But he was out of practice with interpreting human behavior). "There were a lot of things wrong and they had nothing to do with you. But... I suppose they weren't as important as they seemed at the time. No, things are good. And I can't even imagine my life without the children. You have to meet them. God, it's a disgrace that you haven't met them." And she entered into a lengthy narration of Ruth and Jay's lives from birth up to the present. Such stories can sometimes be a bit dull for the listener, but Jan had a great patience for detail, and he was interested regardless. The children seemed to have done well for themselves, and she clearly loved them very much.

After the tale, she was quiet for a while. "I missed you, though. So much. It wasn't until years after I left that I realized I'd been staying here for you," she said very softly. "Now, when I look at the stars, I find solace there instead of dread. I thank *you* for that."

"You do?"

"That night I had the panic attack. The first one that you saw. And the next night, we talked about the stars."

"Of course. I remember. I remember," he said.

"Remembering. That's why I had to leave here. There were too many memories."

Paul didn't know what to say to that. "But... you did come back. Eventually."

"It's my home," she said, "and it's very beautiful. I'm old now. I've done some traveling and rubbernecking and I loved it, and then I wanted to come home," Indira said.

Fearing he trod dangerous ground but feeling brave, he asked, "On that trip back from Mars... when we didn't talk... I was in torpor, so I cannot be sure. But I... I think you called me a coward for not talking to you, back then."

She looked away from him. She said, "Maybe I did. It was a long time ago."

"If we had talked... what would we have said?" he asked.

"I don't know," she said, very quiet. And there was a long, painful wait. Then she said, "Maybe not much, after all. There was... tons to say. But I can't think of anything I would have said."

"Yes," Paul conceded, softly, scarcely more than a mutter. But after a pause, he said, "That... voyage to Mars with you. Seeing the production of *A Funny Thing*

*Happened on the Way to Tau Ceti...* just getting to spend time with you without interruption... It's... the best memory of my life. But then, after... what happened that day on Mars... I'm so sorry." Paul said, "If there are regrets in Heaven, then when the stars have died and the galaxies gone to dust, I will still regret what happened that day."

She laughed and cried a little. He'd probably rehearsed the line. Such a thing to say, and yet such a stupidly melodramatic way of expressing it. Just like him. God, she'd missed that. "Well... Don't. We'll be together up there. And all the painful crap will just seem like a half-forgotten hiccup."

Though Jan do not dream, as such, the following couple of years felt like a very pleasant one to Paul—not self-directed like the lucid imaginings of torpor, but rather an ever-surprising drifting, as he supposed Earthlings' dreams to be.

He moved back to town. In the intervening decades, Jan had become marginally more frequent visitors to the Earth, though still uncommon in temperate zones—and because of this, he was able to arrange for a dwelling to be prepared for him with minimal difficulty. He resumed his writing career. Long-time residents remembered him and welcomed him back.

He and Indira spent much of their days together. Talking, laughing. These years were the twilight of her life, and they both knew it. They set to reacquainting themselves with one another's old mannerisms and becoming acquainted with their new ones.

He met her children briefly, and they reacted pleasantly and politely, as though finally meeting a distant uncle about whom they had heard a lot over the years. *They're her and Tendai's love, in living form,* he realized, and suddenly the human equating of love and reproduction made perfect sense to him, and his long envy of Tendai faded somewhat, though he did feel some envy that his own people could not experience this particular miracle.

Her children had not followed the Plain way and had left home to pursue careers, but through their help and her own savings, she was well-provided for.

She and Paul spent her final years as close friends.

For Jan, death was gradual. Barring accident, Jan died slowly through petrifaction. It was said to be very peaceful, like slowly going into a very deep torpor. Who could say at what point spirit and body parted company? By contrast, human bodies shut down so *suddenly*... that one moment, to still be in the world... and then nothing? Or face to face with God? In a way, it was wondrous. *Like one of our Warriors, dying in battle,* Paul thought.

She was dying now. She and he both knew it. *"Old like in days of yore."* That was all that was really wrong with her, that she was now so far beyond the three score and ten once said to be allotted to mankind. Time passed and she grew weaker and weaker. Finally she was bedridden.

Both the children were off-planet at the time. Jay was serving as robopsychologist aboard an all-robot vessel called the *Galatea's Rising,* and Ruth was pastor of a church on Titan. The distance was too great for either to make it back to Earth in time. Their messages were frequent, full of love and pain. Paul was there for Indira. Everything that he could do, could arrange, to make her remaining time easier, he did without hesitation.

She thanked him and told him that he was dear to her. Still her strength waned. Eventually the time came that every day held danger of being her last.

Among her last words to him were, "We will meet again. But live a long life. Don't get impatient for that reunion." Then she didn't speak for a long time.

He spoke to her a great deal, though he wasn't sure how much she heard, and he was unable later to recall much that he had said.

Then Indira said, "Thank you for not letting me die alone."

Paul stood vigil at her bedside. The doctor assured him she was not in pain. She hadn't spoken all day. Her eyes had opened occasionally, frequently settling on him. She smiled faintly. Her eyes closed.

He prayed for her to wake up.

She did not.

Minutes later, she was home.

She was gone.

For the first day, his mind was free of words for the first time in decades. Words did not come to him. Thoughts barely came.

He experienced an equilibrium of feeling which lasted through the funeral. A stoicism both within and without, probably much as Indira's father had employed to tame his emotions, Paul now realized. He spoke little to anyone, and could barely feel. Then slowly, thought returned, although the unnatural sense of numb equilibrium remained for a time. With this return of thinking, he took stock of things.

He had expected to suffer a crisis of faith after she died. He had steeled himself for it, and was surprised when it did not immediately come. The fact was that he had known their reunion must be painfully brief, and he was overwhelmingly grateful that it had happened at all. And certainly the pain of this second separation would have been far worse had it been compounded with loss of faith in both God and in an eventual reunion with her, but it was more than painful enough anyway. The dull agony of separation had been so long, and the reunion so brief—little more than a coda. But it had been beyond price.

And then, just when he'd accepted that the crisis would not come, it came.

Feeling had returned. And if God is love, then where love had been was now only void.

Adjusting to a universe without Indira in it was bad. He'd kidded himself that it might not be so, since he had indeed lived without her for these past decades. But to be reunited with her, only to have her then so quickly snatched utterly away, seemed cruel and horrid. Never before had he felt genuine *anger* with his Maker. That ferocity he'd found in the early books of the Bible all those years ago, that had led to bloody wars and death on God's command, all of that came crashing back into his memory. He tried to remember his old discussions about such things with Kazuo, and the missionary's responses all now seemed trite and preposterous. Paul marveled at the contradiction that he could simultaneously be angry with God and doubt His existence.

He struggled with it. Even the promise of eventual reunion with Indira offered little solace now. God's seeming absence right then was a terrible torment that Paul could not understand. He had felt imminence before; why, even in Earth's heat, was Creation suddenly turned cold now?

He wanted a sense of God, and of His goodness, His benevolence, His love. And he wanted more than anything to sense *her*.

He wondered how he might have reacted, had she died half a solar system away, without his ever having seen her again. Would he have mourned then as he did now?

"We were just starting," Paul said.

He stepped outside to look at the stars. Alone. He felt the empty space beside him. She who had felt agorophobic and claustrophobic looking at the heavens, and then later found comfort in them. The stars howled and jeered at him tonight, as they once had done at her. He sought the solace they had once offered him, which he had pointed out to her, for which she'd thanked him. The howling grew louder, and his soul writhed beneath the void as the abyss stared through him.

Still he gazed till dawn.

The sun rose. And the light was good.

Dawn on a thick-aired world. Purple and rose and gold and fire, and deep then paling blue, and quiet chirping, and some exceedingly small but nascent measure of peace. And God was there.

Still in pain, but comforted, Paul said a thank you to the Lord.

He opened the door of his house on Indira's world called Earth and went inside.

## ABOUT THE AUTHOR

Jim Cleaveland is a writer, cartoonist, and animator currently living in San Leandro, CA.

Originally from Plymouth Meeting, PA, he attended Penn State where he created the comic strip *The Inexplicable Adventures of Bob!* for *Explosive Decompression,* the newsletter of the Penn State Science Fiction Society (PSSFS*); and where he also acquired a love of the rural Pennsylvanian landscape.

In 2006, he would revive *Bob!* as a webcomic at http://bobadventures.comicgenesis.com, and it is still ongoing.

After attending *VanArts* animation school in Vancouver, BC (in Canada!), he then lived in Los Angeles for a long period – during which time he worked at lots of bookstores, did a tiny little bit of work for Disney, and then finally found work at Animate For the Cel of It Productions in Burbank.

He has been published in the magazines *Mondo Cult, Nova Science Fiction, Kaleidotrope,* and the PSSFS magazine *Hostigos.*

*Alien In a Small Town* is his first published novel.**

*pronounced "Pizz-Fizz"

**Who knows? Someday I *may* publish that old novella about the fungus monster, but second things first…

*A serialized* **WEBCOMIC** *by the* **AUTHOR** *of* **THIS VERY NOVEL!**.

THE INEXPLICABLE ADVENTURES OF BOB

wow!

by Jim Cleaveland

**You LUCKY READER, you!**

http://bobadventures.comicgenesis.com

The Inexplicable Adventures of Bob is the tale of **Bob Smithson,** who was the world's most **average** man until the day he became a **Weirdness Magnet.**

Now, spaceships crash into his roof, unicorns nibble his lawn, & world-destroying bombs get left on his doorstep **every day.**

He's handling it surprisingly **well,** with a combination of **kindness, common sense,** and being **too dense** to be as scared as he should be.

# Comics! by Jim Cleaveland

**BobAdventures Prod.**

## Anthologies of the webcomic *The Inexplicable Adventures of Bob!*

## Available NOW!

### 1. The Penn State Years:
The 1990's stories originally printed in the Penn State Science Fiction Society newsletter! —
- The Fickle Finger of Fate
- Boxhunt
- Molly's Tale
- The Return of Princess Voluptua

### 2. There But For the Grace:
Sweet tempered Molly the Monster encounters a mysterious and volatile doppelganger -- Galatea's origin story!

## Coming SOON!

### 3. Love And Space:
The love triangle between Bob, Jean, and Voluptua gets heated while Fructose Riboflavin attacks Butane, Planet of Dragons!